Prisoner of the Truth

Prisoner
of the
Truth

ERIC FERGERSON

Charleston, SC
www.PalmettoPublishing.com

Prisoner of the Truth

Copyright © 2021 by Eric Fergerson

All rights reserved

First Edition

Paperback ISBN: 978-1-63837-379-7

Dedicated to my mother and all the other individuals
who struggled and continue to struggle
with untold stories of suffering and abuse –

"I'm always amazed
how you stand so very tall,
how you never give in.
You bend, but do not fall."
—by Paul Holmes

I would like to thank the following people for their continuous support and encouragement throughout the creation of this work. In alphabetical order, Toni Brooks, my beloved friend, for her wise literary insights and advice. Wanda Cager, a wonderful counselor and constant source of inspiration and reassurance – my "cheerleader-in-chief," Hortense McRae, a great aunt and natural-born teacher with an unwavering love and dedication to all her nieces and nephews, Esther Kirk, a dear friend and provocateur, always pushing me to go beyond my comfort level in my thinking and doing, Donald Peebles, my trusted comrade and "motivator-in-chief," who constantly tells it like it is and is always willing to give of himself freely, Jade Royale, a good friend and confidant, thank you for the conversations and your listening ear. I also dedicate this book to all the people, places, and situations that have helped to mold me into the person I am today. There is no "testimony without a test." Most importantly I want to dedicate this book to God, the Universe, Creator, and Most High. Thank you for guiding and protecting me and reconnecting me with the source of all things.

The smell of urine and the sight of piss stains, heat, and chipped paint all contribute to creating a dismal and depressing atmosphere in the Hoyt-Schermerhorn subway station. Rich's excitement at becoming a New York City transit policeman has turned into frustration and boredom. Parade duty, fare beating, traffic, and lots of paperwork are his new normal.

Rich thought police work would entail thrilling undercover investigations, exciting covert operations, and high-profile arrests. Rich wanted the exhilaration and adrenaline rush of a push-it-to-the-limit career. Now, he actively wonders if this is the right job for him. Currently looking at his watch, he sees it's fast approaching six o'clock, and work will be over soon.

The station house is located in the Bronx; getting there quickly and changing into his street clothes, his ride home to Far Rockaway will take about forty-five minutes. His kids, Vaughn, seven, and Gerard, ten, are Down South for the summer. He and Brenda will be driving down tomorrow to get them.

As soon as he reaches his door, the smell of dinner greets him. Rich is hungry and focused on his stomach.

Entering the apartment, he yells, "What's for dinner?"

Brenda shouts back from the kitchen, "Smothered chicken, rice and gravy, string beans and candied yams!"

"How'd your day go?" she asks.

"Same old shit, boring and mundane."

"Have you thought about a transfer?"

"They won't transfer me until I come off rookie status."

"Where'd you like to go?"

"Investigations."

"Oh, that sounds exciting!"

"Yeah, that's just what I'm looking for; I'm tired of all this paperwork."

"I know what you mean. It seems like all I do at the IRS is fill out forms; it's like putting circular pegs into round holes. Whoever thought the work of a financial analyst could be so boring?"

Rich says, "Have you spoken to the boys lately?"

"Oh yeah, I called them yesterday. Vaughn is ready to come home. Gerard is still having fun."

"It'll be nice to see them; school is starting soon, I hope they continue to do well. That reminds me, I have a lot of packing to do; I haven't done any all week."

Brenda says, "Me too. I also need to wash a couple of loads."

After dinner, Brenda clears the dishes in a hurry. Rich goes into their bedroom to pack, and for the next two hours, they each go about finishing up their chores for tomorrow. Later they find themselves in the living room watching TV. Before long, the TV is watching them as they both fall asleep on the couch.

The alarm goes off at four; nudging Brenda gently, Rich rouses her from sleep. While she's in the shower, Rich gets up and fixes them both cold cereal and orange juice. Not having much else to do after breakfast, he carries the luggage downstairs and waits for his wife. Brenda gets in the car ten minutes later. Rich knows the route well and doesn't need a map. Still a little tired, Brenda doesn't say much.

After a few moments of silence, Rich casually asks, "Penny for your thoughts? How're you feeling?"

"I feel okay. Just starting to feel a little drowsy."

After a few hours on the road, without much conversation, Brenda starts to drift back to sleep.

Then, just into Virginia, Brenda wakes up abruptly. She turns to Rich and asks in a genuinely perplexed voice, "Who are you?"

After a few more minutes, she mumbles, "You better give me my money."

With concern in his voice, Rich asks, "Are you all right?"

Seeming confused, Brenda asks, "Where's my mother?"

The crease in Rich's forehead turns into a deep scowl. The gravel hits the car as he pulls over onto the shoulder of the road. He knew that something was seriously wrong.

When Rich looked at Brenda again, she had fear in her eyes. She shouts, "That snake is about to bite me; get it away from me!"

Pushing herself away from him, she unlatches the door. Rich grabs at her blouse, but she slips from his grasp and runs screaming from the car. He quickly unlatches his door, and runs around the car to stop her as she flails her arms wildly, shouting, "Don't you hear them? I want them to stop!"

He catches up, grabs Brenda by the arm, and wrestles her to the ground. Rich lay on top of her for what seems like an eternity.

She beat at his chest, furiously screaming, "Make them stop! I want them to go away! Please make them stop!"

After what seems like forever, she gently begins a cry, which eventually turns into a sob. Holding her gently, Rich picks her off the ground and guides her back to the car. He drives to the nearest gas station and asks the attendant for directions to the closest hospital. The man says Kings Cross Medical Center is about fifteen miles away. Rich pulls off. Brenda is silent and staring straight ahead, blankly looking into the nothingness that lay ahead.

They drive for approximately twenty-five minutes. Eventually, the sign for the hospital appears. Rich pulls into the emergency room parking lot, gets out, and walks over to the other side of the car. He opens his wife's car door and carefully takes her hand. Gently helping her out of the car, they walk arm in arm into the emergency room. Rich sits Brenda down and goes to the triage clerk.

He asks, "Where's the psych emergency room?"

The clerk replies, "Oh, it's around back. Just go to the end of this corridor, make a left then a right, and walk all the way to the end of the hall."

Brenda sits in silence and gets up when Rich motions for her to follow him. Eventually, they arrive at the psych emergency room. It is empty, except for three people. The only woman in the room is a nurse. When Rich walks in, they all look up. One of the men asks, "How may I help you?" Rich sits his wife down, walks over, and says, "My wife started exhibiting some strange behavior in the car."

Rich then describes in detail the incident on the side of the road. The man quickly walks over to the nurse, and they begin to converse. With caution, they approach Brenda. They lead her from her chair to a seat opposite a desk with a sign which reads "Intake." The man sits while the woman stands behind him. He then begins to ask questions.

"What's your name?"

"Brenda Wilson."

"Where do you live?"

"55-05 Beach Channel Drive."

"How old are you?"

"Thirty-three."

"Do you know where you are?"

"Yes."

"Where?"

"A hospital."

"Do you know why you are here?"

"Yes."

"Do you hear voices?"

"Yes."

"What do those voices say?"

"I just hear a male voice say to kill myself."

"Do they say anything else?"

"Yes, sometimes I hear them mumble my name: 'Breenddaaa.'"

"Do you want to hurt yourself?"

"Yes, I want to die so I can make the voices stop."

"Do you want to hurt anyone?"

"No."

"Do the voices come from within or outside your head?"

"They come from outside my head."

"Do you see things?"

"Yes, I see snakes."

"How long have you been seeing and hearing these things?"

"For the last few hours."

"Are you on any medication?"

"No."

"Did you take any drugs or alcohol?"

"No"

The attendant says, "Okay, Brenda, those are all the questions we have. You can go and sit with your husband."

Brenda gets up with the rigidity of an officer-in-training and walks back to her seat. The attendant and nurse consult each other. After about five minutes, the nurse walks over to Rich. She needs to speak with him in private. Rich turns to his wife and says, "I'm going to talk with this lady; I will not go very far; please stay here."

With those words, Rich and the nurse walk away.

The nurse begins by saying, "It appears your wife is experiencing psychotic symptoms. We have to keep her for seventy-two hours because she expressed a desire to hurt herself."

Rich did not hesitate to agree. After he signs the form to admit Brenda into the hospital, the nurse speaks with the orderly. Rich walks back to his seat and holds Brenda's hand.

Gently squeezing her fingers, he says, "Brenda, they're going to keep you here for a few days."

Hearing this, she slowly turns to look at him. Tears well up in her eyes. At about this time, the orderly comes back with another man.

Standing before her, they say, "Mrs. Brenda Wilson, we are here to take you to Ward C."

She holds her head down and begins to cry softly. The orderlies stand on either side of her and gently grab her arms. Slowly they lift her. She proceeds to walk with them.

As she leaves the room, she turns to Rich and says, "Take care of Vaughn and Gerard. Tell them I love them."

Rich says, "Of course, I will."

* * *

It takes them about five minutes to walk to Ward C. When they stand at the ward entrance, the nurse opens the door. At the nurses' station, patients in the dayroom and walking the hall all turn to look at the new admittee. The orderlies hand Brenda over to the nurse. The nurse thanks them and says, "Hello, Brenda. My name is Nurse Stryker."

The nurse has already received the dosing instructions. Brenda should take ten milligrams of Haldol and fifty milligrams of Trazadone. The nurse walks to the medication station and gets the medicine along with a cup of water. Brenda swallows the pills. The nurse then leads her to her sleeping quarters. Brenda puts on her dressing gown, lays her head on the pillow, and wearily falls asleep.

As soon as Brenda leaves the room, Rich gets up and takes a deep breath.

He thinks, *How will I tell the boys?*

He runs to the car. It seems running conveys a sense of urgency that walking can't provide. Thoughts race through his head.

"Both of Rich's parents are deceased and he wonders, "Who should I contact first, my aunt or my mother-in-law?"

He decides to call his aunt.

She picks up on the second ring.

"Hello?"

"Hi, Aunt Ruth. You'll never believe what happened."

"What?" she asks nervously.

"Something happened to Brenda."

"Gasping," she asks, "She's not hurt, is she?"

"Oh no, but it appears she's gotten sick."

"What's wrong with her?"

"She's hearing voices and seeing images outside her head. The people at the hospital think she had a psychotic break."

"Oh, my God."

"She just started acting real weird on the ride down, and I pulled over. She ran out of the car screaming, and I had to restrain her forcibly on the ground. Eventually, she calmed down, and I took her to the nearest hospital. We are in Chatham, Virginia. I'm at the hospital now.

"Are you sure you're calm enough to drive?"

"Sure, I'll be all right."

"Don't worry about the kids; aren't they with their grand-mother?"

"Yes, and Aunt Ruth, one more thing. Could you do me a favor?"

"Sure, anything."

"Call Veronica and tell her what happened. Also, tell her I will arrive in Raleigh later tonight. They're going to keep Brenda for a seventy-two-hour observation period."

"Oh, that won't be a problem. What's her number?"

"It's 919-485-8865, and thanks a lot."

"No problem."

After hanging up, Rich immediately gets back on the road. He'd been up since four this morning, but the adrenaline rush of the day's events eclipse his tiredness. He can't seem to slow down and thinks driving would calm his nerves and channel his restless energy. Rich's palms begin to sweat as he holds the steering wheel tight. He worries more about Vaughn; quiet and a little hesitant, he doesn't express himself much. Gerard, on the other hand, is outgoing with no problem expressing his feelings.

A few hours later, Rich arrives at Veronica's house. She's waiting in the living room and opens the door with a quickness. She tells him his aunt called earlier and told her everything that happened. She says, "I didn't mention anything to Gerard or Vaughn about Brenda."

Rich says, "Good."

He then goes on to recount the day's events in exhausting detail. He decides against waking the boys, saying, "It's too late, and I'm too tired. I'll speak with them in the morning."

At this point, Veronica shows him the upstairs bedroom, adding, "We're going to church tomorrow."

Rich changes into his pajamas, and only after he sits on the bed does he realize how exhausted he is, and as soon as his head hits the pillow, he falls fast asleep.

The following day Rich gets up first, still thinking about his sons. The boys were close when they were younger, but distinct differences in their personalities now push them apart. Gerard commits himself to doing something, and he does it; there is no hesitation. He excels at school, and his outgoing personality makes him many friends. People like his leadership qualities and single-minded focus. On the other hand, Vaughn is quiet, speaking only when spoken to and rarely offering anything extra. His sensitivity makes him insightful and more mysterious. Grandma Veronica says he reminds her of his mother, with "wisdom beyond the eyes."

Rich hears the boys in their bedroom. He knocks on their door and says, "Meet me in the living room."

Shortly, afterward, still in their pajamas, the boys rush to see what their father wants. He calls them over to the couch.

Vaughn is the first to ask, "Where's Mommy?"

Rich says, "I'll get to that."

He takes a deep breath before starting. "In school, remember you learned about the different parts of the body, the head, neck, shoulders, etc."

The boys nod in agreement.

Rich continues, "Do you also remember when Vaughn was ill last year? We talked about sickness and how it affects the body? Well, your mother has an illness. It's of the head—you know, where you think. She hears voices and sees things that are not real. She started to do some weird things when we were coming to Raleigh, and I had to take her to the hospital—"

Gerard interrupts, "Will she be coming back?"

"Yes, she should be coming home soon."

"Will she get better?" Vaughn asks.

"I don't know, but they're giving her pills to make her feel better. She did tell me to tell both of you she loves you dearly. Remember, we're still a family."

The boys don't say much or ask many questions. After he speaks with the boys, they wash up then get something for breakfast.

Ten minutes after they start eating, Rich walks into the kitchen, announcing, "It's now ten o'clock. Hurry up and finish. We're going to church today. Your shirts are hanging over the washing machine."

Gerard is the first to finish. He quickly gets up, picks up his shirt, and goes back to his room. Soon after and doing what seems to be a pattern in their life, Vaughn follows his big brother.

The ride to church doesn't take long. When they enter the sanctuary, ushers and deacons mill around. The family finds seats in the third-pew middle section of the church. Shortly after they sit down, service begins. Slowly the choir works its way down the aisle, one foot to the left on the first beat, another step forward on the right foot to the second beat. It's a well-choreographed routine. Arriving at the front of the church, the singers take their place in the choir stand. They continue to stand and sing until the last verse of the hymn is over.

Once the choir is finished, the co-pastor steps behind the podium and calls the church to order. Next, the pastor enters the pulpit and delivers the invocation and responsive reading. Pastor Brown, a tall, dark-skinned, round-faced, middle-aged man in his fifties, wears a custom-tailored blue suit, gold cuff-links, a blue and green tie, and white handkerchief. He finds his place in the Bible and announces, "Today's text will come from 2 Chronicles 15:7: 'But as for you, be strong and do not give up, for your work will be rewarded.'"

Pastor Brown begins his sermon by saying, "Everyone has experienced a difficult challenge. Did it seem like a solution was impossible?"

Then referring to Luke 18:1 in the Parable of the Persistent Widow, the pastor says, Jesus told his disciples always pray and do not give up. He next cites "Galatians 6:9, which states, 'Let us not become weary in doing good, for at the proper time we will reap a harvest if we do not give up.'"

Pastor Brown goes on to ask the congregation, "How many of you have persevered through that problem only to find grace at the end?"

Many congregants nod their heads in agreement, mumbling "um hmm," each reflecting momentarily on the personal dramas of their life. By this time, beads of sweat begin to form on Pastor Brown's forehead.

He steps down from the pulpit and walks from one side of the church to the other, exclaiming, "Jesus had problems, but he didn't give up. The Son of Man knew what the future held for him. He had a mission and a purpose that was clear to him; he wouldn't give up."

Veronica nods her head, soaking up every word, then presses her body forward to check on the boys. Vaughn is sitting at the end of the row. Gerard is listening, but Vaughn has fallen asleep. He sits with his eyes closed, head cocked to the side and mouth slightly open.

Pastor Brown starts to move up and down the aisle, asking, "How many of you have a problem bigger than Jesus? Of course not; he had the world's redemption on his shoulders. No one has a problem bigger than that."

By this time, Pastor Brown is near the Wilson family. He starts speaking in tongues: "Heek a ba sundah hiakunda." Then unexpectedly and without warning, he reaches down and grabs Vaughn with both hands, lifting him high into the air. Vaughn's eyes open wide as saucers.

Seemingly in a trance, Pastor Brown says, "The spirit told me to say touch not mine anointed; do my prophets no harm."

The little boy is petrified. He has a half-second to wake up, a half-second to realize he's in the air, and another half-second to hear words he does not understand. Pastor Brown then roughly places him back in his seat.

Afterward, Veronica leans across Gerard and whispers in Vaughn's ear, "That was a blessing; next time, don't fall asleep in Gods' house."

By this time, Pastor Brown is on the other side of the sanctuary, instructing, "When you feel like giving up, think about God. Remember, dear souls, that through Christ, all things are possible. The Word doesn't say some things or most things work for good for those who love the Lord; it says, 'All things work for good for those who love the Lord.' The Bible doesn't say that through Christ, some things or most things are possible. It says 'And through Christ all things are possible.'"

In closing, he says, "Remember, beloved, there is never any problem too hard for God."

Pastor Brown now faces the church with both hands raised, drenched in sweat. Smiling broadly, he says, "Now let's give the Lord a hand praise."

Thunderous applause echo throughout the church as the choir starts to play, 'You can't beat God's Giving,' and the collection plate is passed around. Then during altar call Veronica thinks about her daughter and walks to the front of the church to say a special prayer for Brenda. Pastor Brown next asks for new members and performs the benediction before dismissing the church.

The family atmosphere and fellowship in the church feels warm. On their way out of the sanctuary, Rich and Veronica shake the pastor's hand, saying, "I really enjoyed the service."

Pastor Brown pats Gerard and Vaughn on the head, saying enthusiastically, "We need to see more young people like this on Sunday morning."

The boys look up and smile respectfully.

In the car, Veronica says, "I so enjoyed the service."

Rich adds, "Pastor definitely preached."

"Did you boys enjoy service?"

"Yes," they say in unison.

For the rest of the ride, there is a comfortable and light feeling in the car but in the back of their mind everyone is thinking of Brenda.

Arriving home, the family immediately changes out of their church clothes. Veronica goes into the kitchen to get dinner ready and the boys turn on the living room TV, channel surfing until they find an old episode of *Star Trek*.

Stepping into the living room, Rich announces, "I'm calling your mom."

Both boys light up and quickly walk to the hallway phone. It takes a long time for someone to answer.

"Hello, may I please speak to Brenda Wilson?"

"Hold on a minute," the attendant says, and after another long wait, Brenda answers the phone.

With trepidation in her voice, she says, "Hello."

"Hi, honey," Rich replies.

He instantly notices a distinct change in her voice. She is speaking lower, slower, and with a slight vocal tremor.

"How're you feeling?"

"Sleepy."

"No, I don't mean that. What do you feel like emotionally?

"I'm okay. I feel kind of emotionless."

"Do you feel at least a little bit better?"

"The voices have stopped, and I do not see snakes anymore."

"So, that's a good thing."

"How're the boys?" she asks.

"They're fine and are right here waiting to speak with you."

He hands the phone to Vaughn, realizing the conversation's brevity belied the complexity and depth of the issues needing to be discussed. Rich knew this would be uncomfortable.

"Here is Vaughn,"

Bursting with anticipation, Vaughn says, "Hi, Mom."

"How're you?"

"Fine."

"Are you ready for school?"

"Yes."

"Are you going to study hard and make good grades?"

"Yes."

"Are you listening to your father?"

"Yes."

Vaughn then asks, "When are you coming home?"

She then responds, "You know mommy is having some problems."

"Yes, Dad told us."

"But I don't want you to worry about me. I am feeling better now and should be coming home soon. Most of all I want you to know mommy loves you."

Brenda desperately wants to see her children, and the wound from not being able to be with them begins to open up.

"Okay, you take care, and remember, I love you; now put your brother on the phone."

"Hi, Gerard."

"Hi, Mom."

"How're you?"

"Fine."

"Are you ready for school?"

"Yes."

"Gerard, you know Mommy is having problems."

"Yes, Daddy told us."

Tears begin to well up in Brenda's eyes.

"You know I'm in Virginia."

"Yes."

Unable to contain her hurt and feeling the wound opening up once again, Brenda ends the conversation, suddenly saying, "Okay, I'm not feeling well and don't want to keep you too long. Remember, I love you."

"Okay, take care, Mom."

After Brenda hangs up, a heavy sadness comes over her, and a single teardrop begins its slow descent down the left side of her cheek.

After hanging up, Gerard rejoins Vaughn in the living room.

Veronica yells from the kitchen, "Gerard, why did you hang up? I wanted to speak to your mother."

"She wasn't feeling well."

Veronica says, "Oh, she's scheduled to come home tomorrow. I can always speak with her then. How did she sound?"

Gerard says, "She sounded okay. She just asked me about school, told me she was in Virginia, and said she loves me."

"Oh, so it was a very brief conversation."

"Yes, she didn't say much."

"Okay, that's fine."

* * *

The boys continue to watch *Star Trek*. A couple of hours later, Veronica tells the boys to wash up for dinner. She then walks upstairs to Rich's room to tell him dinner is ready.

They are seated at the table and eating when the phone rings. Rich picks up immediately. He announces loudly and with excitement in his voice, "It's Dr. Chen from Kings Cross Medical Center."

Eagerly, he asks, "How's Brenda doing? We spoke to her earlier today."

After a relatively brief conversation, Rich says to the family, "Dr. Chen said Brenda was stable, responded well to treatment, and will be discharged tomorrow."

The whole family cheers. The boys get up and do a happy dance. The family finishes their meal with a warm feeling in their hearts. Later, as the evening progresses, the house begins to lull itself slowly to sleep.

The next morning, Veronica gets up at eight, much earlier than she usually would, to prepare a large dinner for this evening. Rich gets ready to leave for the hospital. Vaughn plays with a truck, and Gerard watches TV downstairs. As soon as Rich finishes getting dressed, he exits the house quickly, and without much fanfare, yells, "Have a good day, everyone. See you when I get back."

A few hours later, he pulls into the hospital parking lot.

After he knocks on the door to Ward C, a nurse comes and asks, "How may I help you?"

"I'm Brenda Wilson's husband. Today she's being discharged."

"Oh, oh," the nurse says. "We were expecting someone."

She opens the door wider and lets Rich onto the ward, saying, "Wait here while I get Brenda."

Moments later, his wife appears. She is expressionless, has a glassy look in her eyes and a slight tremor in her hands. She scans the entryway and smiles rigidly when she sees Rich.

He kisses her gently, saying, "We're going to your parent's house today."

Nodding, she asks, "How are the kids?"

"Fine," he responds.

The nurse says, "Mr. Wilson, I have some papers for you to sign."

He dutifully looks over the paperwork and signs each sheet.

As he turns to walk back to his wife, the nurse says, "Wait a minute. Here is her medication and a prescription with three refills. Remember to have her see a doctor as soon as she returns home."

During the ride home, Brenda says nothing.

"How're you feeling?

"Okay," she replies.

Rich then starts to chatter aimlessly, bringing up anything to unsettle the painful silence within the car. The radio serves as an easy distraction.

Upon arrival in the city, Rich hopes for a spark of recognition in Brenda's eyes. However, she remains silent and absent. As he walks up to the house, he can hear the television playing. Upon entry, he sees Veronica and the boys waiting in the hallway. With tears in her eyes, her mother reaches out to hug her as Gerard and Vaughn run and embrace their mother tightly.

Brenda looks down, wraps her arms around both boys, and says, "Hi, babies."

Rich says, "I'm sure Brenda is tired; she's going to need some rest before dinner."

Brenda smiles blandly, says nothing, and walks toward the upstairs bedroom.

Arriving in her room, she quickly changes clothes and gets into bed. A few minutes later, Rich walks into the room with three pills and a glass of orange juice. She swallows the pills and quickly dozes off.

Believing she is dreaming, Brenda imagines herself in a park with snakes all over the ground. They are all manner of shape and size, writhing on the ground around her. She's in a panic. In the distance, she sees a hand. Slowly she gets up from the bed. The hand appears to be motioning her toward it. Continuing to walk toward the hand; Brenda reaches out to grab it. The glass violently breaks as she plunges through the second-floor window to the ground below.

Everyone in the house hears the glass break. There is a half-second pause before the house erupts into chaos and pandemonium. Everyone drops what they're doing and rushes to Brenda's room. Veronica reaches the room first. Opening the door, she runs to the window. Looking down, she sees Brenda's body.

Screaming, "Oh my Lord!" she runs outside. The boys follow her out of the house.

Seeing their mother on the ground, Gerard and Vaughn echo each other's loud, heaving sobs.

The family is in a state of shock. Rich immediately dials the police. They arrive in a matter of minutes. He takes them around the side of the house. A paramedic kneels to check Brenda's pulse, then offers his condolences. The family has now formed a semicircle around Brenda's body. Veronica has her back turned and looks away in stunned disbelief. The boys fix a steady gaze on their mother's body as the coroner places a white sheet on top of her.

Rich answers the policeman's questions, stating, "We arrived home about thirty minutes ago. Brenda recently got out of a mental hospital after a seventy-two-hour observation period. She was diagnosed with psychosis and expressed a desire to kill herself. Brenda reported auditory and visual hallucinations."

After answering the questions, Rich escorts the detectives upstairs. Going back outside, he finds the family in the same place. They do not notice his approach. Coming from behind, he gently divides his sons and wraps his arms around them, leaning into them reassuringly.

Before leaving the house, the investigators walk over to Rich and pronounce the cause of death as suicide. By the time the coroner has put the body into the medical examiner's van, the family starts walking into the house.

Veronica is the first to speak: "I must call the family."

She tries to call her sister but breaks down. The family is still in a state of shock. Eventually, Veronica begins to make calls. As she makes more calls, her phone and doorbell start to ring. Relatives, friends, and neighbors start to fill the house. The crowd makes Veronica and the rest of the family feel embraced.

As the night progresses, the atmosphere in the house begins to shift. Still sad but with more energy. Tearful memories begin to mix with fonder ones. The boys grow tired and eventually fall asleep on the living room couch.

Veronica says, "Go to bed."

Gerard immediately gets up and goes to their bedroom.

Upon waking, Vaughn says, "I saw the devil laughing at me."

Nana asked, "When?"

"Last night."

"Were you sleeping? It was probably just a bad dream."

"No," Vaughn says. "I wasn't sleeping. I was in bed, but I saw his face on the side of my closet right next to my nightstand, laughing at me."

"Did you get the Bible and read it?"

"No. I was too afraid."

"If you ever see the devil laughing at you again, read the ninety-first Psalm and sleep with the Bible under your pillow."

When they get to his bedroom, Vaughn kisses his grandmother good night, lays his head on the pillow, and tries to go to sleep. A few minutes later, Veronica walks back into the boy's bedroom with a burning white candle.

Vaughn asks, "What's that for?"

His grandmother replies, "To usher in the presence of God."

Worried as she walks to her bedroom, she gets on her hands and knees to say a special prayer for Vaughn before climbing into bed, trying not to think about what he just told her.

Morning usually brings forth newness and rebirth, but yesterday's events hang a pall over the new day. This morning Veronica and Rich find themselves alone in the living room. Veronica is the first to speak. "I was hoping we could have her service soon."

Rich says, "I was thinking the same thing. I can call the funeral home and make arrangements with the caterer today."

Veronica says, "I can pick out the flowers and get her dress. We can start after the boys have their breakfast."

Rich and Veronica's voices float upstairs and wake Gerard up first. Vaughn isn't far behind. After washing up, they go downstairs to the kitchen. While eating, Vaughn says, "I miss Mommy so much. Why'd she jump out the window?"

Gerard replies, "I don't know, but you know she is now with God in heaven."

Vaughn remarks, "Yes, with Granddad, Jesus, and the angels."

"Yes," Gerard says.

They want to talk further about their mother, but their conversation is interrupted by Veronica's entry into the kitchen.

"Good morning, boys; we realize how tough this must be for you. Talk to us if you start feeling sad, angry, or just need to discuss anything. We need you boys to be on your best behavior today. I know that's not easy given what's happened, but I'm asking you to try. That means no fighting. We have a lot on our plate today. Both Rich and I will be gone for a while, so we need you to behave. Am I clear?"

Gerard says, "Yes."

Vaughn shakes his head, interjecting, "Gerard told me Mommy is in heaven with God, Granddad, Jesus, and the angels."

Veronica smiles, saying, "Yes, she is. She certainly is, baby."

Tears begin to glisten in her eyes. Looking at the time, Veronica says, "All right, we have to go now. You two take care, and remember: no fighting. We should be gone for a few hours."

After they leave, the boys watch TV and don't say much to each other. The silence in the home creates an invisible wall between them. Eventually, Vaughn goes back to his room to play with toys while Gerard stays in the living room and watches TV. Each within his own mind is thinking about his mother but is speechless in the shock of not having her around anymore.

Around six, Veronica returns and settles in the kitchen. She immediately starts thinking about the service. "I need to handle the insurance first. I know she had a policy. Rich is going to need those papers."

Bearing the weight of what needs to be done is tiresome, and feeling the need for a helpmate, Veronica momentarily thinks about her deceased husband, Joe. Sadness overtakes her for a moment, but she manages to smile on the inside, thinking, *My daughter is back with her dad in heaven.*

As Veronica stares into space and daydreams, Rich walks in, saying, "I was able to confirm with the caterer. It wasn't too pricey."

Veronica adds, "I was just thinking about her insurance. I know she had a policy."

Rich says, "I took one out when we got married. Brenda also has one with her job. I will call them tomorrow. How're the boys?"

"They're okay. Gerard is watching TV in the living room. Vaughn is upstairs in his room."

Gradually daily rituals begin to push aside the hurt of small remembrances. The weight of Brenda's death lifts slightly, and when the day of the funeral finally arrives, the family feels prepared. Putting Brenda to rest is a formality. Tabernacle Baptist Church is packed. A sea of black dresses and navy blue suits fill the church. Flowers line the front of the sanctuary. In his remarks, the pastor mentions "the sweet sting of death," saying, it leaves behind pain for the mourners. Then in citing Corinthians 5:8 says, "We are confident, I say, and willing rather to be absent from the body and to be present with the Lord," is a blessing.

Rich delivers the eulogy, speaking about the love of his life and the wonderful mother of his children. Family members, both old and new friends, and coworkers all offer remembrances of her warm spirit, recalling anecdotes from a short life well lived. The hymns selected echo the sadness of the hour while conveying hope for a brighter tomorrow. Veronica picked out a beautiful beige silk dress, and people remark that Brenda looks like she's sleeping in the casket. During the eulogy, mourners grab tissues and dab at their eyes while sniffles echo throughout the sanctuary. During the ride to the cemetery, Rich, Gerard, Vaughn, and Veronica look out the window to avoid seeing the pain in each other's eyes. At the internment, mourners put roses on the casket as a sign of final respect. Silent tears become audible sobs as the coffin is lowered into the ground. The pastor's last words are "We, therefore, commit this body to the ground, earth to earth, ashes to ashes, dust to dust; in sure and certain hope of the Resurrection to eternal life."

On the way back to the limousine, Vaughn says, "Nana, Mommy whispered in my ear and winked at me in the casket."

Veronica doesn't respond and just bites her lip as she holds Vaughn's hand tighter and closes her eyes in silent prayer.

At the repass, the atmosphere lightens up. People eat, talk, and give their final condolences before leaving. The family arrives home around seven and settles in the living room. Rich says, "You boys have to start school soon."

Vaughn says with pride, "I'll be in second grade."

Gerard chimes in, "I'll be in fifth."

"Yes, you boys are getting big. We need to get you registered for school right away."

Tired and exhausted from the day's events, Veronica announces, "It's been a long day, and I'm ready for an early night."

Rich says, "I'm worn out too. I'll do the same."

The boys stay in the living room but eventually fall asleep on the couch. Fatigue replaces tiredness for the family. The weariness of the mind always weighs heavily on the body.

The boys wish to be home. They want to be near the familiar. It's a place that will give them happier memories of their mother. As things sort of get back to normal, each day rolls into the next until it's time for Rich and the boys to leave. As they're departing, Veronica hugs her grandchildren goodbye and wishes them a successful school year.

In parting, she says, "Have a safe trip home. I'll be praying for you guys."

"Prayer is what we need," Rich replies.

Once home and tired from the long ride back Rich and the boys go straight to bed. Vaughn, however, has a dream this night. In it, he is walking alone in the dark and cold of a dungeon. In bed, his body tenses, and his muscles contract with fear. After walking in this space for an indeterminate amount of time, he comes upon some stairs. He cautiously and methodically makes his way up the stairs. As he moves up each step, something begins to happen. He starts to feel less fear and more peace. With each step, he gets stronger. With each progression, his fear seems to diminish. Finally, he reaches the last step and finds himself standing in a doorway that has no door. There is only pure whiteness and the glow of a white light emanating from somewhere deep within. It's as if Vaughn has arrived at the entrance to a cloud. As he stands there, he feels joy, not ecstatic but peaceful. All the anxiety and tension of the journey is over. As he takes the next step, he feels a hand on his shoulder. He knows it's his mother.

Reversing the pattern, Vaughn is the first to get up this morning. Gerard is not far behind. Rich says, "I have to register you two for school today."

Gerard is openly excited about the new school year. "I wonder who my teacher will be?" he asks.

Later on that day, Rich and the boys walk to school. He meets the boys' teachers and tells them about Brenda's passing. They express genuine sympathy and hope for a good school year.

Later on that evening, Rich thinks it's a good time to call Sherry. The boys are in their room, and his door is shut. Sherry picks up on the first ring.

Rich blurts out, "Those pills really work. Brenda started acting crazy a few hours after I put them in her cereal. You heard she jumped out the window."

"They were talking about it at the stationhouse."

"Where'd you get them?"

"Our investigative team uses them frequently. We utilize all types of drugs in our investigative protocols. We have about 200 of them."

"Wow, I can't wait to get over there. I'm tired of doing street patrol. I want more exciting work."

"Yeah, I know, just give it time."

Sherry now mentions what's most on her mind, and her tone becomes serious. "Rich, what about the baby?"

"I told you I would give you the money for an abortion."

"I don't want an abortion. I want this child."

Firmly, Rich says, "The boys already know you; I previously told you we could get married as soon as Brenda was out of the way. We won't be able to manage with two kids, one newborn, and our busy lifestyle."

"It isn't about getting married; it's about my baby. I don't care how many kids there are or how busy I am. This is my first child, and I want it."

"It's your decision, but I disagree."

Sherry's voice gets louder. "And you can disagree all you want, but I'm keeping our baby. I'm disappointed in you, Rich; I need our child to be wanted and raised in love."

Rich remains resolute, saying, "I will respect your decision, but I disagree with it."

Sherry says, "I'll speak with you later," and slams the phone down.

Trying to forget the conversation, Rich tells the boys, "Dinner'll be ready soon."

At the table, Gerard says, "I can't wait to see my friends at school."

Vaughn says, "Me too."

Rich reminds the boys, "You have all your school supplies and everything you need for the first day, so you're all set."

The boys go to bed eagerly waiting for the new school day to begin.

Mrs. McRae has a childlike, lively personality suited for work with young children. She picks up her new class in the schoolyard. The kids bounce around with the vibrancy and enthusiasm of youth. Mrs. McRae calls them to order. During playtime, students choose to either play with blocks, color, paint, or read.

Vaughn decides to play with blocks. Billy is racing cars in the adjacent play area. With skill, patience, and diligence, Vaughn builds a wall six blocks high. Billy accidentally bumps into him. As Vaughn stumbles into the wall, it crumbles to the floor. Filled with rage, he picks up a block, slamming it into Billy's face. At the sound of Billy's cry, everyone looks up. With unbelievable speed and agility, Mrs. McRae is at the site of the incident. She immediately attends to Billy by pulling his hand away from his face. Mrs. McRae gently guides him to the sink, splashing water on the injured eye, now turning black and blue. She gets the first aid kit, finds a large patch, and holds it over his eye.

Turning to the nearest student, she says, "Take the pass and go get the nurse."

After a few minutes, the nurse rushes in. She finds Mrs. McRae looking after Billy. At the sight of the nurse, Mrs. McRae backs away.

The nurse says, "I'll take him to my office. Give me his official card."

Mrs. McRae finds the card and gives it to the nurse. She then scours the room for Vaughn.

She glares at him, saying, "Come here, young man. You know this is very serious; we're going to the principal's office."

Mrs. McRae writes out a note for the teacher next door: "Mrs. Scott, please look after my class. I have an emergency and need to go to the principal's office."

She chooses the student standing next to her to deliver the note. The student is back in two minutes with the word "Okay" written on the paper. With Vaughn in tow, Mrs. McRae marches down the hall to the principal's office.

After entering the office, she asks, "May I speak with Mrs. Smith? I have an emergency."

The secretary intercoms Mrs. Smith, who says, "Send them in."

"We had an incident in class," Mrs. McRae begins. "Vaughn assaulted another student."

Mrs. Smith looks sternly at Vaughn, asking, "Young man, what happened?"

Vaughn says, "I was playing with blocks, and Billy bumped into me and made me knock them over."

Mrs. McRae interjects, "We went over the rules today. One of our main rules is no fighting. Billy didn't do it on purpose. If you felt he was being mean, you should have told me. There was no reason for you to hit him in the eye with that block. If you were feeling sad or mad, you could have come and talked to me."

Without saying anything further, Vaughn shrinks back in his chair.

Mrs. McRae continues, "In my class, we have consequences and rewards. If you do good things, you get a reward, and if you do bad things, you suffer consequences."

Mrs. Smith adds, "This school has a zero-tolerance policy on fighting and assaults, and the consequence is suspension."

Mrs. Smith asks for Vaughn's father's phone number. His stomach muscles tighten as she dials his cellphone.

"Hello."

"May I speak with Rich Wilson? This is Mrs. Smith, the principal at Vaughn Wilson's elementary school, PS 105."

Rich nervously asks, "Did something happen to Vaughn?"

"Oh no, Vaughn is fine, but he assaulted another student, and this school has a zero-tolerance policy on assaults.

Students who hit other students get suspended. You need to get someone here to pick him up right away."

Rich asks, "What happened?"

"Vaughn was playing with blocks, and a classmate bumped into him and he fell into the wall he was building and knocked it down. Vaughn then hit the student in the eye with a block. *In the eye!*" she repeats with emphasis.

Rich replies with genuine surprise, "This is really out of character for him. You know his mother passed away two weeks ago. I'm not saying that excuses his behavior, but I think that might explain his anger."

Mrs. Smith expresses sympathy and concern but remains convicted in her belief. She states, "I'm truly sorry to hear that, and you have my condolences, but again this school has a zero-tolerance policy on physical assaults. It's the beginning of the school year, and if we let one student slide, that will send the wrong message to the other students."

The annoyance in Rich's voice is evident. His speech becomes strident, and his inflection more pronounced. He states, "I just want you to know I think your policy is unreasonable, cruel, and doesn't take into account what Vaughn has been through. However, I will come and get him. How long will he be suspended?"

"Typically, for a week, but given the circumstances, I will make it two days."

"Ok, I can be there in forty-five minutes."

After arriving, Rich signs in at the school safety officer's desk and asks for directions to the principal's office. He walks into the outer office and finds Vaughn slumped in a chair with a sad look on his face. Once Rich arrives, Mrs. Smith motions for both of them to come into her private office.

She closes the door and says, "Thanks for coming so quickly. As I told you, this school has a zero-tolerance policy on all types of physical altercations. Suspension is our consequence for assaults. Just so we're clear, it wasn't a fight because Billy didn't hit Vaughn back."

"Your suspension is for two days. Mrs. McRae has prepared your lesson packet. Hopefully, you have learned something from this experience and will follow school rules in the future. I want you to think about what you did, why it is wrong, and what you will do differently in the future. Do you understand?"

Vaughn nods his head robotically.

"I hope this is just a one-time misstep."

Mrs. Smith then says, "It has been a pleasure meeting you, Mr. Wilson. I wish it was under better circumstances. I'll also sign Vaughn up for counseling with Mr. Stevens."

Rich says, "That's fine."

Mrs. McRae has left Vaughn's work with the secretary. After picking it up, they exit the building.

In a show of passive resistance, Vaughn ambles. His young, perceptive mind senses his father is not angry. Deep within, he realizes his anger was not at Billy; he just misses his mother. As they walk home, Rich maintains a brisk pace. In reality, he's not upset with Vaughn but sympathetic. He understands that the confusion and resentment associated with losing your mother at such a young age would cause any child to lash out.

Rich reaches the first traffic light, moves his head to the side, and takes a quick look back. Vaughn is walking about five feet behind him. With feigned irritation, Rich says, "Hurry up."

Vaughn looks up, quickens his pace, and grabs his father's hand.

Vaughn then asks his father, "Why did you kill Mommy?"

His father immediately drops his hand, saying, "Where did you hear that?"

"Mommy just told me."

"How could your mother tell you that when she's dead?"

Vaughn is insistent with his facts. "She just whispered it in my ear."

The truth of Vaughn's words produce a range of intense emotions in Rich, most prominently fear.

Perplexed and unnerved, Rich thinks, *What if he tells someone? What if they believe him? What if he saw or heard something? What if he found the pills? What else does he know?*

Rich begins to sweat. Fear stifles his inquisitiveness.

Thinking of a diversion tactic, he says, "You're going to have lots of work to do when you get home. You need to be glad I don't beat your little ass."

Vaughn doesn't say anything, but he doesn't forget what his mother told him.

They get home, and Rich sends Vaughn to his room. Meting out the punishment was simple enough; without TV and video games, Vaughn will spend most of his day studying and working on his lesson packet.

Later that day, Vaughn wakes with a start as his brother enters the room. He feels like he's been asleep for fifteen minutes, but in reality, it's been a couple of hours.

"What're you doing home? I waited fifteen minutes at our usual pickup location."

"I hit another student and got suspended."

Gerard reacts with shock, repeating the words slowly and loudly, "*You hit someone.* What happened?"

"I was playing with blocks, and Billy bumped into me and made me knock down the wall I was building."

"What did Dad say?"

"He said I couldn't watch TV or play with my video games; I have to study all day and do my worksheets."

"Wow, I'm shocked at you."

Vaughn's days prove to be long and boring; each day seems like the day before.

Rich doesn't say much to Vaughn besides "Try that stunt again, and I'll beat your little ass for real."

Rich calls Sherry, asking, "Can you get your hands on some more of those pills?"

Laughing, she asks, "Who're you trying to drive crazy now?"

"I have a coworker who's getting on my nerves. I want to teach him a lesson."

"Which ones do you want?"

"Give me the same ones you gave me for Brenda."

"I'll see what I can do; we have a lot of drugs we use. Everyone reacts to them differently. They can make you anxious, depressed, manic, obsessive-compulsive, angry, emotionally numb, sexually promiscuous, feel like you're falling in love, have cognitive difficulties, and give you cancer or a heart attack; the list is endless."

"Get me as many as you can."

"You're a mess! I'll see what I can do."

Sherry comes over later that evening and gives Rich the pills; the visit is short. She says, "Fun stuff," as she exits the apartment.

Rich puts the pills in a glass of orange juice at Vaughn's placemat. In the middle of the night, Gerard gets up to use the bathroom. Thirsty, he grabs the first glass of orange juice he sees and goes back to bed. Rich gets up, sees the orange juice is gone, and starts smiling on the inside. A few hours later, he gets a message from PS 105 saying they need to speak with him about Gerard. Rich says, "Damn, I just got a call about Vaughn last week; now Gerard."

He calls the school in a hurry.

According to the school secretary, Gerard is in the playground, yelling, "I'm a warlock with special powers to control the weather."

His teacher says he won't calm down or respond to redirection.

Surprised, Rich says, "What? I can't believe it!"

"Yes, this is really out of character for him. We need someone to pick him up. Gerard can stay home until he calms down."

Before hanging up, Rich asks about Vaughn.

"He must be doing okay; I haven't heard anything to the contrary."

Rich realizes what must've happened.

Rich calls Captain Kuntz immediately. Rich knows Kuntz from his previous job as a bookkeeper—where Kuntz was the accountant. He caught Rich stealing money from the company.

Kuntz said, "If I go to the boss, you'll get at least ten years in prison." Kuntz held this over Rich's head as blackmail to someday get what he really wanted. Remembering a very long and uncomfortable conversation, Rich knew what Kuntz wanted in exchange for his silence.

Rich explains to the captain that he needs to leave work to pick up his son from school.

"Didn't you just go up to school for one of your sons the other day?" Kuntz asks.

"Yes, I don't know what's going on. I think they're reacting to the death of their mother."

"Oh, I'm sorry. I forgot. Of course, you can take off as much time as you need."

Rich hangs up quickly, saying, "All right, thanks."

When Rich gets to school, Gerard is seated outside the principal's office. Rich looks at Gerard and thinks to himself, *He seems calm now.*

Once in Mrs. Smith's office, she says, "I'm not sure if this is a psychotic episode, grief, or ingestion of drugs. Children of a young age can react in many unusual and unpredictable ways over the loss of a parent."

Rich says, "He seems to be relaxed now."

The principal confers, "Yes, I noticed that also, which makes me believe he could be coming down off of a drug high. I asked him if he'd taken any drugs earlier. He said no; nevertheless, I'm not sure he's telling the truth."

"A drug trip at ten years old."

Look, it happens. "Now, let's get to the heart of the matter. Do you have any illegal drugs at home?"

"No, just some over-the-counter stuff."

"I'm not sure what's going on, but I've already signed Gerard up for counseling with Mr. Stevens."

Mrs. Smith then intercoms her secretary to send Gerard in.

"How're you feeling?" Mrs. Smith inquires.

"Fine, but a little weird."

"What do you mean?"

"I just feel funny."

"Okay, I'm going to ask you a series of questions. They may seem obvious, but answer them anyway."

"Who am I?"

"Mrs. Smith"

"Who is this?"

"Dad."

"Where are you at?"

"PS 105 in the principal's office."

"Who is your teacher?"

"Mrs. Elliott."

"Did you take any drugs?"

"No, the only thing I had today was breakfast."

"Do you hear voices or see images outside of your head?"

"No."

"Why were you saying you were a warlock with special powers over the weather?"

"I don't know."

Mrs. Smith ends her questioning by saying, "Okay, those are all the questions I have." She then turns to Mr. Wilson and says, "To be honest, I don't know what happened, but it appears Gerard is coming back to himself."

Addressing Gerard, the principal says, "I've signed you up to see Mr. Stevens. Today you can leave with your father."

Speaking to Mr. Wilson, she says, "I'll dismiss Gerard for the rest of the day. Hopefully, tomorrow he can get back on track."

When they reach home, Rich tells Gerard to take a nap. He starts thinking about Vaughn.

The phone interrupts his thoughts.

Sherry says, "I was just calling to find out if the pills worked?"

"I decided not to use them."

"Oh, okay. I know I didn't hear anything around the stationhouse."

"I just got back from the doctor. Rich, the baby should be here in a few months. I want you to change your mind on abortion."

"I've said this before, and I'll repeat it. I love you; I just don't think a newborn can fit into our lifestyle, but I want you to know I'll treat the baby with love either way."

"That makes me feel a little better."

"All right."

"Okay, bye."

Later in the day, Rich visits a botanica. Entering the store, he sees a short, skinny, light-skinned Hispanic woman. He approaches her with a bold request.

"What do I need to do to drive someone crazy?"

The woman shakes her head, saying, "I don't fool with those things."

Rich counters with, "I may go to hell for doing what I'm doing, but the other person will go to hell for their mess."

The woman thinks for a minute, then says, "Follow me."

She points to a black candle and whispers, "Write the person's name seven times on a piece of parchment paper. Place the paper in the bottom of the candle. Write the person's name on the side of the candle seven times, then light the candle.

Once the candle burns out, take it to a cemetery and bury it at midnight."

Once home Rich writes Vaughn's name on the candle and parchment; he then puts the candle on his chest of drawers. Rich keeps his bedroom door locked. The boys notice the light in their father's room one night, and Gerard asks, "What's that light coming from your room?"

"I'm burning a white candle in remembrance of your mother."

Vaughn says, "Grandma burned a white candle when I saw the devil laughing at me. She said it was to usher in the presence of God."

Rich says, "You saw the devil laughing at you. You're always saying something stupid or crazy."

Gerard stays up half the night, hypnotized by the light shining under his father's door. He can't stop looking at it, change shape, and flicker on and off. It keeps him up half the night.

The following morning, while sitting at the breakfast table, Rich asks Gerard, "How do you feel?"

"Just a little sleepy."

"But other than that, are you okay?"

"Yeah."

As the boys walk out the door, Rich says to Vaughn, "You better behave. Don't let me get another call, or I'll come up there and bust your little ass."

After they leave, Rich is getting into the shower when he receives a call.

Captain Kuntz asks, "Hey, Rich. I was calling to find out how your boys are doing?"

"The older one is okay, but I'm having problems with my youngest."

Captain Kuntz says, "When you get a chance, stop by my office. I want to talk to you about a transfer."

Rich's heart leaps with excitement. "Okay, I'll be in around nine."

Rich goes to work with a hopeful smile on his face.

He walks into the stationhouse and goes straight to Captain Kuntz's office. The captain greets him with a big smile and a firm handshake.

"I need to talk with you about your transfer. I know you want to get into investigations. I have some good news for you. We're going to approve your transfer early. Your work has been exceptional, and they're short-staffed in that division anyway, effective immediately. You start shadowing Detective Rodriguez tomorrow."

Rich thinks he remembers Rodriguez. His heart leaps for joy.

"Hey, thanks, Captain Kuntz; I'm grateful for the opportunity to serve in a greater capacity on the force."

The captain then unexpectedly gets up from his desk and closes the door.

He says, "You're welcome, but there's one more thing I want to discuss with you before you leave."

Suddenly, the captain's facial expression and vocal tone change. Rich gets a knot in the pit of his stomach as he senses what the captain wants to talk about.

"I know you remember the favor you owe me."

Rich slowly and hesitantly says, "Yes."

Getting straight to the point, the captain says, "I think it's time you paid up."

Rich instantly starts to fidget, looking down and away from the captain, unable to maintain eye contact any longer.

"All right, I remember our deal. I'll set something up this weekend."

"Okay, just remember our arrangement."

Rich says, "I will. Is that all?"

Captain Kuntz says, "Yes, you can leave now."

Rich swiftly exits the office. Unnerved by what he's agreed to do, he waits a while before calling Sherry.

After fifteen minutes he picks up the phone and dials her number. The first words out of his mouth are, "Guess what? You'll never believe what happened today."

"What?" she replies.

"They're going to start my training in the Investigative Unit!"

"Oh, that's great! We have to celebrate! Who told you?"

"Captain Kuntz."

"I know him, and I like him. He's a good guy. I'm so happy for you! If I weren't out in public, I'd be screaming. We should call ourselves 'The Dynamic Duo.'"

"Yes, we should," Rich says, "I'm so excited I can't sit still."

"I know how you must feel."

"Alright, I just wanted to tell you the good news."

"Yeah, that's great news."

"I'll talk to you later."

"Enjoy the rest of your day," Sherry says.

"You too."

Rich starts smiling on the inside. After hanging up, he starts thinking about his boys.

Gerard and Vaughn have a half day today and are walking home from school.

Vaughn says, "I had a dream about Mommy last night. When I get home, I'm calling Grandma Veronica."

Gerard asks, "Did it scare you?"

"No, I just want Nana to tell me what it means."

"You're always having dreams or saying something weird."

They walk the rest of the way in silence. Upon entry into the apartment, Vaughn immediately throws down his bookbag, picks up the phone, and calls his grandmother. She answers on the second ring.

"Hi, Grandma."

"Hi, Vaughn. How's it going?"

With excitement, Vaughn says, "I had a dream about Mommy last night."

"Yeah, tell me about it. Was it a good dream?"

"Yes, it left me with a good feeling."

"Great, so tell me about it."

Vaughn can't wait to get it out. Anxiously he begins, "She was on a ship, dressed in white, waving goodbye. I was on land. Suddenly, the skies turned black, the seas got rough, and the rain started to pour. The entire time she just stood on the ship's deck, waving at me until it pulled out of port. I just stood there watching her until I couldn't see her anymore. Then I woke up."

With rising excitement in her voice, Veronica says, "Hallelujah. This dream symbolizes your mother's love for you. It means she will be by your side through every problem and difficulty in life. It's not a bad dream. You should feel happy about it. Your mother will be like your guardian angel. Don't you get it?'

"Yes," Vaughn asserts with a smile.

As an afterthought, Veronica says, "I have a necklace with a metallic angel with the words 'He shall give his angels charge over thee' written on it. I found it in your mother's belongings. Remember to wear it at all times. I meant to give it to you before you left. You always reminded me of your mother. You have wisdom beyond the eyes."

"What does that mean?"

"You know things without knowing how you know; God gave you a special power, like a superhero."

"Okay, Grandma. I feel special now."

"You should. I will be sending the necklace right away. You should get it in a few days. Now, where's Gerard?"

"In the bathroom."

"Okay, don't disturb him."

"Vaughn, Grandma has to go. Tell Gerard I love him and to take care."

"Okay, I will, Nana."

In the meantime, Gerard has taken the matches out of his bookbag. One by one, he lights them and watches them burn. He is fascinated by the heat, color, shape, and size of the flame. The flame quickly consumes the toilet paper, leaving it as a pile of ash on the bathroom floor. He feels something inside he can't explain, which excites him.

His adventure is interrupted by the sound of his father entering the apartment. Quickly, he puts the matches away and flushes the ashes down the toilet.

In the living room, Rich says to Vaughn, "I hope you're not in here watching TV without having done your homework or finished your chores."

Vaughn immediately turns off the TV and rushes down the hall to his bedroom.

As Gerard comes out of the bathroom, Rich asks, "How'd your day go?"

"It was fine."

"That reminds me, I never followed up with Mr. Stevens about your meeting."

Rich then goes into the kitchen to start an early dinner. Afterward, they settle in the living room to watch TV. A few hours later, Rich and the boys head to bed. Rich is tired but does not forget to perform his nightly ritual. Gerard stares at the flame shining under the door. He stays up for hours, hypnotized by its light.

In the morning, Rich's mind wanders back to his childhood. Who would have thought a boy from the country who lived in the basement of a church, wore second-hand clothes, and shoes with holes in them would one day become a New York City police investigator.

He says to himself, "No more parade patrol, fare beating, or traffic duties for me."

The real heart of police work is here.

At the stationhouse, he gets to work, immediately seeking out DT Rodriguez. He's not the man Rich remembered. Instead, he's a tall, stocky man with olive skin and medium-length, wavy, black hair. Well-groomed and clean-shaven, he has on dark brown khakis and a beige polo shirt. Rich greets him with a warm smile and a firm handshake.

Rodriguez says, "Just call me, Bruce." He reminds him they'll get started after roll call.

At about this time, Rich gets a call from Captain Kuntz, reminding him about this weekend.

"I'm with you," he says, hanging up abruptly. Once roll call is over, they head to an unmarked police car. Bruce says they have an investigation in the neighborhood and want Rich to begin covert surveillance of the subject.

In the car, Bruce refers to the subject as Doug. He's under general community policing surveillance for possibly being a child molester.

Bruce says, "We have no evidence that he is one; however, we've integrated him into a network of neighbors, coworkers, family, and friends who are all working with us. If he meets individuals who are not actively participating in the investigation, then we start preliminary investigations of them also."

"How do you co-opt family members to work with you on an investigation?"

"We approach the entire family and tell them the subject is being put under surveillance by the police; they have to participate. It's the law. If they refuse or tell the subject, they go to jail; it's mandatory. There's some resistance in the beginning, but over time they typically cooperate."

"Do you tell the family what he's being investigated for?"

"Not initially, but we will if the investigation gets to a certain level."

Bruce drops Rich off at a bodega referred to as "base camp." The undercover detectives meet in the basement, which they refer to as the "war room." Bruce introduces him as "Rich the newbie," then introduces him to everyone on the team; Gary, Tom, Vincent, Whitney, and Logan. Looking at the video monitors on the wall, Rich sees they have about ten spy cams and several listening devices set up in Doug's apartment. Throughout the day, the investigators orient him to their different investigative protocols. They put drugs in Doug's food, monitor his phone calls, use keys to enter his apartment, and put GPS locators in his clothes and personal items.

On this day, Doug doesn't go to work. He answers a few phone calls, makes a run to Starbucks, fixes something to eat, reads for a while, watches a little TV, and sleeps on and off all day.

Rich thinks, *If this is how my days are gonna be, I might as well have stayed where I was, having this boring-ass motherfucker to watch.* Laughing to himself, he says, "It's a living."

When Rich gets off work around 6:30 p.m., he immediately calls Sherry.

When she picks up, he says, "Hi. How you doing?

"I'm all right."

"By the way, how was your first day on the job?"

"Boring as hell; the guy I'm investigating sleeps a lot."

"Where're you working?"

"In the Kingsbridge Heights section of the Bronx."

"Oh, I've worked out of that precinct before, but as you know I'm floating now. It's annoying to not have a homebase, but on the flip side, I meet quite a few people and experience working on the force from many different angles. Who're you investigating?"

"This African-American guy named Doug is under surveil-lance for the possibility of being a child molester."

"Oh, they just have an allegation that he might be one."

"Yes."

Rich remarks, "I had no idea they co-opt family members into investigating their own relatives."

"Man, they do more than that, much more than that. They murder people! That's right; I said murder! Usually, it's some child molester or another degenerate who gets thrown out the window, attacked by dogs, or run over by a car."

"What?"

"Believe me! It's true."

"Wow, that's deep."

"Yep, it's true, but I'm glad your first day went well. How about this weekend? Can I see you?"

"Nah, this weekend is going to be busy."

"It's been a while."

"Yeah, I know, but we talk a couple times a day, every day."

"I realize that, but talking isn't enough; I want to see you in person."

Rich remains firm. "I feel you on that, but this weekend is still not a good time."

"I also want to celebrate your promotion."

"I appreciate that, but I don't have the time."

"Since I can't see you this weekend, I'm still glad you learned some new things on your first day as an investigator. Welcome to my world. All right, talk to you later."

"Okay, enjoy the rest of your evening."

On his way home, Rich returns to the botanica. He speaks with the same lady.

"I burned the black candle, but nothing happened."

"Can you get some of their personal belongings, like a pen or a comb? Something they won't miss?"

"Yeah, I can do that."

"Okay, then burn another black candle. This time bury the items with the candle and parchment."

Rich buys another candle then continues on his journey home.

Upon entry into the apartment, Rich announces, "You guys spend so much time in front of the TV. I'm making a new rule: no more TV on the weekend."

Gerard's face takes on a sad look, and his voice goes up slightly as he pleads, "Some of my favorite shows are on the weekend."

"You'll have to find some other ways to entertain yourselves. What's wrong with playing outside? Most kids your age love to go outside."

"Nothing. I do too, but I also like watching TV and playing video games."

"Too much TV is not good for either of you, anyway."

Gerard is disappointed and starts to pout. Vaughn is quiet and says nothing.

Sensing the boys might be hungry, Rich asks, "Anybody want McDonald's?"

With excitement in their voices, both boys exclaim, "Yeah!"

"We can treat ourselves. We'll leave in a minute, but I have to make a call first."

They get to McDonald's, and the boys run to the counter and order. As they retrieve their trays, a man walks over. Rich hands him a bag, and they part ways quickly. The man looks at Gerard and Vaughn then leaves in a hurry.

Once home Rich tells Vaughn, "Oh, by the way, I received a package for you from your grandmother this evening."

"She told me she was going to send me something."

"Okay, here it is."

Vaughn hurriedly opens the package and pulls out a silver necklace with an angel attached to it. The words "He shall give his angels charge over thee" are written on the wings. Vaughn takes the chain into his room. He asks his brother to latch it in the back, happy he has something belonging to his mother. The boys watch TV for the rest of the evening. On their way to bed, Rich reminds them, "Remember, no TV this weekend."

* * *

In the morning, without television, the boys feel lost.

Gerard goes to his dad and says, "We have nothing to do."

Rich reminds him, "You can go outside and play, read, or study. You like books, take one out and read it."

"But not this early in the morning. Can Vaughn and I take out our bikes instead?"

"Yeah, just don't leave the block."

The boys leave for an early morning bike ride. Once gone, Rich makes a phone call.

After a couple of hours, Gerard comes upstairs.

"Where's your brother?"

"Oh, he was behind me. He'll be coming up soon."

Vaughn comes through the door after a few minutes, saying proudly, "I got a dollar."

Rich asks, "Where did you get that from?"

"A man kissed me and gave me a dollar when I was getting into the elevator."

"Kissed you and gave you a dollar." Rich repeats loudly. "When did this happen?"

"Just now."

Gerard stands in silence, not knowing why he can't speak, unsure of what he's feeling or how to react.

Rich tells Vaughn, "Show me where this happened."

They go down to the first floor. Vaughn points to where it happened, repeating the words, "He just bent down, kissed me on the lips, and gave me a dollar."

"What did he look like?"

"He was white, with a lot of hair, tall, dressed in black, with a hat and dark sunglasses."

Rich takes Vaughn upstairs, saying, "I have to teach you boys to be more aware of strangers."

Gerard goes straight to the bathroom. He lights a match and watches it burn. Feeling excitement at seeing it consumed by fire, he's in somewhat of a trance when the phone rings.

Rich picks up.

"Hey, Sherry, how's it going?"

"I'm okay. Just checking in. How's everything?"

"Everything is fine; Gerard and Vaughn just came in from riding their bikes. I told them no more TV on the weekend; I want them to go outside."

"Yeah, that sounds like a great idea. Kids nowadays spend too much time in front of the TV."

"I was even thinking about cutting down on their TV time during the week."

"I'm sure that wouldn't go over well."

Rich says, "If I decide it's what I want them to do, they'll have no choice but to get used to it. How've you been otherwise?"

"I'm okay. Just a little morning sickness now and then, but other than that, I'm fine."

"That's good. Bruce wants me to work tomorrow."

"That's a bummer."

"It's double-time."

"That's sweet."

"I'm going to need a babysitter tomorrow."

"I can sit with the boys while you're at work."

"Yeah, that would be a blessing."

"Sure, no problem. See you at eight tomorrow."

"That's fine."

"Okay, bye. Enjoy the rest of your day."

Rich goes into his bedroom to rest. After a while, Gerard goes into the bedroom to play with his brother. He takes out a game of checkers, and the boys play in silence. Before long, Gerard goes back into the bathroom.

* * *

An hour later, Rich wakes up coughing and choking; he immediately recognizes the smell of smoke inside the apartment. He rushes out of his bedroom. It appears to be coming from the bathroom. Gerard and Vaughn are busy dousing the flames as Rich runs in. He grabs both boys and yanks them into the hallway.

Looking at the matches, burnt toilet tissue, and water all over the floor, Rich yells, "How'd this happen?"

"Gerard was playing with matches."

Rich immediately slaps Gerard across the face.

At the top of his lungs, Rich yells, "Why were you playing with matches?"

Scared of his father's anger, Gerard says, "I don't know."

Turning to Vaughn, Rich asks, "How long did you know this was going on?"

"I didn't know. I just smelled the smoke and came into the bathroom."

"Oh, so you had no idea Gerard was playing with matches!"

"No."

"Why didn't you come get me?"

"We tried to put it out ourselves."

Rich yells, "You could have burned us all up!"

Furious, Rich rushes into his room and grabs a belt, proceeding to beat both boys severely. After a while, Rich's arms grow tired, and the blows become softer; eventually, he stops.

The boys go to their room, hurt and sad. Still upset, Rich calls Sherry.

"What's up?"

"You'll never believe what happened!"

"What?"

"Gerard was playing with matches and started a fire in the bathroom."

Sherry's voice rises. "What? I can't believe it!"

"Yes, the smoke woke me up."

"I'm so sorry about the fire. How bad was it?"

"It was bad enough to wake me. There was some smoke, burnt toilet tissue, matches, and water all over the bathroom floor. I'm glad the shower curtain didn't catch on fire. Then we would have had a real disaster on our hands. I beat Gerard's ass good. I don't think he'll be playing with that shit anymore!"

"Yeah, he could've burned you all up and set the building on fire."

Still seething with anger, Rich says, "I tell you those kids are too much."

"Yeah, that's too much."

"I wore both their little asses out."

"Why'd you beat Vaughn?"

"For not waking me up first. They tried to put it out themselves."

"What're they doing now?"

"I don't know, but I know one thing: I better not hear any noise coming out of that room."

"Wow, I see you're still angry. Honestly, I would be too."

"I need to calm down."

"Yes, you do. Sorry about what happened, but I've got an appointment at two; I'm still seeing you in the morning at eight."

"Yes, definitely."

"All right, take care."

"You too."

Still fuming, Rich yells, "If I hear a peep out of you two, I'm gonna give you something else to cry about!"

Rich makes a call and says, "Meet me at my door in fifteen minutes."

After Kuntz arrives, he hands Rich the bag through his car window. Looking inside, Rich sees the dark glasses, false beard, and hat. Snatching the sack, he takes it upstairs and puts it in the bottom of his closet.

Alone in their bedroom, the boys don't talk about downstairs, the fire, or the beating. Vaughn pulls out the necklace from his grandmother and retraces the words: "He shall give his angels charge over thee."

Stuck in their room, the boys eventually fall asleep.

After a while, Rich starts fixing dinner. Smelling the food, Gerard wakes up and goes into the kitchen to tell his father he's ready to eat.

"You and Vaughn aren't getting any dinner tonight; that's your punishment."

Rubbing his stomach, Gerard whines, "But I'm hungry."

Rich turns to grimace at Gerard. "Didn't you hear what I said? Don't let me repeat it."

Gerard walks back into his bedroom with his head down, pouting, and his arms folded over his chest. His stomach is growling and empty; he has a fitful night's sleep without food.

Rich is awakened by the phone the following day. The familiar sound of Sherry's voice gives him comfort.

"I thought I'd give you a call as soon as I got up. How're you feeling?"

"I'm still annoyed, but I've calmed down a lot."

"Are the boys awake?"

"No. I'm just waking up myself."

Sherry says, "I'm about to take a shower and make breakfast. I should be there by eight."

"Good, it's going to take me about forty-five minutes to get to the Bronx. I need to be in place by nine. I'll wake the boys now.

"All right, I'll see you in a few."

Rich knocks on Gerard and Vaughn's door, shouting loudly, "Get up! Sherry's on her way."

The boys, startled by their father's voice, wake up with a start. After washing up and putting on their clothes, they enter the kitchen, ready for breakfast.

After five minutes at the table, Sherry rings the doorbell.

She enters the apartment with a warm smile and bright eyes. "Good morning."

"I'll be ready in a few minutes," Rich says.

Sensing their father is still upset, the boys wash the dishes and clean up the kitchen without being asked.

Grabbing his coat on the way out, Rich yells, "*Behave*, and don't let Sherry tell me either one of you was acting up."

Trying to forget the drama of yesterday, Rich gets in his car and thinks about Doug. He'll log into the system and read up on his new assignment. The guys on the team say Doug doesn't socialize much in the neighborhood. He primarily goes to and from work and school.

Arriving at the stationhouse, Rich walks past his supervisor, Captain Kuntz. Without speaking, they exchange furtive glances. Rich immediately goes to his computer and logs in. The first thing that surprises him about Doug is the length of time he's been under surveillance. His father first put him on the police's radar for participating in a burglary of the family home and for inappropriate contact with his sister at the age of eight. The investigation was unsubstantiated. Rich says to himself, "I didn't even know they investigated children that young."

According to his family profile, his mother died of breast cancer three years ago. His father is a retired NYPD sergeant. They were divorced. His older brother Jamel is getting his doctorate at Harvard. Marima, his sister, is currently working for Verizon as a software engineer. She has a history of drug abuse. As a family, they're not very close, and there's a history of abuse, neglect, and violence.

The investigative reports state that Doug is homosexual and lives with a mental health diagnosis of generalized anxiety disorder with mild depression. He's currently seeing a psychologist and is on medication for this condition. His psychological profile lists him as intelligent with a high level of integrity.

Neighbors describe him as friendly and quiet. Two of his friends, Darryl and Ryan, have installed audio/video surveillance equipment in his apartment and on his phone. Two members of his friend circle are actively spying on him. His coworkers call him "Smiley" and state he has a good work ethic—conscientious and hardworking.

After spending a couple of hours reading the investigative reports, Rich decides to call Sherry and check on the boys.

"You're going to live a long time. I was just getting ready to call you."

"What's going on?"

"Ahh, nothing. The boys are in their room, and I'm in the living room, watching TV."

"How've they been behaving?"

"Oh, they're fine. How's your workday going?"

"It's fine. I'm actually at the stationhouse, doing some background research before I go up the hill."

"Oh, I certainly know about that."

Rich says, "Sherry, this guy we're investigating has been on the police's radar since the age of eight. He's now twenty-seven. Why would they investigate someone for that long?"

Sherry says, "A lot of times, when they close an investigation as unfounded, they still put you under what's called general community surveillance. They always keep one eye on you. I've seen some people investigated their entire life."

"Oh, wow, that's deep."

"Yeah, these investigations are no joke or anything to be played with or taken lightly."

"In any event, I was just checking in. I have to go up the hill now. Enjoy the rest of your day and remind those boys no misbehaving. I'm still pissed about what happened yesterday."

"They'll be all right. Okay, bye."

Rich hangs up. After logging off the computer, he goes to the bathroom then leaves for base camp.

Doug resides on the third floor of a seven-story apartment building that sits at the top of a long, winding hill in the Bronx's northwest corner. His is a small L-shaped studio with parquet floors, white walls, and one big, three-paned window. The team assumes he will eat and read at his favorite hangout, Starbucks, this morning. Sensing Doug is about to leave, the base camp team calls over to the super of Doug's building, Sal. He's a bad-tempered, ugly, middle-aged man who nobody likes working with but who they all must deal with in order to do their job. Sal monitors Doug on the computer in the first-floor utility room. Everyone gets in place—neighbors, shopkeepers, and social acquaintances on the street. No one says anything, but they all keep one eye on Doug as he walks down the hill. After about two hours away, Doug returns, turns on the TV, and eventually falls asleep.

Typically, Doug doesn't do much on Sunday. However, today he picks up the phone and calls a friend.

"Hey, Ron, want to go to Unity Fellowship Church this afternoon?"

"Yeah, sure. I haven't been there in a minute; what time does service start?"

"I think around twelve."

"Nothing better to do."

"We'll be late, but that's okay," says Doug. "Call Sidney and see if he wants to go also."

"I will."

Going over the game plan, Doug says, "Okay, we can meet at twelve-thirty at the 168th Street train station near the token booth."

"That's fine. I'll hurry," says Ron.

"Okay, see you in a few."

Doug hangs up and immediately gets in the shower. He then goes to his closet to pick out an outfit. Once dressed, he leaves quickly. The "neighborhood spy network" is already in place. Doug stops in the bodega across the street to get something to drink. They secretly watch him as he walks down the hill. Ron calls Bruce to confirm he's meeting up with Doug.

After a ten-minute ride on the 1 train, Doug takes the elevator to the downtown A train platform.

Five minutes later, Ron arrives.

Doug asks, "Sidney couldn't make it?"

"No, he said he was tired and didn't feel like going."

Doug has known Ron for approximately seven years. Ron has worked for a downtown accounting firm for the past three years. He's also a classically trained violinist who aspires to get his PhD in music composition.

During the ride into Brooklyn, Ron tries to get as much information out of Doug as possible.

"How's work going?"

This question releases a pressure valve. Doug starts to complain bitterly about a recent occurrence with his supervisor.

Recounting the incident, Doug says, "One day, that bitch told me between Italy and Africa I'll never get any work done around here. You believe that shit. Racist fucking bitch said that to me."

Doug then starts to grumble about his performance review, shitty salary, lack of a promotion, and being given work below his level of ability.

"Welcome to my world," Ron says.

"Working there is giving me the motivation to strive harder in school. I want to leave that fucking cesspool one day."

"You'll be able to one day. Don't worry," Ron says reassuringly.

"How's your family?" Ron asks.

Doug's eyes glaze over as his expression suddenly turns pensive.

Ron remarks, "You look sad; what's wrong?"

"Just thinking about my mother. You know I miss her a lot."

"Yes, I remember you and your mother were very close."

"Yeah, man. I miss her and think about her all the time." Doug then says, "My brother and sister are doing well," and sucking his teeth, he says, "My father is still the asshole he always was."

By this time, they're close to Unity and will be changing to the local any minute now.

"That's enough about me," Doug says. "How about you, Ron?"

"Nothing much going on; just trying to make it day by day."

At about this time, their train pulls into Liberty Avenue, where they exit and meet other worshippers headed in the same direction.

Upon arrival at church, Doug looks at his watch and realizes Bishop Cooper must be more than halfway through his sermon. In the bulletin, it states his text comes from John 14:27: "Peace I leave with you; my peace I give to you; not as the world gives do I give to you. Do not let your heart be troubled, nor let it be fearful." Doug listens intently for this week's theme.

Bishop Cooper makes it plain by saying, "Everyone must deal with their health; mental health is as important as physical health. I don't care how normal you think you are; everyone must live with an awareness of their mental health. It's just that some people's mental health is closer to one, and others are closer to ten, and that changes daily if not hourly, but we all must live with an awareness of our mental health."

Bishop goes on to say, "In Romans 8:18, the Word says, 'For I consider that the sufferings of this present time are not worthy to be compared with the glory that is to be revealed to us.' God gives a troubled mind comfort, even in the darkest of hours. We can always seek refuge and find relief in him and his Word." Bishop Cooper next cites John 14:1: "Let not your heart be troubled: ye believe in God, believe also in me."

Bishop Cooper stays on this topic: "Do not be afraid; find peace, renewing strength and comfort in the Lord." Then returning to his central theme, he says, "The two are not mutually exclusive; you can believe in God and also believe in your doctor. Jesus walked with a physician, Luke, and doctors are God's miracle workers on earth. The knowledge and skill they possess is a spiritual gift, not from man but from God." In closing, he says, "Take care, beloved, and that means mind, body, and soul. There is no crime in seeking help for yourself. But it is a crime to let pride and ignorance get in the way of finding the supports you need to live a better, healthier, and happier life." The bishop then instructs the congregation to, "give the Lord a hand praise," as the congregational offering starts.

Doug turns to smile at Ron, saying, "Bishop preached."

The church must have agreed, as thunderous applause echoed throughout the sanctuary.

After they leave, Ron asks, "Wanna go to dinner? I'm a little hungry."

"Sure, let's go."

Doug remembers a local restaurant where the food was excellent, and they made the best chopped barbecue this side of the Carolinas.

Walking to the restaurant, Doug says, "I so enjoyed Bishop's sermon. I'm glad he used scriptural references to discuss mental health. It spoke to me. People used to say all you needed was prayer, reading your Bible, and getting close to God to heal your mind. Sometimes it takes more than that."

"I agree," Ron says.

After a while, they come upon the small, unremarkable "greasy spoon" located on the corner of Atlantic and Saratoga. It's called the North Carolina Country Kitchen. The C in Carolina and the K in Kitchen are below the other letters and look like they're about to fall. Doug guesses the restaurant can only seat about twenty-five. The steam from the trays obscures the view of the freshly made and succulent food. The smells overwhelm Ron and Doug's taste buds as they patiently wait to be served. The workers seem to be moving at a fair pace; however, it takes about twenty minutes to place their orders.

Shortly after taking a seat, Ron says, "I know I asked about your job and family, but I didn't ask how you're doing, Doug."

"I see Dr. Ehnis tomorrow. I'm looking forward to our appointment. I have some things I want to discuss with him. I trust you like a brother, Ron, and being honest. I'm having some terrifying thoughts about my father. I feel my hatred for him is getting worse. It's getting to the point where it's about to boil up and over in a big way."

Ron's ears perk up. "What do you mean? Why now? What's going on?"

"You just don't understand how wicked that man is."

Doug stops eating and averts his eyes as he begins to speak, "To be honest, I've been planning on killing my father."

Doug lifts his shirt and shows Ron the handle of a knife tucked into his waistband.

"When did you get that?"

"I purchased it last week. I plan to see him next week at a family gathering. That's when I was going to walk up to him and stab him in the chest."

"Are you serious?"

Doug replies sarcastically, "You see the knife, don't you?"

"Remember, 'God is love, and love is for everyone,'" Ron says.

"I don't care. It's been on my mind for a while. You just don't understand how much I hate that man."

"C'mon, speak to Dr. Ehnis about it. Are you still taking your meds?"

Annoyed, Doug replies, "Yes, and I intend to speak with Dr. Ehnis about it, but I don't think he can dissuade me."

"Okay, if that's how you feel. That's how you feel. However, I do hope you reconsider."

Ron searches Doug's face for a few seconds, intently noticing his resolve and look of certainty. They don't say much to each other as they continue to eat. Doug seems to be intensely focusing on his thoughts, and Ron doesn't know what to say. So they finish their meals in relative silence.

As they start walking to the subway, Ron remarks, "I have to come back here. They can really burn."

Doug is mentally absent and distracted. Ron notices the change in Doug's attention, and when they depart, all he can think about is calling the stationhouse.

Once they part ways, the first thing Ron does is call his supervisor.

Bruce picks up immediately.

"Hey, how's it going, Ron?"

"You'll never believe what Doug told me."

Bruce eagerly asks, "What?"

"Doug is planning on killing his father."

"What?"

"He just said his father is wicked, and he plans to stab him at the next family gathering."

"Wow, that's serious. When is this gathering?"

"Next week."

"So he plans on doing it soon. Did he say why?"

"No, just that his father is evil."

Bruce says, "Well, he's said that before."

"Yeah, I know."

"Is he still taking his meds?"

"Yes, and he's going to see Dr. Ehnis tomorrow."

"That's good."

"If he's serious, we'll have to bump up his level of surveillance and change the investigative protocols."

"Yeah, I know."

"How was he otherwise?"

"Oh, he was fine. We went to church and then got something to eat. Once we started eating, he began talking about how much he hated his father. He showed me the knife he was carrying around to kill him with; I was genuinely shocked."

"I'm glad you told me. That's very serious. I have to call up to base camp to tell them to keep an extra eye on him."

"Thanks, Ron. Talk with you soon."

"All right, Bruce."

Everyone gathers around the phone when they see Bruce's number.

Bruce says, "Keep an extra eye on Doug; we've got some information he's planning to stab his father."

Gary asks, "What's the backstory? We noticed he's been carrying a knife around for the past week but assumed it was for his protection."

"No, he told Ron he's going to stab his father at a family gathering."

Logan says, "That's serious; we'll keep an extra eye on him,"

Bruce says, "Remember, keep me in the loop if you see or hear anything of note."

"Will do," Whitney says.

"All right, talk with you later."

Tom says, "Okay, bye."

Meanwhile, Sherry has been in the living room watching TV most of the day. She notices the boys have been quiet for too long. She knocks on the door before entering their bedroom. Vaughn is assembling a puzzle while Gerard is reading a book. Gerard is the first to ask, "Can I touch the baby?"

"Sure, be very gentle."

Gerard puts his hand on her stomach and gasps with delight as the baby moves. Vaughn has jumped up from the floor by now, asking, "Can I touch it?"

"Of course, you can. Just be gentle; touch it as your brother did."

Vaughn softly places his hand on her abdomen.

Leaving it there for a couple of minutes, he asks, "Why did you give Dad those pills to hurt Mommy?"

Sherry is barely able to contain her shock. Her voice and hands start to tremble. The baby doesn't move. Sherry's eyes grow wide, and the tension in her voice rises.

"What're you saying? I didn't give your father any pills to hurt your mother."

Vaughn doesn't respond. He just keeps his hand on her abdomen.

"That's enough touching," Sherry says anxiously.

Still perplexed, and in a slight daze, she asks, "What do you boys want to eat?"

Vaughn says, "A ham and cheese sandwich."

Gerard says, "Pizza."

"I'll make dinner in a couple of hours."

Sherry exits their bedroom and goes back to the couch, trying hard to forget what Vaughn asked. Once Sherry is gone, Gerard questions Vaughn: "Why did you ask Sherry if she gave Dad some pills to hurt Mommy?"

Vaughn replies, "Mommy told me she did."

"When did Mommy say this?"

"Now. She whispered it in my ear."

Gerard rolls his eyes and says, "You know our mother is dead, don't you? You're always saying something crazy or weird."

"But I know what I heard," Vaughn repeats.

With exasperation in his voice, Gerard gives up, saying, "Okay, Vaughn, whatever you say. Go finish your puzzle."

The boys stop discussing the incident, and Gerard continues reading his book.

Later that night, when Rich arrives home, the house is quiet, and everyone is asleep. He tiptoes into his bedroom and quickly gets ready for bed.

"What a weekend," he says to himself as his head hits the pillow.

Sherry gets up in the middle of the night and leaves for her apartment.

The following day Rich is still tired from yesterday's shift but drags himself to the shower. Once the hot water hits him, he slowly starts to come alive. After a few minutes of letting the water cascade down his body, Rich reaches for his washcloth and soap. While lathering up, he hears the door close as the boys exit the apartment. Jumping out of the shower, he puts on his clothes, grabs a breakfast treat, and heads back up to the Bronx.

Doug doesn't go to work today. He'll have just enough time to make his Starbucks run before hopping on the subway for the long ride into Brooklyn. He's been seeing Dr. Ehnis, a psychologist, for approximately five years. Located in Prospect Heights on a quiet, tree-lined street full of potholes and old brownstones, Dr. Ehnis is a tall, white man with a slight paunch and thinning black hair styled in a comb-over. He wears glasses neatly placed on his face. His manner is serious and thoughtful.

Doug waits for ten minutes before entering Dr. Ehnis' office. After some routine pleasantries, the session begins.

"I've had something on my mind for the past couple of weeks," Doug says.

Dr. Ehnis asks, "What?"

"I've been carrying around this knife because I want to kill someone."

Doug lifts his shirt to show the doctor the knife's handle in his waistband.

With apprehension in his voice, Dr. Ehnis asks, "Who?"

Without hesitation, Doug says, "My father."

Dr. Ehnis says, "You've talked a lot about your father being mean to you. You also described hating him intensely when you were growing up, but I didn't know it rose to this level, to the point where you want to kill him."

"I've been thinking about it for a long time. I've finally gotten up the courage to do it. We have a family gathering soon. That's when I plan to stab him."

"Why now? What's going on?"

"My father is a lot worse than I told you. There are things he did that I haven't mentioned here. He's just a straight-ass nasty and wicked man."

"What did he do?"

At this time, Dr. Ehnis notices a distinct change in Doug. He shrinks back in his chair, tears well up in his eyes, and he looks at the floor. His face muscles become tense and drawn.

"I've been thinking about my sister's drug abuse. We became closer after she got into rehab. She shared a few disturbing things about him with me."

"Let's talk about it."

Doug starts to wring his hands nervously, fidgeting with each finger.

"My father molested my sister, and I just feel pure rage whenever I think of him."

"That's a normal reaction."

"If I have to spend the rest of my life in prison for taking off his cloak and revealing who he is, then so be it."

"So, you're not afraid of the consequences?"

"No! I don't care. I know what I must do!"

Dr. Ehnis tries to dissuade him.

"I wish you'd change your mind, my responsibility is to help you hear what you're saying. It's up to you to choose the path you want to take."

"Exactly. I know this; my mind is already made up."

"That being the case. I think that's the wrong choice, but if that's how you feel, that's how you feel. What else is going on?

"Nothing much, except the anger I feel toward my father."

"Well, on that note it's about time for us to close; however, I have one more thing I need to mention. I will be moving to Michigan soon, so this will be our last session. I'm sorry for the short notice. I have thought about a good referral for you; her name is Judy Sonnovia. Here is her card. She works out of the Bronx. Every therapist has their own style, but I know her to be competent and compassionate, and I think she'll be a good fit for you.

"All right"

"There's nothing more you want to talk about?"

"No"

"It's been a pleasure working with you, and I hope it works out with Ms. Sonnovia."

"Okay, thanks, Dr. Ehnis."

"All right. Bye, Doug."

Ten minutes after Doug leaves, Dr. Ehnis doesn't hesitate to call Investigator Bruce.

"Hi Bruce."

"Hello, Dr. Ehnis."

"I have some alarming news to report."

"What?"

"Doug is planning on killing his father at a family gathering soon."

"We heard similar information from another source on the case. This means we're going to have to bump up this investigation."

"He also said his father sexually abused his sister."

"Do you think those are credible allegations?"

"I don't know, but he seemed sincere, and I know him to be an honest person. I know his father is a retired NYPD sergeant."

"What's his name?"

"Robert Jordan."

"I'll start looking into him right away. Glad you told us."

"No problem."

"Bye"

"All right, take care."

* * *

Rich is at base camp when the call from Bruce comes in.

"We have corroborated some information from one of our other agents. Doug is planning to murder his father. We're going to have to increase his level of surveillance, which means we're going to use more potent drugs and increase the level of surveillance within his work, neighborhood, family, and friend networks."

"When will this start?" the team asks.

Bruce says, "Right away."

"We want you folks to watch for any changes in his behavior."

Before hanging up, Logan says, "Thanks for the update."

Afterward, the first thing Rich does is call Sherry.

"Hey, Sherry."

"What's going on?"

"They're going to bump up the level of our subject's surveillance."

"I've seen that happen a couple of times. The subject usually becomes very paranoid."

"Really!"

"Yes, they start letting everyone in the investigation—and I mean family, friends, coworkers, and neighbors, everyone—listen to their phone calls, tell them what they're being investigated for, watch private videos of them in their home, read all the investigative reports, begin to use more powerful drugs, and follow them everywhere—and I do mean everywhere."

"Bruce told us a little about it."

"Why did they do it?"

"He plans on murdering his father."

"Wow. It's starting to get real up there."

"Yeah, I know."

"Good luck with everything; you wanted to be in investigations."

"Yes, this is what I asked for."

"On another note, how're your boys?"

"Oh, they're fine."

"By the way, Rich, something happened with Vaughn over the weekend; I tried to push it out of my mind, but I can't."

"What?"

"I was letting the boys touch my stomach to see if they could feel the baby move. When it was Vaughn's turn, he put his hand on my abdomen and asked, 'Why did you give my father those pills to hurt my mother?'"

Rich is speechless for a moment, stunned into silence.

After a couple of minutes, he says, "That boy is always saying something crazy."

"So, you don't think he saw or knows anything?"

"No, he's too young to understand. Who knows what might come out of Vaughn's mouth."

"I was going to have him put in special ed; I think something is wrong with him; if I were you, I wouldn't worry about it."

"It just shocked me when he said it."

"Don't pay Vaughn any mind."

"If you say so, I thought Vaughn might know something, to say something that specific."

Rich tries to cover up his unease.

"No. I wouldn't put too much stock in what comes out of that boy's mouth."

"All right, if you say so..."

Wanting to get off the phone and collect his thoughts, Rich says, "Wow, we've been on this phone for a minute. Gotta run; something just came up. We'll talk later."

"Okay, enjoy the rest of your day."

"You too."

After hanging up, Rich thinks about his next move. He thinks to himself, *The black candle and drugs didn't work. I'll call his counselor to see if I can have him placed in special ed; I need to speak to him anyway.*

Rich dials the school immediately.

"Hello. May I speak to Mr. Stevens?"

"This is he."

"This is Vaughn and Gerard Wilson's father."

"Oh, I remember your two sons; how may I help you?"

"This is a sensitive topic, but I don't know how to say it without saying it bluntly; I think Vaughn needs to be put in special education."

Mr. Stevens is taken aback, surprised at the request's boldness and directness.

"I remember your son; he had the altercation in Ms. McRae's room. After that, I looked into his school records. He's only seven years old and is doing very well academically. I know he assaulted another student, but that was probably due to mis-placed anger over the loss of his mother. To be quite honest, I'm a little shocked. Most parents fight to keep their children out of special ed."

Rich says, "I think he has a problem. He gets into frequent fights with his brother, the kids in the neighborhood don't like him, and I have to spend so much time going over his homework with him."

"Hmm, this is interesting, particularly because he does so well at school, academically and socially. However, those facts alone are not enough to put him in a special placement."

Rich repeats, "I know you're the professional. I respect your opinion, but I want Vaughn to get the help he needs as soon as possible."

"I appreciate that and will consider it, but I don't think you need to be concerned at this time."

"I know I have to accept your decision, but I want you to know I don't agree with it."

Mr. Stevens pauses before saying, "Well, that is your choice, but I don't think Vaughn needs to be put in a special placement at this time. On another note, the conflict resolution session went well. I had the two boys meet in my office to discuss the incident with the blocks. Vaughn apologized, they shook hands, then they signed a Peace Contract."

Uninterested, Rich asks, "How did your session with Gerard go?"

"It went well. There were no issues."

"That's good. At least I don't have to worry about that one."

"Yeah," Mr. Stevens says, "both your kids will be all right. Vaughn just got a little angry and lashed out, but he'll be fine."

"Yes, I hope so. Well, that's all I wanted to discuss. I must get back to work."

"Okay, Mr. Wilson. Thanks for the call. Enjoy the rest of your day."

"Okay, bye."

By this time, Doug has come home. After settling in and making something to eat, Doug pours himself some lemonade. Within the hour, he's at the bodega, buying a white candle. He starts walking around his apartment in circles with the burning white candle, mumbling, "God will protect me. He shall give his angels charge over thee."

Agitated, he sits on a chair in the living room. Suddenly jumping up, he says, "Oh shit! I'm under investigation."

The investigators at base camp listen intently, stunned by what they heard. They wait for him to repeat it. A few minutes later, he repeats it, saying again, "Oh shit! I'm really under investigation."

The team calls Bruce.

Putting him on speaker, they huddle around the phone. When Bruce picks up, Tom says, "You'll never believe what just happened?"

"What?"

Tom says, "Doug came home, ate dinner, had something to drink, came over here to buy a white candle, and started walking around his apartment with the candle saying, 'God will protect me. He shall give his angels charge over thee.' After doing that for about fifteen minutes, he sat down and said, 'Oh shit, I'm under investigation.'"

"You must be kidding me," Bruce says.

Whitney says, "No, we're not joking! He said it twice."

"This is serious. Who has Doug been in contact with?"

Gary says, "The last people he met with were Ron and Dr. Ehnis."

Annoyed, Bruce says, "Someone must have told him something. When he leaves his apartment, I'll get some more agents in there to look for something we might have overlooked, like an extra phone or something."

"By the way, what are those new drugs supposed to do?" Rich asks.

"They do a lot of things; typically, they increase the level of the neurotransmitter dopamine in the brain, making the subject feel like he or she is going crazy. If we start using truth serum, the individual becomes very suggestible and drowsy. Their pupils dilate, and sometimes their speech becomes a little slurred. They start to present as someone drunk. Usually, when an investigation gets to this level, the subject gets extremely paranoid."

Rich interrupts, saying, "Now he's on the internet, looking up the Bronx District attorney's office."

Bruce asks, "I wonder what that's about?"

"Now, he's writing something on his computer," Logan says.

"It's a letter to the DA's office," Tom says.

"To whom it may concern:

My name is Doug Jordan, and I reside at 6945 Grady Avenue, #3d, Bronx, NY 10463. Under the Freedom of Information Act, I would like to request any documentation your office has about any criminal activity investigation, either concluded or ongoing, of myself. Please forward all documentation to me as soon as possible. If you have any further questions or comments, please contact me at the above address or call me at (718) 432-6530.

Sincerely,

Doug Jordan"

Bruce yells, "What the hell is going on? We have to get some more agents into his apartment to check things out. I'll have them try a different drug cocktail. Maybe we'll titrate him up differently next time. I've never heard of anyone reacting to our enhanced drug protocols in this way!"

Doug puts the correspondence to the DA's office in an envelope and puts a stamp on it. The agents get in place. They assume he's going to the downstairs mailbox, but he starts walking toward 231st Street. They don't know where he's going or what he's going to do. They continue to follow him. Doug senses he's being followed and gets on the downtown 1 train. The undercover detectives continue to shadow him. He takes the train to 34th Street and walks to the main Post Office.

He deposits his letter into the postal box and comes back home. Once in his apartment, Doug relights the white candle and starts writing some more letters.

After getting off work, Rich hurriedly calls Sherry.

"Sherry, you'll never believe what happened!"

"What?"

"Our subject knows about the investigation."

"How?"

"We just gave him the new drugs, and he burned a white candle and started talking about God and had like an epiphany. He was just sitting in a chair and said, "Oh shit, I'm under investigation. It was just that plain. He even wrote a letter to the Bronx District attorney's office about it."

"Wow, I've never heard of that happening."

"Yeah, it's weird; Bruce said the same thing. I wonder how they're going to deal with it."

Sherry says, "I suspect they'll start preliminary investigations of his surveillance teams, friends, family, neighbors, and coworkers to see if there's a leak."

"This is getting very interesting, but it's what I asked for."

"It's what you requested."

"Yep, sure is."

"It's time for me to get back to work. I'm still on the clock."

"Okay, I just wanted to fill you in on the latest."

"All right, talk with you soon."

"Okay, take care.

"All right, Bye"

Rich hangs up and starts his journey home.

After hanging up with "base camp," Bruce immediately goes to the captain. The first words out of his mouth are, "You'll never guess what's happening with that guy we're investigating up the hill."

"What?"

"I told you we upgraded his investigative profile. It sounds weird, I know, but according to the agents, the first time we gave him the new drugs, he started burning a white candle, talked about God protecting him, sat in a chair, and said, 'Oh shit. I'm under investigation.'"

"You must be kidding me," Captain Kuntz says.

"No, I'm serious, all jokes aside."

"So, what's the game plan?"

"We'll probably try some different drugs. By the way, his psychologist also reported that he said his father sexually molested his sister. His father was a cop."

"Does the doctor think it's a credible allegation?"

"Yes."

"So, you're looking into it."

"Definitely."

"What's his name?"

"Robert Jordan."

"Haven't heard of him."

"Excuse me, captain; I'm getting another call from base camp."

"Keep me informed. I want to know how this turns out."

"Okay, will do. Bye."

Bruce quickly answers his phone.

He listens for a couple of minutes and repeats what the team is telling him: "So he believes God anointed him with a gift of discernment with the ability to look into someone's eyes and know what they're thinking."

"Does it seem like he's becoming mentally ill? I've seen subjects on these drugs get delusional, paranoid, or just become unhinged in general. They might start isolating, stop eating their food for fear of being poisoned, walk around their house in the dark for fear of being watched or discontinue using their phones and computers. In addition, they might become suicidal or homicidal, leave their job, lose their home or become homeless; really, anything could start happening. Remember, keep an eye on him. We have him on some powerful stuff. Is he sleeping now?"

Logan says, "No, he's still up."

"The drugs should be wearing off pretty soon, and he should be getting tired. All right, keep me informed. Bye. Talk with you later."

During the week, the investigators notice a pattern. After each dosing, Doug will typically burn a white candle, write nasty letters to either his father, friends, coworkers, neighbors, and family, accusing them of plotting against or spying on him.

This night, Doug goes to his refrigerator for some iced tea. After several sips, he immediately becomes paranoid and decides to go to the nearest police precinct to complain about his neighbors.

After arriving there, he shouts at the policeman on duty, "My neighbors are coming into my apartment and putting drugs in my food!"

The policeman asks, "Where's your evidence?"

After that question, Doug's chest muscles tighten, and the knot in his stomach starts to grow larger; he replies, "I don't have any proof, but I know they're doing it!"

Calmly, the policeman replies, "If you think this is happening, you need to get a toxicology report from the hospital."

Without saying anything further, Doug walks out of the precinct, goes to Broadway, and hails a cab to Bronx-Lebanon Hospital.

Doug arrives at the hospital in under twenty minutes. He tells the triage nurse that he believes his neighbors are coming into his apartment and putting drugs in his food. The nurse looks at him inquisitively and gets up to speak with a colleague. A few minutes later, another nurse arrives and asks Doug to follow her into a room. She brings a cup of water and asks him if he wants to sit on the bed. After drinking the water, he starts to relax. A few minutes later, an orderly comes in and asks if he wants to take off his shoes and lie down. Doug agrees with every request to get more comfortable. After a few more minutes, another nurse walks into the room. Doug immediately sits up as the nurse starts talking to him. She puts her arm around his shoulder. A few seconds later, Doug feels a pinch in his right arm. The nurse sticks him with a needle. She then leads him to a locked room with a bed and some pajamas. Nonresistant, he takes off his clothes, puts on the pajamas, then falls asleep.

His sleep is peaceful; however, he doesn't sleep long. He wakes up at five in the morning and starts to reflect on his current life situation. A couple of hours later his daydreaming is interrupted by an attendant with a breakfast tray.

About thirty minutes after eating his meal, Dr. Chandora and an attendant walk into Doug's room. The doctor has a clipboard with some papers and a pen. The attendant stands behind the doctor, carefully monitoring Doug. The doctor pulls up a chair and begins the assessment with questions about Doug's family life, health history, social activities, and daily living activities.

Dr. Chandora asks, "Do you have a therapist?

"My psychologist just moved away, but he gave me the card for a therapist at Riverview Mental Health Center named Judy Sonnovia."

"Would you agree to let me speak to her?"

"Yes, but I haven't seen her yet."

"But, you were planning on scheduling an appointment soon, weren't you?"

"Yes."

"That's fine; I want to debrief her on your current hospitalization."

"Is that still okay?"

"Yes."

"Are you taking any medication?"

"Yes, an antidepressant."

"Would you be willing to take an antipsychotic?"

Doug says, "No, absolutely not."

"It might help you."

"I haven't lost my mind, and I refuse to take an antipsychotic."

"Do you have the card for your new therapist?"

Doug takes the card out of his wallet and hands it to the doctor.

The doctor goes into a nearby room and dials Ms. Sonnovia. He gets her on the line.

"Hello. May I speak with Ms. Sonnovia?"

"This is she. How may I help you?"

"This is Dr. Chandora from the Bronx-Lebanon Mental Health Emergency Room. I have one of your clients here. He gave me verbal authorization to speak with you. His name is Doug Jordan. He received your business card from Dr. Ehnis. I know he hasn't seen you yet, but he plans on scheduling an appointment this week."

"That name does sound familiar. I believe Dr. Ehnis called me recently about a patient referral. Oh yes, I remember the name now."

"Yes, Doug came here yesterday, very paranoid. We kept him overnight. He seems stable now, but we'd like to put him on an antipsychotic and have him schedule a follow-up with you. He's on an antidepressant and is very resistant to the idea of taking an antipsychotic."

"May I speak with him ?"

Dr. Chandora says, "Yes, hold on a minute."

Doug picks up the phone.

"We've never met, but I know Dr. Ehnis referred you to me. My name is Ms. Sonnovia. How're you feeling?"

"I feel fine now."

"Yes, Dr. Chandora told me. They have some new medicine they'd like to put you on."

"I know."

They want you to take an antipsychotic for the paranoia.

"I told Dr. Chandora I'm not taking an antipsychotic."

"That's okay, but let's talk about it in your first session."

"I don't promise anything."

"That's fine. When can you come in for your first appointment? I have tomorrow at eleven open."

"I have a pretty open schedule tomorrow, so I can do eleven."

"All right, I'll see you tomorrow at eleven."

"Okay, bye."

As soon as she hangs up, Ms. Sonnovia calls Bruce.

"Hello."

"Hi, this is Judy. Doug is coming for his first appointment tomorrow."

"Great, I know he went to the hospital last night. How's he doing?"

"Our conversation was brief, but he sounds fine. The ER doctor suggested he start taking an antipsychotic, but he's resistant to the idea."

"Yeah, let's keep our fingers crossed. We have to convince Doug he's mentally ill and his beliefs about being investigated are delusions because as long as he keeps talking about being investigated we have to maintain this higher level of surveillance. Gaslighting him is the only way we can lower his investigative level back to general. He's reacting to our new drug protocols in a very unusual way. He's causing problems for himself and a lot more work for us."

"Yes, I know," says Judy.

"All right, I have to go now, Judy. Talk with you later."

"Okay, Bruce. I will see you at our next staff meeting."

Dr. Chandora discharges Doug thirty minutes after hanging up with Ms. Sonnovia. After leaving the hospital, Doug decides to take a bus instead of a cab back home. He starts to feel calmer. Arriving at his apartment, Doug immediately calls his office and quits his job. He also takes a leave of absence from school.

It all comes back to Doug in waves of remembrance, insight, and intuition. He believes his father faked a break-in of the family home when Doug was around eight to have him placed under surveillance by the police. Afterward, his father has been building a case against Doug by continuously lying to them. He has been telling them all these years that Doug was touching his sister when in fact it was his father who was molesting her. This setup has been going on for years.

Doug shakes his head and reflects on the adage "What's done in the dark will always come to the light," trusting and believing he now has a clear understanding of the scheme. With the heaviness of these new realizations, Doug closes his eyes and takes a nap, which eventually turns into a deep slumber.

After Doug falls asleep, Rich calls Sherry.

"Hello."

"Hi, you'll never believe what's going on with Doug."

"What?"

"This guy is something else! Everyone on the team thinks he's some kind of god or psychic. In Doug's letters, he's methodically uncovering the plot against him. It seems his father set him up to fail. Vincent and Logan heard Bruce say a lot of what he puts in his letters is being corroborated by our other investigators. They're tending to believe him."

Sherry says, "So, they're reviewing old case files?"

"Yes, I believe—as well as going over all the past investigative reports, and it seems his father has been trying to frame him all these years."

Sherry says, "A target has figuratively and, in a sense, literally been placed on your back once they start investigating anyone. Everyone who's worked on one of these investigations knows that it's true."

Rich says, "It seems that's what his father tried to do. He placed a target on his son's back at eight years old."

With disbelief in her voice, Sherry says, "Wow, that's so fucked up."

"This is too crazy to believe."

"Yes, it is, but what you said about your subject makes me think about what Vaughn said when he put his hand on my stomach and asked me, 'Why did you give my father those pills to hurt my mother?' It makes me think Vaughn could be gifted in some way."

"As I said before, Vaughn is just a problem child; he's not going to amount to much. I don't expect much from him; he'll probably grow up to be a drug addict."

Sherry's tone changes, and her voice becomes louder as she asks, "Why would you say that?"

Rich shrugs his shoulders.

"You're something else; I just know our baby won't grow up to be a drug addict."

"By the way, how's the pregnancy coming along?"

"I haven't seen the doctor this week, but our little bundle of joy should be here any moment now. Previously, the doctor said the baby was doing fine. I can't wait."

Wanting to skirt the issue, Rich says, "I haven't seen you in a minute."

"Yes, it's been a while. We haven't been on a date in a long time. When it's our time, we'll do it the right way."

Rich laughs and says, "All right, if you say so, but I've really got to go now. Take care and have a good evening."

"You too. Speak with you soon. Bye."

While Doug is sleeping the mood in the war room changes. The team unwinds and doesn't do much for the rest of the day. When Rich leaves for home Doug is still in bed. After arriving home he looks in on the boys, gets ready for bed, and is asleep in minutes.

The next day, Doug wakes up feeling relieved. Since he doesn't have to work, his day feels empty and unscripted; dirty clothes are strewn all over the floor, dust covers the furniture, and papers are scattered all over the kitchen table. Doug thinks to himself, *This apartment needs a lot of work,* but since he doesn't feel like cleaning up, he only thinks about his eleven with Ms. Sonnovia.

Doug arrives at his appointment fifteen minutes before his scheduled start time. The Riverview Mental Health Center is located in a nondescript four-story, rectangular, utilitarian-looking building, all concrete, metal, and glass with little ornamentation besides the words "RMHC" written on the outside. The Center is on the second floor. Since it's Doug's first time in the building, he takes the elevator. The office has slightly worn chairs and a couch with cushions that look like they've seen better days. Pictures of the inside of subway cars, flowers, and scenes of ocean waves crashing along the shore of some tropical island hang along the wall of the waiting room. Old issues of *Harper's Bazaar*, *Cosmopolitan*, *Self*, and *Ebony* sit on a table. Doug walks up to the receptionist and says, "I have an eleven with Ms. Sonnovia."

The receptionist takes his information and instructs him to have a seat. On the table are also issues of a newspaper Doug's never heard of called *New York Visions.* The cover states, "This newspaper is written by and for consumers of mental health services."

Doug takes a copy to finish later.

After ten minutes, Ms. Sonnovia opens the waiting room door. She is an average-sized, attractive brunette woman, with a firm handshake, and a slight smile. They go to a small room with two chairs. There is a mirror opposite Doug's chair. An East Indian textile print hangs on the left wall, a small table with flowers is in the corner, and Ms. Sonnovia's desk, with her chair turned around to face him, is on the right side of the room.

Ms. Sonnovia says, "Hello. Nice to meet you."

Doug replies, "Thank you. Nice to meet you also."

Ms. Sonnovia begins with a question: "One of the first things I like to ask my clients is, 'What are your goals for therapy?'"

Doug responds matter-of-factly, "I just want my life back. I think I'm under investigation, and everyone in my life is more or less part of a spy network."

Ms. Sonnovia's eyes grow wide. She appears eager to hear more.

"What makes you think you're under investigation?"

"It's a long story, but I know I'm right."

"I'm open to hear whatever you have to say."

"I'm being drugged."

"What makes you feel this way?"

"I can tell when they're doing it."

"Who's investigating you?"

"The police."

"Why would they be investigating you?"

"I believe my father both initiated and propagated an investigation of me to cover up the fact he molested my sister. My father was a police sergeant, so it would be easy enough for him to do. I also feel that most of my family, friends, neighbors, and former coworkers are part of a spy network."

"How do you know this? It sounds like paranoia. What's your diagnosis?"

"Generalized anxiety disorder with mild depression. I believe what I'm going through is real."

"Do you know why you got your diagnosis?"

"No, I just assumed Dr. Ehnis had to put something down for insurance purposes. I've never asked about it.

"So, you never discussed your diagnosis with Dr. Ehnis?"

"No."

"You do realize that sometimes symptoms change for individuals with mental illness, and you do understand that one of the symptoms of schizophrenia is paranoia and fixed delusions."

Doug replies, "I'm aware of that. I've never heard voices or seen images outside my head."

"All people with schizophrenia don't hear voices and see images outside their head."

Doug says, "I know I don't have that disorder. I believe I'm under a police investigation, and drugs are one of the things they use when they put people under surveillance."

"You do know a common belief among people with schizophrenia is that they're under investigation."

I know this sounds weird, but I believe, when the police drug me, it enhances my natural-born 'gift.' It's biochemical, but it's also spiritual. I believe God gave me a gift of discernment in which I can look into someone's eyes and know what they're thinking. I also feel and sense things deeply."

"Tell me. What am I thinking now?"

"It doesn't work like that, and it doesn't work all the time."

"Do you think I'm a spy?"

"Yes, I do."

"Wow, this is a lot to take in. How do you know these things?"

"Basically, through my God-given gift and intuition. I've been writing letters to certain individuals outlining what they've done to me and how much I hate them. Those letters pretty much tell the story."

"Maybe we can discuss those letters if you would like."

"Sure, we can talk about them whenever you want to."

"However, there is something more important I would like to discuss with you, the antipsychotic medication Dr. Chandora would like to prescribe."

"*I'm not crazy!*"

"You don't have to be crazy to take them. It's your choice, but I wish you would reconsider. Things might get better for you if you do."

"I'll think about it, but I do not promise anything."

"You put forth a lot of suppositions. What proof do you have for all the things you believe?"

"I don't need proof. I know what I believe. Some people believe in God; others don't; some people are even willing to die for that belief, yet there's no scientifically verifiable proof that God even exists."

Ms. Sonnovia looks at the clock and realizes it's almost time for their session to end.

Abruptly, she says, "You're right, but we'll have to continue this discussion at our next session. Our time is up for today. I'll see you next week at this same time if that's good for you."

"Yes, that's fine." Doug says.

He forces a smile through his scowl and gets up to leave.

Once he exits the building, Judy calls Bruce.

"Hey, Judy."

"Hi, Bruce. My session with Doug just ended."

"How'd it go?"

"It was all right."

"Is he going to take the antipsychotic?"

"He was emphatic in saying he's not crazy and won't take the pills, but I'll continue to press him on that. He's also resolute in his belief that he's under investigation."

Bruce states, "He quit his job. If he accepts that he's mentally ill and his beliefs are delusions, we could lower his surveillance level and get him on Social Security Disability. Because as long as he keeps talking about being investigated, we're not going to be able to lower his investigative level back to general. We have to 'gaslight' him into doubting his perception of reality."

Judy says, "I've got an idea. I know he's not working. I'll use that as an 'in' at our next session to put pressure on him to let us apply for Social Security Disability for him. I'm sure he's stressed trying to find a new source of income."

Bruce says, "I'll have our forensic accountant look into his finances."

Judy says, "Doug also mentioned some angry letters he's been writing to his father and other people outlining what they've done to him."

"Yeah, he's been writing a lot of letters lately. I haven't had time to look at all of them."

"Doug also mentioned his father lied to have him investigated for child molestation. What's that about?"

"We're looking into that now. There are a lot of moving parts. It's a shame that a father would do that to his son. We're inclined to believe him, though!"

"I also have to go over his case files when they arrive from Dr. Ehnis's office. That's going to be a lot of work. He saw Dr. Ehnis for quite a while."

"All right, Judy. I'll let you get back to your day."

"Okay, take care, Bruce. Talk with you soon."

Doug tries to figure out who the undercover agents are on the bus ride home by playing a three-card monte mental mind game. After doing this for a while, he attempts to read the newspaper *New York Visions* but can't concentrate. Pondering his future, he thinks, *I quit my job; tomorrow, I'll begin my job search at a temp agency.*

Arriving home, Doug immediately looks through his desk for some old business cards from employment agencies he's worked with previously: Olsten, Kelly and Cosmopolitan. Doug starts making calls to set up appointments for this week. The account execs Doug met with before are no longer there. However, he's still able to schedule something at Kelly Services for tomorrow.

Doug wonders if the temp agency will find something for him right away. Also, in the back of his mind he thinks, *How am I going to live with this level of surveillance in my life? Will the investigators be at the temp agency?* Doug turns on the TV, not to watch or listen but as a distraction to drown out the cacophony of thoughts, feelings, and questions in his mind. His daytime TV choices fall into three main categories: cable news, soap operas, and talk shows. Doug settles on CNN. Present in the body but wandering in his mind, Doug makes something to eat before falling asleep.

After Doug falls asleep, the team chews the fat for the next couple of hours. After talking for a while Rich takes a break outside the bodega. After standing out there for five minutes, Sherry calls. "Hey, what's up?" he says.

"I was thinking about the last time we saw each other. I have a plan; how about we pencil something in this weekend."

"I have to find someone to keep Vaughn and Gerard. In the past, I might've let them stay by themselves but not since the fire."

"Then how about the four of us go out for lunch. It's not ideal, but it's better than just talking over the phone all the time. At least, I'll get some face time with you."

Rich remembers his schedule is open. "Just so happens I have both days off this weekend. Let's make it at one on Saturday. Meet at my place."

Sherry says, "All right, that sounds like a plan. By the way, how's that crazy case of yours?"

"Still crazy, but nothing much going on today."

"I guess that's a good thing."

"Yeah, it kind of is."

"All right, gotta run. Talk with you later."

"Okay, see you soon. Bye."

Rich hangs up and thinks about the boys. They should be coming home from school about now.

The neighborhood candy store is their regular after-school meeting spot.

After walking in silence for a few minutes, Gerard says, "You're mighty quiet. What's going on?"

Distracted, Vaughn doesn't answer.

Gerard gives him a soft elbow in the ribs. "What's up? Didn't you hear what I said?"

Vaughn replies, "You know Mommy is angry. I can feel it."

Gerard rolls his eyes and takes a deep breath, sighing, "You at it again. I thought I told you mommy was in heaven with God, Jesus, Granddad, and the angels."

"I know you said that, but she's still mad."

"Okay, Vaughn. Mad at who, and how do you know this?"

"She's mad at Dad and Ms. Sherry."

"Why?"

"I can't tell you."

"Then shut up about it."

"I felt it in my dream last night."

"You had a dream about Mommy last night?"

"Yes."

Vaughn recounts the dream: "Mommy was dressed all in white. She was barefoot, wearing a long white dress, and white beads hung around her neck. In front of her, a white candle burned. She was at a cemetery, standing in front of two freshly dug graves with outstretched arms."

"What do you think it means?"

"I don't know."

"You should tell Grandma Veronica."

"Yeah, I think I'll call her as soon as I get home."

The boys walk the rest of the way in silence.

When they reach the apartment, Vaughn takes off his jacket, throws down his bookbag, and immediately grabs the phone.

Veronica recognizes the number and picks up on the first ring.

"Hello?"

"Hi, Grandma."

"Hi, baby. How're you and Gerard doing?"

"We're fine."

"Grandma, I have a question."

"Sure, what is it?"

"I had a dream about Mommy last night, and I don't understand it. Could you tell me what it means?"

"Definitely."

"All I remember is that Mommy was angry and she was dressed in white. She was barefoot, wearing a long white dress, and white beads hung around her neck. In front of her, a white candle burned. She was at a cemetery, standing in front of two freshly dug graves with outstretched arms."

Veronica thought for a minute, then said, "I think it's saying someone is going to be with God, and your mother is going to meet them when they transition over."

"You mean someone is going to die?"

"Yes, but don't worry because we're all going to die one day. It doesn't mean it will happen today or tomorrow; it could be fifty years from now. It doesn't even have to be someone you know. Anyway, only God knows the true meaning of a dream. So, don't worry about it."

Vaughn feels reassured by his grandmother's words. "I won't, Nana," he replies.

Changing the subject, Veronica asks about school.

"You continuing to make good grades?"

"Yes."

"I'm so proud of you guys. Keep up the good work."

"Is your father around?"

"No, he hasn't come home from work yet."

"Okay, let me speak to Gerard."

"Okay, Nana."

Vaughn puts the phone down and yells for Gerard, who quickly picks up the receiver.

"Hi, Nana."

"Hey, baby. Nana just wanted to shout at you. How's it going?"

"Everything's fine."

"You still doing well in school?"

"Yes."

"You and Vaughn getting along and not giving your dad too many headaches?"

Gerard giggles and says, "Yes."

"All right, I just wanted to holler at you. Take care now and enjoy the rest of your day."

"Okay, Nana, I will."

"All right, goodbye."

This afternoon they change their clothes, get a snack, do their chores, and complete their homework. The boys intend to live up to their grandmother's expectations. For the rest of the afternoon, Vaughn and Gerard read books.

Once home, Rich opens the door and is immediately struck by the quiet in the apartment. He enters the kitchen and sees that it's clean. He then proceeds to the boy's room, when he opens their door, they stop what they're doing, look up and say, "Hi, Dad."

Before slamming the door, Rich says, "Dinner'll be ready in a few."

Within the hour, Rich puts the food on the table. The boys gobble down their meal then clean up the kitchen. Later, they join their father in the living room. Eager to learn about the world, the boys watch the evening news with rapt attention. Time slips by as Rich starts to nap on the couch. Secretly grateful and not wanting to wake him, the boys take control of the remote. Around 9:30 p.m., Rich wakes up with a start. Finding the boys up past their bedtime, he orders them to their room and continues sleeping on the couch. About twenty minutes later, he goes to bed.

After a relaxing night's sleep, Rich awakens, feeling refreshed. He goes into the bathroom to shower. *TGIF*, he thinks to himself. *And I have the weekend off too; sweet.*

Following the well-choreographed morning ritual, Gerard and Vaughn walk around bleary eyed and say little as they wash up, eat breakfast, put on their clothes, then leave for school. Ten minutes later, Rich exits the apartment.

He arrives at base camp within the hour. Doug is still sleeping, and the team discusses his plans for the day, remembering he has an appointment with a temp agency.

Doug eventually starts waking up around the time Bruce begins his weekly supervisory staff meeting. Bruce conferences in everyone who can't be there in person.

"Al, present on the phone."

"Rommie, present on the phone."

"Ron, present on the phone."

"Judy."

"I would also like to introduce Michael, our forensic accountant."

"Captain Kuntz."

Bruce says, "This is getting to be a very complicated and involved case. As you know, our subject realizes he's under investigation, which complicates matters. We upgraded his surveillance level per our guidelines. It seems that Doug performs a particular ritual every time we give him certain drugs. He burns a white candle, talks about God and being investigated, and then writes accusatory letters to primarily his father and others he believes are part of the spy network. Judy met with him this week, and I'd like her to debrief us on the meeting. But first, I'd like to make sure everyone saw the video of the session.

"Is there anyone who hasn't?"

After a minute of silence, Bruce continues with the meeting.

Judy begins, "Our therapy session went well. Doug wasn't angry or hostile. He was very firm in his belief that he was under investigation, and everybody in his life is more or less part of a spy network. He even told me, 'I believe you're part of the spy network too.' Doug then referenced some letters he wrote his father and others, outlining what they've done to him. Doug also believes God gave him a 'gift' of some kind."

Bruce asks, "Did he go into detail about what his gift is?"

"Yes, a little. Doug said he gets feelings, and when he looks into someone's eyes, he can read their mind. He also said the drugs enhance his natural God-given gift, and he senses and feels things very deeply."

Al asks, "Did he mention his family? Because since he's talking so much, we had to tell them why he's being investigated."

Bruce interjects, "How did they react?"

"Some of them were angry, but others didn't say much."

Judy continues, "No, he didn't discuss his family; however, he talked about a 'grand conspiracy' in which his father has plotted against him."

Bruce says, "You all know Doug told Dr. Ehnis his sister told him their father molested her?"

Judy says, "Yes, he told me that also but didn't go into details about it."

"How does he know about these schemes against him?"

"Doug said through his gift, intuition, and memory, he realized what was being done to him."

Al responds, "It seems like he's using his 'gift' but also figuring some of this stuff out on his own."

"Yes."

Bruce says, "We've already corroborated some of the information in his letters. If his father initiated and propagated an investigation of him based on untruths. That's a felony, and lying to police investigators and conspiracy are all against the law. We've been granted a court order allowing us to open previously closed investigations. The information in these reports help us validate some of the information we're receiving from other sources. I would also like to know from Al how his family is responding to the increased surveillance level?"

"They're still cooperating."

Bruce says, "Now I would like to ask Ron and Rommie, have you had any contact with him lately?"

Ron says, "We just recently went to church together, and I already told you about the knife."

Bruce says, "The team at base camp said he stopped carrying it around."

"How about you, Rommie? Have you heard from Doug lately?"

"No, and he's stopped returning my calls."

"So it appears he's isolating a little, sleeping a lot, and not going out much. We have to get him more socially engaged. We can't have an investigation if he's not leaving his home much."

"Judy, does he show any signs of depression?"

"No, he seems fine."

"Has he mentioned being gay?"

"No, he hasn't talked about that yet."

"Al, did his family talk about it?"

"A couple of them mentioned it, but they only saw him at family gatherings and rarely spoke with him over the phone. So, it was not really an issue for them."

Bruce says, "I'd also like to hear from Michael about Doug's finances?"

Michael says, "Doug makes a decent salary but isn't wealthy. He has a moderate amount of savings, isn't in debt and has a fully paid for cooperative apartment, so he has a pretty sizable financial asset at his disposal. His spending profile is practical, and he typically stays within his budget."

Bruce adds, "Doug also quit his job recently. He's going to a temp agency today. I want Ron and Rommie to start reaching out to him more aggressively, and Al, I want you to tell his family to do the same. We have to get him more socially engaged. Those are all the things I had on the agenda. Does anyone have anything else?"

No one responds.

"Okay, so the meeting is adjourned."

By this time, Doug is ready to leave his apartment. He only needs to grab a few copies of his resume. Sarcastically, he thinks to himself, *I wonder what kind of adventures they're planning for me today.* He remembers to light a white candle before departing, saying to himself, *I hope they at least have some respect for God.*

* * *

The subway ride downtown goes by quickly. On the fifth floor of a forty-story office building, the big, green, and white "Kelly Services' sign" smacks him in the face as soon as he walks off the elevator. Doug immediately notices the office's busy energy: multiple conversations, copy machines churning out paper, and phones ringing off the hook. About ten people are in the waiting area. Doug goes to the receptionist desk and asks for an application. Barely looking at him, a woman hands him a clipboard with about fifteen pages on it. He groans as he fills out the paperwork.

It takes about twenty minutes to complete. Doug hands the clipboard back to the receptionist then returns to his seat. He starts feeling a little nervous and begins to play a three-card monte mental mind game, trying to figure out who the under-cover detectives are in the room.

After waiting about twenty-five minutes, a thin, white woman with long, blonde hair and a cheesy grin introduces herself as Amy Grobin. Ms. Grobin escorts Doug to her desk. After sitting down, she immediately starts to pepper him with questions about his work history and what kind of job he is looking for. She asks, Why did he leave his last employer? Does he want short or long-term assignments? What were his previous job responsibilities? What is he looking to get paid? After an approximate thirty-minute interview, Ms. Grobin hands Doug a pamphlet listing all of Kelly Services' policies and procedures, along with her business card. In parting, she says, "Call me regularly to see if any work comes in."

The experience leaves him feeling unimportant as just another cog in the wheel of the temp world. However, he knows he needs a job.

* * *

Rich is sitting outside of base camp when Doug arrives home. After about fifteen minutes, Bruce calls and says to the team, "I spoke with his employment counselor at the temp agency. She said the interview went well, and they expect to place him at a financial services firm."

Logan says, "Well, that's good. At least, I don't have to watch him sleep all day."

"We've not drugged him in a while," Rich says.

"Yes, we're being more strategic in how we use them. Meaning, we're going to start monitoring how Doug reacts to particular drug cocktails, since he doesn't have a normal reaction to them. They seem to give him more insight. By the way, that also reminds me, I think our investigation is getting a little unfocused. We're supposed to be looking at Doug for plotting murder against his father and potential child molestation. Yet, we are getting hung up on all this other stuff."

Vincent says, "He stopped carrying that knife around. Maybe he isn't thinking about killing his father anymore."

"That's a possibility," Bruce says. "If that's true, we still need to continue investigating him, per our guidelines, as he knows he's under surveillance. Those are all the updates I have for now, and I see it's about time for a shift change. Does anyone have any further questions?"

After a couple of minutes of silence, Whitney says, "No, we're good."

"All right, then I'll speak to you guys later."

Rich is glad he'll be off-duty soon. He's looking forward to this weekend and getting some much needed rest. When it's his time, Rich says his goodbyes and swiftly heads out the door.

Entering the apartment, Rich sees the boys are in the living room watching TV. Barely acknowledging their presence, he washes up and goes into the kitchen. The gulf between Rich and his kids grows wider every day. Vaughn has stopped bringing permission slips home from school, assuming his father will only say no. Gerard focuses intensely on his schoolwork, almost to the exclusion of everything else. They're not a family anymore; they're only three people living in the same apartment. The evening ritual doesn't change much. They eat dinner in silence, and after finishing their meals, the boys clean up the kitchen. Rich turns on the news, watches it for a little while, then falls asleep. The boys, not wanting to wake him, take the remote and turn to their favorite shows. Rich wakes up a few hours later, and sends them to their room, reminding them, "No TV this weekend."

After a good night's sleep, Rich wakes up feeling rejuvenated. This morning's relaxed pace allows him to observe things he often overlooks: the dappled morning sunlight streaming through the blinds, the eerie quiet of the house, and dust mites floating in a ray of sunshine.

After enjoying this peace for a few minutes, Rich decides to make breakfast. He goes into the kitchen and searches the cupboard. He finds the bacon, eggs, and bread. After a while, the bacon's hickory-smoked smell and the sound it makes as it's frying wake Vaughn up first. Reversing the pattern this morning, he's the first to wash up. Gerard is wide awake and sitting on his bed when Vaughn returns to their room. While Gerard is in the bathroom, Vaughn quickly puts on his clothes and heads to the front of the apartment. His eyes hunt for the source of the unfamiliar but inviting sounds and smells. His stomach growls. He watches his father perform a culinary juggling act; bacon frying, eggs waiting to be scrambled along with bread being toasted.

Gerard bounces into the kitchen a few minutes later. They smile at each other as they sit at the small, rectangular table, rubbing their hands together in anticipation of their meal. To occupy their time, they play with silverware and anxiously turn their heads in the direction of the meal being prepared. Rich says, "Perfect timing," as he finishes cooking. Hungry, they get up and run with their plates to get their meal. The orange juice, milk, and butter are already situated on the table.

In contrast to the boys' nervous energy, the quiet at the table is deafening, interrupted only by the sound of forks and knives clinking on plates. After a few minutes, Rich breaks the uncomfortable silence: "We're gonna have lunch with Sherry this afternoon."

The boys say nothing in response.

Halfway through the meal, Rich's phone rings. Without looking at the number, he picks it up, expecting Sherry to call sometime this morning.

"Good morning, Sherry says."

"Yeah, good morning."

"What's up?"

"I'm just eating breakfast with the boys. I got up early and fixed some bacon, eggs, and toast."

"Sounds good. I hope it doesn't spoil your appetite for later today."

"No, it won't."

"Anyway, I was just calling to find out where'd you like to go."

Immediately, Rich says, "Applebees."

"I see you already had a place in mind. Well, that was really all I was calling about. So, on that note, I've got a couple of errands to run, so I'll see you this afternoon. Don't forget to tell the boys I said hello."

"Okay, will do."

After hanging up, Rich tersely relays the message. "Sherry says hi."

The boys smile obediently.

Rich asks, "You guys going outside this morning?"

Vaughn says, "Yes."

Gerard asks, "Can we take out our bikes?"

"Yes, and come back upstairs by twelve-thirty."

Hearing this, the boys hurry up, finish their meal, and clean up the kitchen; Gerard takes all the silverware and dumps it in the sink. Vaughn puts the butter, milk, and orange juice back in the refrigerator. He then takes a dishcloth and vigorously wipes down the table. This morning they don't argue over who will wash and who will dry and put away. Gerard fills up the dishpan with water and liquid soap while Vaughn stands at the drying rack, ready with his towel. The kitchen assembly line runs like a well-oiled machine today.

While the boys are getting ready to go outside, Rich jumps in the shower. He hears the bicycle wheels' squeaky noises on the linoleum as the boys make their way down the hall. A couple of minutes later, the door slams shut. Walking back to his bedroom, he notices the black scuff marks on the wall. Annoyed, he shakes his head, making a mental note to remind them to be more careful next time.

Once outside, the boys breathe a deep sigh of relief, sensing but not knowing why there's always tension in the house. On this early fall morning, the sun is shining bright; it's neither cold nor hot, and the leaves have not entirely changed color. The boys get on their bikes and immediately head for the playground. The rubber padding in the playground is torn in some places and missing in others. Several broken swings no longer have chains supporting the seats, and broken seesaws are scattered throughout the park.

Disappointed that no one else is outside, the boys feel sad and alone. However, they maintain hope that their friends will show up soon. In the meantime, they race their bikes around the expansive housing project, riding up and down the pavement as fast as they can, careful to avoid inconspicuous cracks in the concrete. After a while, the boys become tired and rest on the chain-link fence in front of their building. Checking the time, Gerard is the first to realize an hour and a half has passed; wondering where the rest of their friends are and what they can do for the rest of the morning; they start to think of ways to entertain themselves.

Vaughn says, "We could go to the store, but I have no money."

Gerard says, "We could sit here and wait for someone to show up or go home and play some board games."

Contemplating their choices, the boys wait for a little while, but no one shows up, and they decide to go back upstairs and play some board games.

The sound of Gerard and Vaughn entering the apartment wakes Rich from his nap; checking the time, he sees it's 11:37 a.m. Curious, he asks, "Why did you come upstairs so soon? We have an hour before we leave."

"Nothing to do. No one outside," Gerard replies.

As an afterthought, Rich says, "Be careful with your bikes; you're messing up the walls."

Once inside their room, Vaughn suggests they play Monopoly. Gerard searches the jumble of dirty clothes, shoes, books, and book bags at the bottom of their closet. For the next forty-five minutes, they become engrossed in the competitive nature of the game. Gerard wins the first game. As they start the second game, their father knocks on the door, snapping, "It's almost time to go."

Looking forward to going out, the boys get ready quickly. They sit in the living room, bored, without their favorite distraction. After a while, they hear a knock at the door. Gerard opens the door enthusiastically, knowing that it's Ms. Sherry. It is, and she greets him with a warm, welcoming smile. Dressed casually in a blue maternity dress with white tennis shoes, she walks into the living room and asks, "Where's your dad?

"He's in the back," Gerard says.

Vaughn adds, "He's not ready yet."

"We have time; we can wait. How're you guys doing in school?"

Vaughn says, "I'm making A's and B's."

Boasting, Gerard says, "I'm making all A's."

"Yeah, that's what your father tells me. Keep up the good work."

Both boys smile with pride. "Thank you," they say in unison.

Not knowing when Rich will be ready and searching for something to do, Sherry automatically goes to turn on the TV. Suddenly remembering the new rule, she stops midstride just as Rich enters the living room. He says, "I thought I heard a knock at the door."

"I came in about five minutes ago."

"All right, I'm ready. We're still going to Applebees."

"You guys like Applebee's, don't you?" Sherry asks.

"Yes," they say in unison.

"We can go to the one in Brooklyn at King's Plaza; it's only about twenty-five minutes away," Rich says.

The boys jump up from the couch, excited to begin the journey. Rich stands with the door open as the boys and Sherry leave the apartment in single file. Sherry seems to stick out her belly even farther in a show of maternal pride. Her baby bump is getting bigger, and she glows with the joy of impending motherhood.

Once in the car, Gerard and Vaughn talk about Monopoly. Vaughn vows to avenge his loss as soon as they return home. Rich turns on the radio, and Sherry casually looks out the window. They arrive at the restaurant in fifteen minutes. The mall is an assortment of colored lights, neon signs, loud sounds, and enticing smells; its energy seems to heighten the boy's excitement. Crowded this afternoon, the line for Applebee's is long.

The restaurant is a jumble of flashing advertisements, blaring TVs, sports, movie and music memorabilia, and loud conversations. Situated in the middle of the restaurant, Rich takes his seat on the inside of the booth. Sherry sits on the outside, making it easier for her to maneuver her baby bump, and the boys take seats across from them. Without introducing herself and appearing to be in a hurry, the waitress comes over quickly and drops four menus on the table. After looking at the menus for a couple of minutes, Sherry says, "The Cajun chicken pasta looks good."

Rich says, "I think I'll try the fish tacos." Looking at his sons, he says, "What are you'll having?"

Without giving it a second thought, Gerard says, "Hamburger and fries with a Coke."

Vaughn says, "I'll have the same."

After a few minutes, the waitress arrives. Dressed up like an umpire with black pants, a black and white striped shirt, and a whistle around her neck, she puts four glasses of water on the table. She asks, "You'll ready to order?"

Rich speaks for the group: "One fish taco, one Cajun chicken pasta, and two hamburger deluxes. I'll also have some water with lemon and two cokes."

Sherry adds, "I'll have a Sprite."

The waitress picks up their menus and rapidly walks away.

Sherry sits with her arms folded over her belly, appearing to protect her baby from the noise and chaos of the restaurant. Everyone seems to be in their own world. Rich looks over Gerard's head at a TV situated on a shelf lining the wall. His only interest is the football game. Sherry continues to people watch while Gerard looks at the signed pictures of movie, music, and sports stars hung up behind his father's head; Vaughn just stares at his father. Sherry eventually breaks the silence, saying with a smile, "Rich, the boys say they're doing well in school."

Seeming to be interested only in football, he dismissively replies, "Yeah, they are."

Sherry notices the searching look on Vaughn's face as he stares at his father. She asks, "How's it going with no TV on the weekend, Vaughn?"

"It's okay."

"What're you doing instead?"

"This morning, Gerard and I went outside and rode our bikes; we then came upstairs and played some Monopoly."

Before Sherry can ask another question, the waitress returns with the food situated on a gray, large, round plastic tray; she quickly places the silverware on the table. Remembering Vaughn and Gerard ordered the burgers, she asks, "Who had the fish taco?"

Rich raises his hand. Once all the food is situated on the table, Sherry says a quick grace, and everyone digs in.

Sherry asks, "How're your burgers?"

Still chewing and between mouthfuls, the boys say, "Good."

"Yeah, my food is tasty too," Sherry says.

Distracted, Rich keeps his eyes on the football game. Everyone eats with their eyes averted, looking down at their plates instead of each other.

Rich is the last to finish, Sherry feels uncomfortable with the distance and silence at the table so she asks, "Are you ready for the bill?"

Before Rich can answer, Sherry waves her hand in the air, to grab the waitress's attention, and asks for the check. In a fast, single-handed motion, the waitress puts the bill on the table. Rich looks at the total, takes out his wallet, and gives the waitress his credit card. She comes back in a couple of minutes and waits for Rich to sign the receipt. She then gives a half-hearted smile, says, "Thanks; enjoy the rest of your day," and swiftly walks away.

Rich signals he's ready to leave and Sherry gets up, as the boys start maneuvering out of the booth. In an unusual display of affection, Rich grabs Sherry's hand as they walk out the restaurant. The boys bounce ahead, taking in all the sights, sounds, and smells of the mall. In their hearts, they want something, a token of the visit, a piece of clothing, something sweet to eat, or a pair of shoes, anything to remind them of this outing. Unwilling to ask and silent in disappointment, they realize their father will only say no.

* * *

Gerard and Vaughn change their pace as they near the parking garage. They stroll as a way to prolong the experience. The mall is crowded, and the boys feel like they're leaving the party early. Subtle signs of sadness and disappointment begin to echo on their faces. Full from their meals, they say little in the car. The traffic is light, and they arrive home in under twenty minutes. As Sherry gets out of the vehicle, Vaughn gently places his hand on her stomach. Initially distracted and unaware of what he's doing, she doesn't say anything. After a while, she notices and quickly moves his hand away, unsure of why fear overtakes her for a moment. Vaughn turns away and begins to walk upstairs, uncertain of why he did it.

Plans change, as the boys no longer wish to play games; they feel sleepy and decide to nap. Rich turns on the TV. At which time, Sherry says, "Let's do something different. How about some music?"

Pleasantly surprised, Rich says, "Sure, who're you feeling?"

"I'm in the mood for slow jams."

"How 'bout some old school?"

"That's fine. Surprise me."

Rich looks through his CD collection, stopping at Marvin Gaye. The soulful crooner's voice begins to fill the room. A sly smile creeps across Sherry's face.

"Good choice," she says.

"Let's Get it On," one of Marvin Gaye's classics from the early seventies sets the mood. Rich extends his hand, inviting Sherry to get off the couch. Sherry manages to stand up, and Rich pulls her into him, grabbing her by the waist; they start to slow dance. Sherry hugs him and puts her head on his shoulder, lingering there for a long time. As she lifts her head, they stare into each other's eyes and begin a long, wet, and passionate tongue kiss. Holding her tightly, Rich slowly moves his body into hers. Their embrace becomes tighter, and eventually, they move to the couch, where they continue to kiss. Rich utters words he doesn't say often: "I love you," to which Sherry responds, "I love you more."

She starts to gently rub her stomach in a show of love for her baby and the man she adores. At this moment, Sherry feels like no one else in the world matters besides the three of them. They continue to hold one another and kiss.

As the CD ends, so does the intensity of their romance. Sherry says, "That was good."

With a smile on his face, Rich jokingly replies, "Yeah, you're all right."

With the music playing in the background, they talk about their future together.

Reassuringly, he says to her, "You know I want to marry you."

Sherry smiles broadly, and says, "I can't wait."

At about this time, Gerard wakes up. Wanting a snack, he goes into the living room to ask for some ice cream and cake.

Rich says, "Yeah, that's a good idea; I think I'll have some too."

Sherry says, "Me three."

Hearing noise in the kitchen, Vaughn wakes up and walks to the front of the apartment.

Sherry asks, "Do you want some ice cream and cake also, Vaughn?"

Vaughn eagerly replies, "Yes."

Sherry smiles inside as she looks around the table, fantasizing that soon this will be her reality. She imagines fixing dinner for her new family, helping the boys with their homework, getting them off to school, taking care of the new baby, and making sure Rich is happy.

After they eat, the boys go back to their bedroom to finish playing Monopoly. Rich and Sherry settle in the living room and turn on the TV. After a while, they each nod off. About ten minutes into her nap, Sherry wakes up, experiencing sharp pains in her stomach. The sudden movement on the couch awakens Rich, and he notices the pained expression on her face. Seeing that she has both hands wrapped around her abdomen, Rich asks, "What's wrong?"

Sherry replies, "I had a sharp pain in my stomach, but it's gone now."

"I'm glad you're feeling better now; you scared me for a minute."

They resume their nap on the couch, but a few minutes later the pain returns with more intensity. Sherry loudly screams, "Oww!" and instructs Rich to take her to the bathroom.

Rich immediately grabs her arm and helps her off the sofa. They walk arm in arm down the hall.

Sherry stays in there for quite a while, and just as Rich starts to get nervous, she yells loudly, "Call an ambulance!"

Rich runs to the bathroom and shouts, "What's wrong?"

"I'm bleeding," she says.

Rich runs to the phone and dials 911.

The operator asks, "What's your emergency?"

Breathing heavily, Rich says, "My girlfriend is pregnant, and she's having bad stomach cramps and bleeding."

"What's your address?"

"55-05 Beach Channel Drive, #3C, Far Rockaway. Is there anything I should be doing to help her in the meantime?"

"No, just try to keep her calm; I've alerted the EMTs. They should be there any moment."

"Okay, then I'm hanging up."

"No, stay on the line with me until the EMT's arrive."

Rich says, "okay," and takes the phone to the bathroom door. He doesn't hear any noise, so he knocks, asking, "How're you feeling now, Sherry?"

"A little less pain, but more bleeding."

Rich tries to reassure her. "The EMTs should be here any moment now."

Hearing the commotion, Gerard and Vaughn step into the hallway.

Vaughn asks, "What's going on?"

Rich shouts, "Go back in your room; Sherry isn't feeling well!"

The boys comply; however, they stand on the other side of the door, listening, eager to know what's going on. Sherry starts to moan as Rich, with rising anxiety in his voice, tries to keep her calm. He says, "They'll be here any minute now."

Tiny beads of sweat start to appear on his forehead. Not knowing what to say, Rich keeps repeating, "Just hold on, baby; just keep holding on."

After about five minutes, Rich hears a succession of loud, rapid knocks at his door. He yells, "They're here!" and runs to open the door. The EMTs walk in swiftly, asking, "Where is she?"

Rich directs them down the hall as he hangs up the phone with the 911 operator. They knock, then enter the bathroom. Seeing Sherry seated on the toilet, they first check her blood pressure and pulse. Then they begin to examine her. After a few minutes, they decide she needs to be hospitalized. As the gurney makes its way down the hall, Vaughn quietly steps out of his room. Unnoticed, he stands with his hand on his necklace, fingering the words, "He Shall Give His Angels Charge Over Thee." The EMTs assist Sherry as she gets up. They place her on the gurney. She is moaning, and her eyes are closed as they wheel her out of the house. Rich is silent but notices Vaughn standing there. He furrows his brow and starts walking toward him, gritting his teeth, while saying, "Didn't I tell you to stay in your room?" Vaughn quickly opens the door and goes back inside his room as Rich turns around to follow the stretcher outside. The boys plaster their faces to the window and watch as Sherry is placed in the ambulance. The red and white lights swirl as the siren blares and the ambulance speeds away.

Rich comes back into the house, visibly shaken. He grabs his jacket and is getting ready to leave when he remembers Gerard and Vaughn. Rushing to their room, he knocks on their door. Gerard opens it quickly.

Talking fast, Rich says, "Look, I'm going to the hospital. I don't want you and Vaughn fighting, playing with matches, or doing anything you know you're not supposed to do. If I come back and find anything out of order, I'm beating both your little asses. Am I clear?"

Gerard says, "Yes."

Rich then runs out the door and heads downstairs to his car. Sherry arrives at the hospital, and they immediately take her into emergency surgery. The doctors and nurses feverishly work on her for the next three hours. Unfortunately, they can't save the baby. Sherry isn't told of her baby's death right away. However, after approximately forty-five minutes, a doctor and nurse come into the large maternity ward to tell her the news. Intuitively, Sherry knows something is wrong.

Dr. Flores says, "Ms. Martin, I have some bad news to tell you."

Sherry's tear ducts begin to fill up.

The doctor continues, "I'm sorry to report we lost the baby."

Sherry starts sobbing. The nurse puts a tissue box on the table next to her bed.

"Can someone tell Rich?" she asks.

The doctor replies, "Do you give me verbal consent to speak with him about what's going on?"

Sherry says, "Yes, you have my permission."

The doctor reassuringly places his hand on Sherry's shoulder. She reaches across her chest to put her hand on top of his.

"How're you feeling?"

"Numb."

"That's to be expected. You've been through a very traumatic experience."

After standing in silence for a long time, the doctor says, "I must go now, but the nurse will remain with you."

As the doctor walks out of the room, he turns and takes one last long, lingering and sympathetic look back at Sherry.

Dr. Flores walks out of the ward and finds Rich is the only person in the waiting room. The doctor asks, "Are you Rich Wilson?"

Rich nervously replies, "yes."

"I'm Dr. Flores. Sherry has given me verbal authorization to speak with you about her condition."

Rich's eyes grow wide, "How's Sherry?"

"I'm sorry to inform you that she lost the baby."

Rich holds his head down, grimaces, and closes his eyes tightly. "How is she doing, though?"

"As best as can be expected under the circumstances. Sherry's vitals are stable; however, she is despondent, as you might expect. "

"I must see her."

"That would be a great idea. I'm sure Ms. Martin would appreciate it."

He quickly walks into the maternity ward and scans the room for Sherry. Once he locates her, he runs across the room and gives her a tight hug. Sherry sobs into his chest.

"I so wanted this baby," she cries.

"I know you did."

"I wanted us to be one big, happy family."

"We still can be. I plan on marrying you in six months."

Sherry cries, "But I wanted this baby so much."

While continuing to hug her, Rich keeps repeating, "I know you did. I know you did."

Sherry slowly stops crying as she and Rich continue to embrace.

After a few moments of silence, she says, "You know Vaughn put his hand on my stomach as we were getting out of the car."

"Let's not go there," Rich says with irritation in his voice.

"But he did, as I was getting out of the car. He reached over and touched my stomach."

"So, what's that supposed to mean?"

"I don't know, but I think it means something. I told you, the last time Vaughn touched my stomach, he asked me point blank, 'Why did you give my father those pills to hurt my mother?'"

Rich begins to break out in a cold sweat.

"Can we change the subject? I'm not in the mood for this conversation. You've just lost a baby you loved dearly and wanted very much. I can't begin to imagine how much pain you must be in."

Sherry holds her head down as more tears begin to fall from her eyes. Rich wraps his arms around her and says, "We'll get through this."

As they hug, Dr. Flores enters the room.

"I'm sorry. I know this is a challenging time for both of you, but we need to run some more tests."

Rich slowly lets go of Sherry, kisses her gently on the forehead, and softly rubs her arm, saying, "I understand."

He then turns to walk out of the room, content he's done everything he could for the time being.

* * *

The next day Rich sleeps late. The boys play outside for a few hours. Afterward, they come upstairs, get some lunch, and take a nap. Rich thinks about Sherry and calls the hospital to see how she's doing.

Dr. Flores says, "She's doing as well as can be expected. The tests came back clean. She's been sleeping on and off all day."

Rich says, "I'll be in close contact."

Dr. Flores says, "That's good. I'll let you know if there are any changes."

After getting off the phone, Rich hopes for the day to be over soon and tomorrow to roll around quickly. Sundays are usually uneventful, and Rich goes into the living room to watch TV and read the paper. Eventually, he falls asleep on the couch and wakes up around six to fix dinner. After eating, Rich decides to turn in early, reminding the boys to go to bed at nine.

The following day Rich hopes for a peaceful workday. Still unnerved by the events of the weekend, he feels distracted and distant and rides to the Bronx in a foggy haze. Once at base camp, Gary picks up on his mood and asks, "How'd the weekend go?"

Rich nonchalantly shrugs his shoulders and says, "It was all right."

The team knows that Rich and Sherry are seeing each other. He assumes they have figured out he's the father of her baby. Deciding not to tell them about her miscarriage, Rich walks outside for some fresh air.

Outside, Rich begins to think about Doug. He remembers he's going to his temp work assignment today.

Shouting back into base camp, Rich asks, "Hey, when is Doug getting that call from the agency?"

Vincent yells, "Bruce said in about forty-five minutes to an hour!"

Rich asks, "What about the drugs? Are we using them today?"

"Remember Bruce said we're using the drugs sporadically from now on. It's causing too many problems."

Rich says, "Damn, that's one of the most interesting things about this assignment. Other than that, he's boring as hell."

By this time, Gary has come outside. "Hey, you don't seem like yourself today, man. What's really going on?"

"Uggh, nothing. Just got a few things on my mind."

He hands Rich a beer. "Here, try one of these; maybe this will help."

Rich opens the can and takes a big gulp. The cool drink feels refreshing going down his throat. Rich shouts, "Damn! we're turning into a bunch of alcoholics, drinking this early in the morning."

Their loud laughter echoes into the street.

Time moves slowly as Rich and his teammates shoot the breeze, waiting for Doug to get up. The call from the agency comes in around eight. Groggy and half asleep, Doug picks up the phone and immediately recognizes the happy white lady's voice from Kelly Services: Ms. Grobin.

"Hello, may I speak with Doug Jordan?"

"Yes, this is he."

"This is Amy Grobin from Kelly Services with good news. We've found you an assignment at JP Morgan Chase. Are you available to work today?"

Doug eagerly replies, "Yes."

"Well, this is a long-term administrative assistant position. The address is 60 Wall Street. The dress is corporate, and your pay rate is twenty dollars an hour. You must first report to Security for your picture and ID badge before meeting the office manager, Irene Olivio, in Private Banking on the thirty-seventh floor. When can you arrive?"

"I can be down there by ten."

"Okay, I'll let them know, and good luck on your assignment."

Ecstatic, Doug says, "All right, thanks, Ms. Grobin."

"All right, bye, Doug. And enjoy the rest of your day."

"Okay, I will. And you do the same."

After hanging up, Doug jumps out of bed and heads to the shower. He's dressed and ready to go in under twenty minutes. Before walking out the door, he remembers to grab the paper *New York Visions*. Outside, the surveillance team is in place. They covertly watch him as he exits the building. The train ride is slow—the local creeps along the tracks. Changing for the congested but faster express at 96th street lessens Doug's anxiety about being on time. He even forgets about his three-card monte mental mind game.

As the train pulls into Wall Street, Doug excitedly gets up and walks to the door. The station is located directly beneath the office building. Doug takes the escalator upstairs and walks to the building entrance. He is directed to a nearby room at the security desk to have his picture taken and get his ID card. He then takes the elevator to the 37th floor. He instantly notices the office has an open floor plan with a slew of floor-to-ceiling glass windows, small rectangular cubicles, and little decoration. Doug finds the office manager, Mrs. Olivio, who introduces herself with a handshake. She next introduces him to the four officers he'll be working with. Doug enthusiastically takes his seat, ready to begin his first day of work.

As the minutes and hours tick by, Doug realizes there's not much to do besides answer the phone and take a few messages; he twiddles his thumbs most of the day. In the afternoon, he receives two calls, one from Ron and another from Rommie. He doesn't answer or return them.

With so much time on his hands, Doug starts to analyze and question everything about his life, including his friendships, neighbors, family relationships, and even his coworkers on this job. After pondering his situation for a while, Doug decides to call his sister and brother. He's confident they couldn't be part of the investigation or plot against him; he picks up the phone to call his sister first.

"Hi, Marima."

"Hey. What's up, stranger? I haven't heard from you in a long time."

"Yeah, my mind has been preoccupied."

"That's fine. I'm just happy to hear from you."

"So what you been up to?" Doug asks.

"Ehhh, nothing much, just working hard.

"Have you spoken to Jamel lately?"

"No, that reminds me. I need to speak with him. Every time I call, he never picks up or returns my message."

"Yeah, I know what you mean, but I plan on calling him right after I get off the phone with you."

Marima asks, "How's work?"

Hesitantly, Doug replies, "I quit my job. I'm temping now."

Shocked, Marima asks, "Why?"

"It's a long story."

"I've got time."

Doug says, "I just got tired of their racist bullshit."

"I certainly can relate, but in this economy, you don't just walk away from a job to start temping."

"I couldn't take it anymore."

"Anyway, it's your life. You have to do what's best for you."

"Yep, that's what I'm talking about."

Changing the subject, Marima says, "We need to get together for dinner soon."

"That sounds like a great idea. It's been so long since I last saw you. How's the rest of the family doing? I know I've been missing in action."

"Oh, they're all fine."

Doug asks, "You dating anyone?"

"No, I'm happily single. How about you?"

Doug tersely replies, "The same."

The superficial nature of the conversation is starting to disappoint Doug and make him slightly angry. He remembers the three things he never discusses with his sister: her previous drug addiction, their father, and his homosexuality. He decides to end the conversation abruptly.

"All right, well, you were on my mind, and I decided to give you a ring. I'll let you get back to work. I also have a few things I need to finish up around here."

"Okay, I'll talk with you later."

"All right, bye. Enjoy the rest of your day."

"Will do."

As soon as Marima hangs up, she calls Al, tears start to collect in her eyes.

Al picks up on the second ring.

"Hello."

"Hi, this is Marima, Doug Jordan's sister."

"Oh, hi. How are you?"

"I'm fine. Doug just called me."

"That's great. We wanted you all to start reaching out to him more aggressively anyway. What was on his mind?"

"We discussed his job, calling our big brother later today and setting a future date for dinner together. He also wanted to know how the rest of the family is doing. All told, it was a relatively brief conversation, about fifteen minutes long, but Al somethings been on my mind. Can I now ask a question?"

"Sure. What?"

"How long is this investigation going to last?"

"I don't know. Did Doug mention anything about being investigated?"

"No."

"We already told you he's been talking to people and writing letters about the investigation. Whenever that happens, per our guidelines, the level of surveillance increases, and the investigation becomes more invasive."

"How'd he find out? Who told him?"

"I told you before; honestly, we don't know. We believe Doug has some kind of special psychic abilities."

"Come on; you must be kidding me, for real."

"Yes, that's what everyone is saying. The investigators can't figure out how he found out so much."

"I can't speak to that, but to be honest, this investigation is tearing our family apart. Since you told us what he's being investigated for, everyone in the family seems to be turning against him. I'm worried, and I know I've asked this question before, what started this investigation in the first place?"

"I told you I'm not at liberty to discuss that with you. So, tell me, what're you worried about?"

"The toll this is taking on Doug and how the family is starting to feel about him."

"How're they starting to feel about him?"

"Most of them say they can't stand him because they think he's a child molester, given you told them what he's being investigated for."

"We didn't tell them he was a child molester, just that he's being investigated for being one. In any event, I'm sorry about that, but it's the law; once an investigation gets to this level, we have to initiate certain protocols. Doug seems to be handling everything fine."

"Yeah, but the difference you mentioned gets lost in the translation."

"Honestly, there isn't much more we can do about that. So, do you have any other new information about Doug or questions for me?"

"No."

"All right, then I'll let you go. You take care and enjoy the rest of your day."

"You too."

By this time, Marima's tears have begun their slow and lonely descent down her face. She softly weeps after she hangs up the phone.

After getting off the phone with Marima, Doug immediately calls his brother Jamel.

"Hello."

"Hey, bro," Doug says.

In a surprised and excited tone, Jamel says, "Oh, how've you been?"

"I'm fine. I just got off the phone with Marima."

"How's she doing?"

"She's fine, just working that nine-to-five and living life. She's been trying to reach you."

"Yeah, graduate school is a bear. I always have something big on my plate."

"Well, give her a call when you get a chance."

"I'll try."

"Don't try; do," Doug says.

Jamel asks, "And by the way, how's work with you?"

"I know you didn't know this, but I recently quit my job."

Shocked, Jamel says, "You did what?"

"Yep, I quit my job. I got tired of the racist bullshit."

"So, what're you doing now?"

"I'm temping at JP Morgan Chase. Today's my first day."

"How's that going?"

"It's boring as hell, but it's paying the bills for now."

"How long do you plan on staying there?"

"I have a long-term assignment, but I'd be willing to leave immediately if something with more money and permanency came along."

Trying to take the focus off himself, Doug asks, "How much longer do you have at Harvard?"

Forcing his breath out in exasperation, Jamel says, "One more year. Thank God!"

"How's Boston been treating you?"

"I don't get out much. It's not treating me at all right now. I'll be glad when this is all over."

"What're you planning after school?"

"I want to teach in my field, public health policy."

Jamel suddenly remembers Doug is in school and asks, "By the way, how's school going for you?"

"I'm not in school anymore. After I left my job, I took a break this semester."

"But you're planning on going back. Aren't you?"

"Yeah."

"That's encouraging."

"Oh, by the way, Marima said the rest of the family is doing well."

"That's good because I haven't spoken to anyone in a minute."

Having covered the basics, both brothers run out of things to say. There is a long and awkward pause on the phone.

The silence starts to make Jamel feel uncomfortable, and he says, "I'm sorry to have to do this, bro, but I've got class soon."

"I understand. You take care and don't be such a stranger."

"I won't. Enjoy the rest of your day."

"All right, you too. Bye."

After the call, Jamel immediately phones Al.

"Hello, this is Al."

"Hi, this is Jamel, Doug Jordan's brother."

"Wow, that was fast. I just hung up with your sister a few minutes ago."

"Yeah, my brother told me he just finished speaking with her."

"What's he talking about?"

"He just talked about quitting his job and temping at JP Morgan Chase. He also inquired about my schoolwork and asked me what I planned to do after I finished my doctorate.

We just chatted for a few minutes, basically about life in general. It was a fairly short and routine conversation."

"Okay, that's similar to what he discussed with your sister. So, there's no new information."

Jamel says, "I was glad to hear from him, though. As you know, I don't speak to my siblings or my family that much."

"We want you all to start reaching out to him more frequently. In any event, I'm glad you spoke to him, and I appreciate you keeping us in the loop. You sound busy, so I won't keep you long."

"Okay, enjoy the rest of your day."

"You too. All right, bye."

After hanging up, Jamel starts to prepare for his next class.

* * *

Once Doug hangs up with his brother, he looks for something to occupy his mind. His day is long and boring. After a while he starts rummaging through his briefcase, and finds the paper *New York Visions*. Eager to see what's in this newspaper, Doug enthusiastically opens it but keeps it slightly hidden so no one around him can see what he's reading.

Doug looks through the newspaper, searching for anything of interest. The first thing he notices is a full-page ad for the National Alliance on Mental Wellness (NAMW). They're a grassroots mental health organization headquartered in the New York City area. The organization is nationwide and has affiliates all over the country offering consumer and caregiver support groups, psychoeducational classes, guest speakers, art and music therapy, and writing classes. The newspaper's subsequent pages contain poetry, art, editorials, and political commentary, all from individuals living with a mental health diagnosis. Near the middle of the paper is an article on a man trying out a new medication for treatment-resistant depression. Right under that is an essay on a man living with schizophrenia who goes from homelessness to work. Doug begins to read about this man's journey. As he's completing the third paragraph, Ms. Olivio starts walking toward him. He quickly closes the newspaper and turns it over.

Ms. Olivio's only been at his desk a couple of times today. Doug frowns as he wonders, *What could she possibly want from me at four-thirty this afternoon?*

Approaching his desk with a smile, she asks, "How was your first day?"

"It was quiet, not much to do."

"Yeah, that should change as the week progresses. The beginning of the week is always a little slow." Ms. Olivio then says, "I came over here for a reason; I have a favor to ask; could you please type up these two memos for me?"

Annoyed he can't finish his article, Doug replies, "Yes."

At that point, Ms. Olivio turns to walk away and says over her shoulder, "After you finish, you can leave."

Doug looks at the memos and believes he can knock them out in under ten minutes. He finishes them in five. Eager to go home, he puts the newspaper back in his briefcase and rushes out of the office.

Meanwhile, the guys at base camp receive a call from Bruce telling them Doug's on his way home.

"Hey, team, we plan on drugging Doug tomorrow morning. We'll have agents at his neighborhood Starbucks. I'm calling to remind you to be on the lookout for any different or unusual behaviors. We're using a new drug cocktail, one we've never used before, so we're unsure how he'll react. Any questions?"

"No questions. We'll keep an extra eye on him," Whitney says.

"On that note, I'll let you go, and we can talk later. It's almost time for you to change shifts anyway. Take care and enjoy the rest of your evening."

"All right. You too, Bruce," says Gary.

* * *

Today Doug takes the bus up the hill. The team gets in place. Doug gets off the bus, crosses the street to his building, and is on his way upstairs when Rich decides to go outside and make his call, stepping away from the store for more privacy.

He dials Dr. Flores, who picks up on the first ring.

"Hi, this is Rich Wilson, Sherry Martin's boyfriend."

"Yes, I remember you."

"How's she doing?"

"Sherry's physical condition is stable; however, her mental state has deteriorated. Earlier, she was crying to herself every now and then, now she's mumbling to herself and sobbing all the time. We've given her a couple of shots and some PRN medications, but they haven't been very effective. We intend to put her on some antidepressants, but they can take weeks to kick in. We're going to give it a few more days before we consider transferring her to the psych unit for further evaluation and treatment."

"Wow, I had no idea she was this bad."

"Remember, she's been through a very traumatic experience. It will take a while for her to get over this, and that's if she ever gets over this. Losing a child is something you carry with you for the rest of your life."

"Yes, I know you're right, Dr. Flores. I intend to visit her right after work. I'm about to get off soon and can be there within the hour."

"That might help. I'm sure Sherry will be glad to see you. Do you have any further questions for me?"

"No, that's all."

"So, I'll see you in about an hour."

"Yes. All right, talk to you later, Dr. Flores."

"Okay, I'll see you when you get here."

Worried, Rich hangs up and goes back into base camp. Keeping one eye on the clock and one eye on the monitor, Rich sees Doug has turned on the TV and is sitting on the couch, watching the evening news. As the minutes tick by, Rich's thoughts turn to Sherry and her condition. The tightness in his upper chest intensifies as he worries about his future wife's health.

Wandering in his thoughts, Rich loses track of the time. Abruptly waking up from his daydream, he looks at his watch and realizes it's five minutes past six. Hurriedly saying goodbye, he departs the bodega quickly. In the car, Rich begins to zone out and unwittingly surpasses the speed limit. Eager to get to the hospital, Rich suddenly remembers his sons and decides to go home first.

Entering the apartment, Rich finds both boys watching TV. Forgetting to check to see if their chores are done, he starts talking in a very rushed and clipped manner.

"Look, I'm going to the hospital to check on Sherry. She's not doing well. I need you boys to behave and do what you're supposed to. There's food in the fridge; you can get something to eat when you get hungry. I don't know when I'll be back. I should be home before your bedtime, but if I'm not, remember to go to bed at nine and not a moment later. Do you understand?"

Vaughn says, "Yes."

Gerard asks, "What's wrong with Ms. Sherry?"

"I told you she lost the baby. She's still having some problems. The doctors don't know what's wrong; she's just very, very sad. I don't have much time to talk," Rich says, "Am I understood?"

Both boys nod their heads in agreement.

"I'm going to leave now. Remember what I said."

Rich rushes out of the apartment and arrives at the hospital in under ten minutes. He finds the doctor's office and asks the receptionist, "Where is Dr. Flores?"

She replies, "He's making his rounds."

Rich quickly turns around and says, "Tell him Rich Wilson will be in the maternity ward."

He scours the big room and locates Sherry in a matter of seconds. She doesn't discern his approach. Slightly shocked by her appearance, he immediately notices her hair is standing up wildly all over her head; her skin looks dry and patchy, and her eyes are puffy and vacant. Without saying anything, Rich walks up from behind and gives Sherry a tight hug, whispering in her ear, "I couldn't wait to get here."

Surprised, Sherry starts to cry. After holding her for almost five minutes, Rich hears Dr. Flores voice.

"I'm glad you got here so soon. I was going to wait in my office, but I had to make some rounds."

"I got here as quickly as I could," Rich says.

Dr. Flores looks at Sherry and asks, "How're you feeling?"

Sherry murmurs, "I don't know, I just really don't know."

Dr. Flores asks, "Did the pills help?"

"No."

"In a couple of days, we might have to transfer you to another unit if things don't improve."

Sherry's eyes grow wide. "Where?"

"It appears you're slipping into depression, and we might have to move you to the psych unit for closer monitoring and treatment. It's for your own good."

A slight scowl appears on Sherry's face.

Sensing Sherry's disdain, Rich offers, "It could help you feel better."

Dr. Flores says, "Let me give you and Mr. Wilson some privacy. I'm going to go now, but I'll check on you one more time before the night is over."

Sherry nods her head slightly as Rich says, "All right, Dr. Flores. I'll talk with you later."

The doctor replies, "Enjoy your visit."

Rich now turns to Sherry and asks candidly, "What do you need from me?"

Sherry says, "You've been perfect this entire time. There's nothing more I could ask of you. It's just that I have these overwhelming moments of sadness that come out of nowhere, and all I want to do is cry and end it all."

Rich says, "I understand; you've been through a lot."

"When you call or visit, it means so much to me; even if we don't talk long or you don't say much, your presence alone helps to soothe me."

Rich gently kisses her on the forehead and asks, "Do you want anything from the snack machine?"

"No."

"Then I'll pull up a chair and sit here with you. You don't have to feel any pressure to speak. We can just sit in silence."

"How're the boys?" Sherry asks.

"They're at home watching TV. I told them to eat when they get hungry and reminded them to go to bed at nine. I can stay for a couple of hours."

"That won't be necessary. I know you have work tomorrow, and you're probably tired."

Rich says, "No, don't worry. I can stay awhile. We can and we will get through this. You know I still intend to marry you."

For the first time in a long time, a slight smile appears across Sherry's face, and she replies, "I look forward to it."

Sherry begins to feel warm and secure with Rich by her side. They don't say much but silently enjoy the reassuring presence of each other's company. Heavily medicated, Sherry slowly starts to drift back to sleep. Rich tries hard not to wake her as he quietly gets up to leave.

On his way out of the hospital, Rich glances at his watch, surprised it's past nine o'clock. He expects the boys to be in bed and asleep by now. Arriving home minutes later, Rich opens his apartment door, pleasantly surprised the TV is off.

Going farther inside, he notices all the lights are out. After checking the kitchen, Rich walks down the hall to his bedroom. Content that the boys have done everything he asked, he takes off his clothes and is asleep as soon as his head hits the pillow.

The following morning the boys follow their well-rehearsed weekday ritual. Approximately fifteen minutes after Gerard and Vaughn leave for school, Rich's alarm goes off. Well-rested and relaxed, Rich enjoys the peace and quiet of an empty apartment. He doesn't distract himself with the TV or radio this morning. Instead, he gets ready in silence and leaves for the Bronx within the hour.

On his ride to work, Rich thinks about Sherry, deciding today is as good a day as any to tell the team about her miscarriage. As an afterthought, he also remembers today's the day they'll restart drug protocols with Doug. Arriving at base camp, Rich assumes Doug is awake and preparing for work. Rich finds the team in the war room, looking at the monitors. Doug is currently in the shower.

"Good morning, guys," Rich says.

The guys on the team say, "Good morning."

Rich says, "Guys, there is something I need to talk to you about."

Everyone turns away from the monitors and looks at Rich, eager to know what's on his mind.

Logan is the first to speak: "Tell us what's going on, man."

Whitney reiterates, "Yeah, what's on your mind, bro?"

A little anxious, Rich looks at the floor, and after a moment's pause, he gets up the nerve to speak, saying slowly, "Sherry lost the baby."

Gary says, "Ah man, I'm so sorry to hear that."

Vincent says, "Yeah, man, I feel for you."

Tom says, "Wow, man. Let us know if there's anything we can do."

"How's she doing?" Whitney asks.

"Not well. Physically she's okay, but mentally she's still struggling a lot."

Gary says, "Damn, I remember how much she wanted that baby too."

Logan says, "It's going to take a while for her to heal from that. Don't forget to let us know if there's anything you need from us, and I do mean anything."

Rich says, "Thanks a lot, guys. I appreciate your support."

"No problem," Tom says.

After a few moments of reflection, the team turns its attention back to the monitors. Doug is almost finished getting dressed. The surveillance team is in place, and as Doug exits the building and starts walking down the hill, Vincent makes the call down to Starbucks. He tells them Doug is on his way.

The coffee shop is located around the corner from the 231st Street train station. The agents recognize Doug the moment he walks in. Unaware of what's about to happen, Doug orders his usual chai tea latte with soy milk. The drug cocktail has already been placed in the soy milk. Doug searches his wallet for some cash while the barista makes his drink. The cashier takes his money and hands him the beverage with a very broad "customer service" grin. Oblivious to what's transpired, Doug takes his first sip of the "pick-me-up" as he walks out the door.

Before boarding the train, Doug makes one final stop at a local convenience store for his newspaper. He then heads upstairs to the downtown train platform and arrives at his job a half hour later. Doug steps off the elevator and greets the receptionist. Turning the corner, he runs into Ms. Olivio, who smiles and says, "Good morning. I've already placed some work on your desk."

Doug politely returns the smile, glad his day will start off busy. Once seated, he begins to type up memos and send out telexes and wire transfers. Not rushed but relaxed, Doug is quickly settling into his day-two work routine.

His day appears to be going well. Then, seemingly out of nowhere, he starts to feel distracted and has difficulty concentrating. Doug begins to feel a slight shiver go up and down his body and gets a queasy feeling in his stomach. Thoughts typically in the back of his mind begin to dominate his thinking. Ideas such as *I'm under investigation, They're all spies, I'm being watched, My phone calls are being listened to, This office is a setup,* and *My computer is being monitored* cause Doug to become restless and nervous. He leaves his desk and goes to the downstairs snack shop.

New thoughts begin to enter his head: *I've got to leave, Home is the only safe place for me, They're out to get me.* After a few minutes, his internal dialogue becomes louder and more distinct and seems to command him. Frantic, Doug rushes back upstairs to get his belongings and leaves the office in a hurry.

He is hyper-vigilant, suspicious, and a little disoriented on the train ride home. He senses he is being watched and followed. The trip home leaves him in a muddled state. Bruce receives the call from Amy Grobin right after Doug leaves the building. She reports, "Doug just got up from his desk and left without saying anything to anyone."

As soon as Doug arrives at the 231st Street station, he walks swiftly up the hill, stopping at the neighborhood bodega to purchase a white candle.

As soon as Doug is inside his apartment, he lights the candle and lies on the bed. Eventhough, he doesn't fully understand why or how the candle gives him comfort and reassurance, he feels better with it burning, nonetheless.

Doug rests on his back, with his eyes closed and one hand on his forehead. He stays in this position for a while, merely facing the ceiling and thinking. A couple of hours later, the phone rings. Doug recognizes the number from Kelly Services but doesn't answer it.

* * *

At base camp, Bruce calls in and asks, "What's Doug doing?"

The team replies, "It looks like he's either thinking or praying."

"But he's not sleeping?" Bruce inquires.

"No. He came over here and purchased a white candle before going into his apartment. He's burning it now."

"Did he do anything strange or unusual?"

"No."

"Okay, the drugs should fully wear off in about five hours. Doug's probably feeling doped up right now, but after the drugs wear off, he'll be very sleepy for the rest of the day and possibly into tomorrow."

"Okay, team, so he's not going to be doing much for the rest of the afternoon; that's fine; I was just checking in."

"All right, Bruce."

"Okay, bye."

Doug's mind is peppered with thoughts about the investigators, who they are, and what they've been doing to him. Some of the specifics remain vague, but his negative feelings toward them remain strong. Many of his friends, officers of the cooperative, family members, neighbors, and coworkers all come to mind. Anger overtakes fear as Doug begins to believe they're all spying on him. Doug tosses and turns for the next few hours, unable to get comfortable in his body or his mind. Nevertheless, over time he begins to grow weary and slowly drifts off to sleep.

Once Doug is asleep, Rich decides to check on Sherry. Going outside, he calls her doctor first.

"Hello, this is Dr. Flores speaking."

"Hi, this is Rich Wilson, Sherry Martin's boyfriend. I'm calling to find out how she's doing?"

"Oh yes, I remember you. Ms. Martin's mental state is about the same. She's still very discouraged and continues to mumble to herself occasionally. In a day or two, we're probably going to transfer her to the psych unit."

Rich says, "If that's what you think is best, then please go ahead and do it."

"Yes, it's for her own good. Her physical condition is the same. Her heart rate and blood pressure are stable. Beyond that, I have no new information to report."

"Okay, that's fine. May I please speak with Sherry now?"

"We don't have a direct line to the maternity ward; I'll transfer you to the receptionist first."

"Okay, Dr. Flores, and thanks for everything."

"Sure, it's my pleasure. Enjoy the rest of your day."

"Okay, bye."

"Hold on a minute."

After a slight pause, Rich is transferred to the receptionist.

She answers, "Peninsula General Hospital. How may I help you?"

"May I have the maternity ward?"

"Sure, hold on a minute."

After three rings, a woman picks up.

"Nurse Robinson speaking."

"Hello, may I speak to Sherry Martin?" Rich asks.

"Oh, this is a bad time. The nurses are on the ward, checking vitals right now. If you can call back in a couple of hours, I can let you speak to her then."

"That's fine. I'll try to call back later."

"Okay, bye. Enjoy the rest of your afternoon."

"You too."

Before going back into the bodega, Rich looks at his watch and sees it's 3:35 p.m. He thinks about calling his sons but decides against it.

Gerard and Vaughn have been home for the last thirty minutes. Their day at school was uneventful, and the boys don't say much on their walk home. Once in the apartment, they change clothes, do their homework, and complete their afternoon chores.

* * *

For the last hour, Rich has been bored senseless watching Doug sleep. The conversation is sporadic in the war room. Rich takes a deep breath as the phone finally rings, ready for someone or something to break the uncomfortable silence. The team sees it's Bruce and puts him on the speakerphone.

"Hey, team, I know Doug is most likely sleeping right now, and it's probably boring as hell in there, so I called to say you can change shift early today. Go home as soon as your replacements arrive. That's all I was calling about. Enjoy the rest of your day."

"All right, Bruce, will do. And thanks," says Logan.

Rich goes outside. Lucky today, Rich's replacement, Investigator Gomez, reaches base camp earlier than usual. As soon as Gomez's car pulls up, Rich says, "Bruce said the team could go home early."

Investigator Gomez says, "No problem. Whenever you're ready."

Rich gets in his car and leaves, grateful for being ahead of the evening rush hour.

Rich walks in and finds Gerard and Vaughn exactly where he thought they would be. The first words out of his mouth are "I hope you did everything you were supposed to."

Gerard says, "Yes, we finished our chores and did our homework."

"Okay, dinner will be ready in an hour."

The boys don't pay much attention to their father. They sense he typically talks at or through them and not to them, not wanting a conversation, just barking commands and orders. Usually, the boys don't look at him when listening; it would appear too warm. Continuing down the hall, Rich goes into his bedroom and changes out of his work clothes, washes his hands then goes back into the kitchen.

Looking in the refrigerator, he decides to fry some fish this evening. The rest of the side dishes, rice, cabbage, and corn-bread, are leftovers. After about fifteen minutes, he places the steaming hot plates on the table. Rich calls Gerard and Vaughn into the kitchen. The boys wash their hands first and, after a quick grace, start to eat. Except for the sound of crunching fish, smacking lips, and silverware clinking against dishes, the table is quiet.

After dinner, Rich feels sleepy and decides to turn in early, reminding the boys to clean up and go to bed at nine. Gerard and Vaughn do as they're told and don't argue over chores this evening. Easing the ever-present tension in the house, the boys are inwardly happy their father is in his room early tonight.

* * *

Rich's alarm goes off at seven-thirty the next morning. Still a little groggy, he hears Gerard and Vaughn getting ready for school. The boys leave while he's in the shower.

The ride to base camp has Rich thinking about Sherry. Yesterday, he forgot to call the hospital back to find out how she was doing. He makes a mental note to do that once he's settled on the job. Arriving in front of the bodega thirty minutes later, he finds Logan and Vincent smoking outside. Rich says good morning and goes downstairs to the basement. Looking at the monitors, he sees Doug is still sleeping.

Gary says, "He's knocked out. Slept straight through the night, didn't even get up to pee."

Tom replies, "Yeah, those drugs really put him into a coma."

As the morning progresses, Rich says, "Damn, he's sleeping like he's dead."

Then suddenly remembering he needs to call the doctor, Rich goes outside to make the call in private.

"Dr. Flores speaking."

"Good morning. This is Rich Wilson."

"Good morning, Oh yes, I intended to call you today. It looks like Sherry's condition hasn't improved. She's still crying a lot and mumbling to herself. We've discussed moving her before and I've decided to transfer her to the psych unit tomorrow. We've done all we could do for her here."

Rich says, "Whatever is best. I respect your decision. Do you think she'll improve?"

"I am hopeful that medication and therapy should help, but I can't guarantee anything. Other than that, I don't have anything else to report. Sherry's physical condition remains the same."

"Well, okay. On that note, I'll let you go and check back in a couple of days."

Dr. Flores says, "All right, you enjoy the rest of your day."

Rich replies, "You do the same."

After hanging up, Rich goes back into the war room. Everyone is looking at the monitors.

Whitney says, "You'll remember Bruce said Doug could sleep a very long time."

Rich says, "Yeah, I know. Sometimes this job can be so fucking boring."

"I know," Logan reiterates.

The other members of the team search for things to do. They smoke cigarettes, drink beers, and read the newspaper, doing anything to make the time go by faster.

Gary asks Rich, "By the way, how's Sherry?"

"Thanks for asking, but she's not doing well. They're going to transfer her to the psych unit."

Whitney says, "Wow. Really, man."

"Yeah, the doctor told me she's still crying a lot and mumbling to herself."

Logan says, "I'm so sorry to hear that. Maybe we can send her some flowers or something."

"That would be nice. I'm sure Sherry would appreciate it. Thanks, bros."

"Anything to help you out, man," Vincent says.

Tom says, "Sorry for your troubles. Damn!"

Rich feels supported by his team and smiles contentedly.

As the hours tick by, Doug finally begins to stir around 12:30 p.m. Feeling as if he just woke up from anesthesia, Doug sits on the side of his bed for a couple of minutes. He looks at the white candle burning, then looks out the window, realizing that it's light outside; he checks his clock and sees that it's past noon. Doug eventually goes into the bathroom to pee and look at himself in the mirror. After washing his hands, he goes into the kitchen to make coffee. Still groggy and sitting on his couch he watches and hears the TV but doesn't listen to it.

After a few minutes, Doug goes back into the kitchen to fix his cup of coffee. Returning to the couch, he takes a couple of sips and begins to feel revitalized. He starts to think about yesterday. Doug says to himself, "They gave me some powerful shit." He remembers getting paranoid, leaving the job, coming home, buying a white candle, and passing out. Pondering his future, he asks, "How will I survive with no source of income and not being able to work?" Worried, he continues to look at the TV with his eyes in one place and his mind in another.

Doug doesn't know what to do. Eventually, he turns off the TV and goes back to bed, not to rest but to think. A million questions enter his mind. The most prominent being, "How will I survive this investigation?" Feeling agitated, he gets up and stands in front of the white candle, in quiet contemplation, trying to quiet his mind. One thought comes into focus, *You've got to stoop to conquer.* Unsure of what it means, Doug continues to stand in front of the candle, *You've got to stoop to conquer.* After hearing this thought a second time, Doug begins to meditate on its meaning. He goes back to bed, lying on his back, with his eyes closed and one hand on his forehead.

The team observes Doug in this position for hours.

Rich says, "I wonder what's on his mind?"

Logan replies, "Yeah, he's been in that position for a very long time."

Eventually, Rich looks at his watch. He gets off early today and realizes it's almost time to leave. He starts to gather his things. As Rich says goodbye to the team, Logan says,

"Goodbye, man, and give Sherry my best."

Gary says, "Yeah, tell Sherry I hope she feels better."

Whitney chimes in, "All right, man. Enjoy the rest of your day; I'll be praying for you."

Vincent says, "Peace, man."

Tom adds, "You and Sherry will be in my thoughts and prayers."

Rich smiles and says, "Thanks, guys," before walking out the door.

On his ride home thoughts typically far in the back of his mind begin to surface. As Rich ruminates on his dilemma with Vaughn, his heart beats faster; his hands shake, and tiny beads of sweat appear on his forehead.

On the one hand, the conflict of trying to believe he's a decent person, coupled with the guilt of what he's done to his son, makes him nervous and anxious. Unsure of how to resolve this contradiction, Rich decides to ease his mind by picking up a bottle of vodka. Five minutes from his apartment, he goes into the local liquor store and comes out with a package. Placing it on the seat next to him, he continues home.

Rich opens the door and finds his sons in their usual spot, on the living room couch watching TV; the boys say, "Hi, Dad."

With his mind preoccupied with other thoughts, Rich doesn't respond or look at them. He walks to his bedroom, then goes to the bathroom to wash his hands before going into the kitchen. Rich sees there are leftovers in the refrigerator.

He yells to Gerard and Vaughn, "When you get hungry, make yourself something for dinner. There's some food in here you can warm up!"

Rich shakes the orange juice container. Not hungry for food tonight, Rich decides to have a liquid dinner instead. Going back into his bedroom, he gets in bed and lies on his side.

Thinking back, Rich remembers something from his childhood. There was an elderly woman in his neighborhood who people called crazy and senile. Rumor had it that she kept her dead husband in the garage. She was short, skinny, brown-skinned, and balding, with flat flaring nostrils, sagging skin, and deep creases in her face. At the time, he thought she was one hundred years old, but in reality, she must have been in her eighties. Rich and his friends mounted a campaign of terror against her. They would ring her doorbell and run away, throw rocks at her house, break her window, put dead pigeons by her door, and open her mail and push it through her mail slot.

They would laugh as she cursed the unknown persecutors. One day Rich was chosen to deposit the open mail back into her mail slot. This day, as he put the mail through the opening, the door opened with a quickness that startled him. The woman reached through a hole in the screen door and grabbed him. She held him with her crippled and arthritic hands and said, "So you're the one." Rich felt a chill race up his spine, and her piercing eyes seemed to look deep into his soul. Her gravelly and throaty voice spit out the words, "I curse you."

Her head jerked back, she laughed loudly, and her mouth opened wide. Dropping the mail, he stumbled as he ran down the steps, seemingly shocked by electric current. Her laugh haunted him for hours, reverberating somewhere deep within his being. His friends refused to touch him for the rest of the day. Rich never went back to that house, but that experience always stayed with him.

He's unsure of why he remembers that incident now. Nonetheless, he does, and his eyes fill with tears as he thinks back on that day with sadness and regret. Rich continues to lie on his side and eventually dozes off. Waking up a couple of hours later, he goes into the kitchen to fix himself a drink. Gerard and Vaughn are still in the living room. He gets his drink and goes back into his bedroom, sipping it for the next thirty minutes. Once done, Rich puts the glass on his night-stand and gradually falls asleep. Not knowing what time it is, he hears the boys coming down the hall during the night. Feeling a sense of relief that they're going to bed, he drifts into an even deeper sleep.

The following day his alarm goes off at 7:30 a.m. Rich has a slight hangover, so it's a little more difficult getting up this morning. He touches the snooze button a couple of times before finally sitting up and putting his feet on the carpet. On his way to the bathroom, he hears the boys getting dressed. After about ten minutes in the shower, the sound of the door slamming shut reverberates throughout the apartment, and he knows Gerard and Vaughn are off to school. After coming out of the bathroom, Rich goes back into his bedroom to get dressed. He makes some coffee, has some cereal with a banana and orange juice, then leaves for his job.

On his way up to base camp, he listens to the radio while thinking about Doug's plans for today, suddenly remembering Doug's therapy appointment at eleven.

Arriving at base camp, Rich sees Logan and Whitney outside smoking cigarettes. He greets them then goes downstairs to the war room. Looking at the monitors, Rich sees Doug is still sleeping. Checking the time, he sees it's 9:30 a.m. Doug should be getting up soon. Rich also remembers Sherry will be transferred to the psych unit today and makes a mental note to call the hospital sometime this afternoon.

In the meantime, the guys at base camp watch the news, read the newspaper, drink coffee, and talk about their family, all to pass the time. Doug awakens around ten o'clock. Bruce calls in shortly after Doug gets up.

"Hi, team. I know Doug has his therapy appointment this morning. We've decided to drug him. He usually gets his chai from Starbucks. We're hoping he stops in there this morning before getting on the bus to Riverview. We've already placed some agents in there to put the cocktail in his beverage."

Rich asks, "Why're you doing it now?"

Bruce says, "I've come up with a plan. We're going to try something different today. I'll give you more details when he gets back home. We'll need you guys to report how he reacts when he returns. That's all I want to say. All right, take care."

"Okay, Bye, Bruce."

After hanging up, the guys refocus their attention on the video monitors. Doug's getting dressed and is almost ready to leave. Logan says to the team, "I'm gonna fuck with Doug this morning y'all. Watch me."

Rich asks, "What're you gonna do?"

Logan replies, "He's always looking over here anyway. You'll see," as he walks outside to stand in front of the bodega. Whitney and Gary go out to see what Logan is going to do.

Doug leaves his apartment, gets on the elevator, and goes downstairs. After exiting his building, Doug starts walking down the hill. He looks over at the bodega and sees Logan standing outside. As Doug looks across the street, Logan makes a vulgar gesture with his hand as if he's masturbating.

Doug rolls his eyes, thinking, *I should go over there and tell him, "Why don't you have your mother do it for you."*

Doug pauses momentarily, almost tempted to cross the street and say it to the guy, but decides against it. Slightly annoyed, Doug continues down the hill, saying to himself, "These fucking investigators."

Gary and Whitney laugh when they see what Logan does. Gary says, "Man, you a mess."

As Doug continues down the hill, the guys go back into the war room.

Once at 231st Street, like clockwork, Doug stops at Starbucks then gets on the bus to Riverview. Fifteen minutes later, he arrives in front of the RMHC. Doug walks upstairs and tells the receptionist he has an eleven o'clock appointment with Ms. Sonnovia. Looking at the clock, Doug realizes it's ten minutes to eleven. He takes a seat, starts to flip through an *Ebony* magazine, and waits for Ms. Sonnovia.

She opens the door to greet him ten minutes past the hour. They walk into her office, and Doug takes his seat.

Ms. Sonnovia asks, "How are you?"

Doug replies, "Best as can be expected under the circumstances."

Ms. Sonnovia asks, "What's going on?"

Doug responds, "I'm tired of these spy networks following, drugging and harassing me. I also quit my temporary job and I need a new source of income."

"Yes, I remember you said you believed the police were investigating you. We can talk about that, but first, I want

to discuss the antipsychotic medication Dr. Chandora pre-
scribed."

"Okay."

"You do know that you don't have to be crazy to take these
medications. They can help with paranoia, anxiety, and even
focus. I was looking through your case files and see you wanted
medication to improve your concentration. These medicines
can help with that also. It appears that your symptoms are getting worse. If you agree to take the antipsychotic medication,
we can help you apply for Social Security Disability."

At first, Doug is offended by the idea that he is disabled and
needs government assistance. Then he remembers the phrase
"You've got to stoop to conquer."

Thinking for a couple of minutes, he takes a deep breath
before answering, "Okay, I'll take them."

Ms. Sonnovia's eyes grow wide, and she appears somewhat relieved. She says, "I'll consult with our psychiatrist,
Dr. Feinstein, about getting your Social Security Disability
application started. We'll use some of your case notes from
Dr. Ehnis and your prescription records. Who was your previous psychiatrist?"

"Dr. Black."

"Okay," Judy says.

Doug is angry that his life has come to this. He decides to
call this his "Incognito" mode. *I'll have to play crazy just to
support myself.* Doug thinks, *Oh well,* as he mentally shrugs
his shoulders.

Ms. Sonnovia says, "This is a good thing. I think you'll find
your symptoms will start to improve."

Doug unintentionally rolls his eyes, annoyed but resigned
to his fate.

Ms. Sonnovia says, "All right, I'll get right on this. But you
were talking about your belief that the police were following,
drugging, and harassing you. You mentioned something about

a spy network. How have the people in these spy networks been harassing you?

"They come into my apartment and create mischief all of the time. These investigators put oil in my door lock, scratched all my CDs, created a gas leak in my stove, cracked an egg in front of my door, put sleeping powder in my medication, put red paint on my linoleum, unscrewed the faceplate on my electric light sockets, put stuff in my food, broken my window-pane, cut the cord for my blinds, put bleach in my clothes, etc. My window's been broken the entire time I've lived there. I guess if they decided to throw me out the window, the excuse would be I fell out of it due to a faulty window frame."

Sarcastically Doug says, "Then I would meet God with a broken neck and a cracked skull. One time I remember coming home after getting something from the store. I came into my apartment, and the middle window was wide open, which I never do. My grandmother lived in a twenty-four-story build-ing, and one day, a pigeon flew into her apartment. So, I never leave my window open. I always put in the screen. So, I put down the window and get something to drink. Suddenly, I start to feel very depressed, almost like a bowling ball dropped inside me. Depression is something I never feel. So, I knew it was the drugs they put in my drink. I guess the window being open was to encourage me to jump out of it. I shook my head and said, such evil people. I just closed the window and went about the rest of my day. The list of things they do to me is end-less. I think they aim to drive you crazy, have you kill yourself, or just plain out murder you. Anyone's greatest asset is their mind and the ability to think and reason intelligently. If you want to destroy a person, typically, the first thing you do is try to make them believe they're either crazy or dumb. I find that people in these spy networks try to convince you of both, but I am neither. It didn't work with me; I understand too well the context in which I live and why all these things were happening to me, so it's easier for me to not let it get to the heart of me. I also believe many people in these spy networks—and I mean all of them, family, friends, neighbors, and coworkers—have tried to use goofer work against me.

"What's goofer work?"

It's voodoo or rootwork. Goofer dust is dirt from a graveyard used to cast spells on people. Whenever I would find dead bugs in my house, my shoes would be cut in the heel, or I would feel the presence of unclean spirits around me, I would burn a white candle, read the ninety-first Psalm, and anoint myself with oil, while saying, 'Return to sender. Go back to you and yours.' I have no respect for rootworkers. First of all, it's stupid because you're inviting the devil into your home, and the devil is a trickster. I've always heard using 'devilish functions' will backfire on the person who uses them, meaning what you try to do to someone else usually winds up happening to you.

I've been told people who use those things live to be very old, suffer a lot in life, create a generational curse for their children, and their souls never find peace after death. What idiot wants to leave that type of spiritual legacy to their descendants. I'm not afraid of voodoo in the least, but I think people who use it are senseless. I probably have a million reasons to use rootwork on a million people, but I would never fool with that stuff for fear of what it would do to my life. God sits above all that nonsense. Most of the individuals in these spy networks I wouldn't spit on when they get to hell to quench their thirst, and as for these 'job' spy networks, in particular, all they do is try to document lies and untruths. Then they go to a judge to get them substantiated and added to your investigative record. Sometimes I look at the people in these spy networks and see wickedness and cruelty in their eyes, sometimes nothing, and sometimes sympathy and kindness. Even as a child, I would look at people very boldly and obviously in a way that might have been considered disconcerting. As a young child, my mother told me to stop staring at people like that. She said it was rude. I continued to do it, and she gave me a beating for it one time. I don't remember believing I was spiritually reading people at the time but maybe that's what I was doing. Even as a teenager, my friends would tell me I had a habit of looking people up and down. I wasn't really aware of it. I am also a descendant of people who were Gullah with the gift of second sight."

"What are Gullah?"

"They are descendants of the last slaves to come directly from Africa. They worked on the rice plantations along mainly coastal south Carolina in the Sea Islands. My great-grandfather was born on Saint Helens Island and went to school in Beaufort. They were isolated from the mainland, so they kept alive many more African traditions. They were different from other Southern Blacks in food, clothing, spiritual traditions, and speech. A lot of them believed in, and some practiced, rootwork. I grew up hearing lots of stories about the culture. I was told that the only way those things can work against you is if you practice it yourself, but if you keep your hand firmly planted in God, no harm will come to you."

Ms. Sonnovia asks, "You've mentioned a lot of things and put forth a lot of suppositions. What proof do you have that any of these things are true?"

"None, but I know I'm right. I can feel it, and I see hatefulness in many of these investigators' eyes. One of the main ones is that lunatic super downstairs. It's very personal for him and the coop board president who lives across the hall from me—but generally all of them on that floor, and many other people. Look, if you can give a person a negative label or make them inhuman in some way, you can feel justified in doing anything to them. I feel that's what they try to do with me. Make me a bad person to not feel guilty about all the shit they've put me through. A biased belief about a person or group of people, a loudmouth, or a strong personality can sway a group to do atrocious things. For example, what has happened to enslaved Africans and Jews. If you say anything loud enough or long enough, people start to believe it even if it's not true. I know how groupthink works. Rare is the person who will stand up in a group and risk alienation from that group by saying this is wrong. That type of person is one in a million. Most people just go along to get along. I know this."

"So, you feel all your neighbors are harassing you."

"Yes, more or less everyone in these spy networks. These investigators also try to frame you."

Ms. Sonnovia asks, "What are they trying to frame you for?"

"I believe they will try to pin anything on you. In these spy networks, I believe they create the facts from the story they tell themselves about you. Instead of creating the story about you from the facts of who you really are. I feel they integrate you into these spy networks to ruin your life in any way they can and probably laugh about it later. I think a lot of these investigators are wicked and sick."

Ms. Sonnovia remarks, "You feel all these people are conspiring against you."

"Yes, I do. I believe it's a despicable process, a kind of oppression."

"It sounds like paranoia."

"I know it does; it's probably set up to make you feel that way, but as I've said before, I know what I believe. I might call myself paranoid but my paranoia is real. I sense and feel things very deeply. I can look into someone's eyes and get powerful thoughts in my mind about them. Not all the time, but sometimes."

Ms. Sonnovia asks, "Do you get those thoughts about me?"

"No, not yet."

"Do they come from inside or outside your head?"

"They come from inside my head."

"Do you see images outside your head?"

"No, I don't."

"You know all individuals living with schizophrenia don't have visual and auditory hallucinations."

Doug says, "Really? I have a question?"

"What is it?"

"How can you be my therapist if we don't have a consensus on what reality is and you challenge the validity of my experiences?"

"That's a good question. I need to think about that for a moment. You also told me you think I'm part of the spy network too."

"Yes, I still do. I'm the client. Isn't my view of reality or what I perceive as factual the only thing that matters here? I'm not saying little green men from Mars are coming through the wall and talking to me. All I'm saying is that I'm under investigation and God has allowed me to peek behind the curtain."

"I guess you're right. So, I'll change my line of questioning. How do you feel about what's going on in your life, given your perception of reality?"

Doug replies, "I get angry for about ten minutes, I get annoyed for five, then I give it to God. I also tell myself I have no proof for what I believe and there's nothing I can do about it. Therefore, I try to release it, but my beliefs never change."

"You told me you are certain your father put you on the police's radar by lying about you molesting your sister."

Doug responds, "Yes, I do, and I believe through the years he's been building a case against me based on lies he's been telling them about me. He was a police sergeant."

"What would he have been telling them."

"I don't know."

"That would be a very, very long investigation."

"I know."

Ms. Sonnovia asks, "Why are you just realizing it now?"

"I don't know. God's timing."

"You did say you believe you were born unique in some way, and when the police use drugs on you, it enhances your natural-born gifts."

Doug responds, "Yes, I do."

Ms. Sonnovia says, "It seems you didn't know this was happening. However, once you get drugged, you develop greater insight into what's going on and what's gone on and reevaluate all of your past experiences. Like a series of 'aha' moments."

"Exactly."

"I read in your case notes from Dr. Ehnis that you hate your father and have had some pretty traumatic and abusive experiences with him. Talk a little bit more about that."

Doug says, "Yuck, do I have to?"

"It would help me understand you and your life better."

"I remember my sister told me she heard our mother say he pressured her to have an abortion when she got pregnant with me. But she told him she would never abort any child of hers. She was dead set against it. He's been an idiot from day one, and I have never liked him from day one. As a very young child, I can remember looking in the back of comic books and reading how to make a voodoo doll. I would try to make one of him and stick pins in it. I also remember, as a very young child, having very violent fantasies of him being tortured. One time, my brother and I were in the kitchen, and my brother was at the sink. My father came upstairs and started yelling at him about something and hit him. I was standing in front of the refrigerator. As he walked out of the kitchen, he slapped me and pushed me into the refrigerator for no reason. I can also remember him slapping me off a stool one time. He was very violent toward me, both of us really—but toward me mostly. When he wasn't violent, he was emotionally cruel and abusive or very negligent and unconcerned.

"At a very young age, I stopped wanting to be anything like him. He would routinely put me down. One time, our mother asked the three of us if we wanted to watch this show on PBS called *I Claudius* with her. I was the only one who said yes. So, we were watching the show in their bedroom when he came home. After he came in the room, he said, 'Doug doesn't understand that.' My mother got angry and said, 'At least he's trying to understand it,' and she said she was tired of him always talking down about, and to me, it was getting on her nerves. I also remember going to school with holes in my shoes, underwear, coats, and pants because I was too afraid to ask him for anything. The answer was always no or some nasty or rude response. We were firmly middle class because he was a police sergeant, and my mother was an engineer. So, there was money in the house, but neither my brother nor I benefited from any of it. There were times we would go weeks without seeing him because of his schedule. He would be at work when we were home, and when we were at school, he would be home sleeping. When he finally saw me, my hair would be very nappy and overgrown; he would ask me why I didn't leave him a note saying I needed a haircut. I would respond I didn't know. I started giving one-word or few-word answers to questions they would ask me about why I was doing some of the things I was doing, but I was afraid. I remember never giving him any of my permission slips for school trips because he would always say no."

Realizing Doug has talked a very long time, Ms. Sonnovia interrupts him by saying, "This is all very sad, but continue if you want to."

"I also believe my father started drugging me from birth. I can remember feeling drugged as a very young child. I remember, in all the pictures of me as a toddler, I just looked strange, blank, and very sad. Through the years, people told me it was like a 'deer in the headlights, poker face, blank look, etc.' My brother would look normal in those same pictures. I remember getting very sick as a young child after dinner one evening, having severe stomach pains and violently throwing up. My mother told him to take me to the hospital, but he refused. However, I remember him coming upstairs and standing by my bed, checking my pulse. This behavior seems strange to me now, given that I was having severe stomach cramps. You check someone's pulse for their heart rate. He never said one word to me after taking my pulse. He just went back downstairs. We all ate the same meal at the same time that day. I think he tried to poison me.

"I also remember going to the eye doctor as a young child because I had a lazy eye. I remember hearing the doctor say to him they should patch my other eye. He never did it. As I got older, I would go to the eye doctor to see if it could be corrected. The doctors would all be surprised that I was never given a patch for it. I think he wanted my eye to wander to support a narrative he was trying to create about me."

Ms. Sonnovia says, "This is all so interesting. Given you told me your sister said he sexually molested her. Did he ever sexually abuse you?"

"No, the only thing I can remember is saying 'monsters would get in the bed with me,' but I thought they were nightmares. I do not remember any sexual abuse. I started doing bizarre things as a young child, like tiptoeing around the house and going to the bathroom in the upstairs storage unit instead of the downstairs bathroom. I didn't want anyone to know I was home. I also started eating raw food. I believe I was doing these things because of the drugs he was giving me. Probably the same or similar drugs to the ones the police are using on me now. I also think he wanted me to grow up disabled, partially for the disability check and also to be a fall guy for the molestation of my sister. Then he could've pinned anything on me because I would've been unable to defend myself as a person with developmental challenges. I believe he is the worst type of child molester, if there is such a thing. He was very strategic in what he tried to do to me. He went on the offense from birth and tried to undermine and stunt my growth from day one. That's really why he started the investigation of me in the first place and treated me the way he did. He was well aware of the impact it would have on my life. He was a policeman before I was born.

"The jackass that he is, I genuinely believe he had the whole family investigated. Headquarters was the house next door. They were Jamaican. My mother would tell him I frequently needed therapy. He would just brush it off or shrug his shoulders. In seventh grade, I took seven Excedrin pills with vodka because I read in *Jet* magazine that one of the Supremes died from pills and alcohol. Nothing happened, so I drank bleach and started throwing up all over the place. I also remember running away from home in seventh grade. When the police found me, he and my mother had to come to the precinct to pick me up. When we got home, he took me to the basement and beat me.

"Are you suicidal now or live with depression?"

"No, I don't have any suicidal or depressive thoughts. I get annoyed or angry at what I'm going through now and have been through in the past."

Ms. Sonnovia asks, "How was school?"

"I did very well in school. I was an A or B student with quite a few friends, and I was well liked. I always felt safer in school. Though I can remember starting to check out mentally in high school."

"What do you mean?"

"I would be in class and look straight at the teacher and seem like I was listening but have not heard one word he or she was saying the entire hour. Even now, I can look at the news for sometimes a very long time and not hear what's being said because I've mentally checked out and started thinking. People say that even now, they can see in my face that sometimes I'm not really listening. I'm often not fully present, meaning my body and eyes are in one place, but my mind is elsewhere. I also told Dr. Ehnis one time I believed I had one brain but three minds. A mind where I could be present and focused, another mind where God would speak to me, where my intuition and insight reside, and another mind where I go when I mentally check out after being triggered."

"Your ideas are compelling, but you've said you've never heard voices or seen images outside your head."

"No, I haven't."

"I saw in your case files that your grandmother took you to a therapist around the age of fourteen or fifteen. Talk about that."

"Yes, I lived with her after my parents divorced. I think at the time, it was more because she and others thought I was going to be gay. In the beginning, I was not too fond of it; however, it made me seek help for myself in later years when I thought I needed more support. It made me unafraid to submit to therapy. I remember one of the first conversations I had with Ms. Euma was 'Am I crazy?' She told me you don't have to be crazy to go to therapy."

"How did your family react to you being gay?"

"Most of the time, it wasn't mentioned, but if there was a conversation, it was about me acting too gay instead of me being gay. My family thought I was 'putting on,' particularly in the way I walked and talked. I remember hearing Aunt Barbara say, 'I could hire a hitman to kill Robert. I remember when Joyce had those boys. They were two bright, beautiful baby boys who Robert just fucked up and fucked over, and that's why Doug turned out to be a faggot.' I also remember Aunt Margaret saying, 'I used to see Robert on patrol at the train station where I worked. He would speak to me, and I stopped getting off at the train exit closest to my job, where I would see him, and instead I got off at the exit farthest from my job so as not to see him.'

"I also remember Aunt Margaret saying to Aunt Barbara one time, 'Doug gets on my nerve because he always seems too nice.' My Aunt Barbara responded, 'Ignore it.' She said it was because I was gay, like a gay Uncle Tom. Through the years, people have called me phony, holier than thou, bleeding heart, etc. I've always viewed myself as a very moral and kind person. It's one of the things I'm most proud of about myself. I feel the average person is walking on street level in terms of integrity and personal decency. I think I'm at the top of the Empire State Building, if not the clouds in that regard. No demon from hell could ever convince me I'm a bad person.

"My mother's side of the family would frequently get disgusted with him for not doing anything with or for us. We never told them the actual depth of his abuse and wickedness. They knew some of the things but not all of them. In that household, our sister was treated the best, then my brother and me last."

"That's interesting. How do you feel about your father now?"

"Typically, I don't think about him, but I used to say I only wished to see him one last time, when he was dead, so I could spit in his face in the coffin. One therapist told me I have to learn to forgive, but honestly, in that respect, some days are better than others, but in general, I'm just not there yet."

Ms. Sonnovia asks, "Given your perception of reality, what keeps you going?"

"My firm belief that I have a powerful anointing on my life and I have a special relationship with God. He has preserved me in all these situations. Humble people become servants of God, and that describes me to a T. God is the most powerful force in the world. He sits above any building super, rootworker, coop apartment board of directors, coworker, supervisor, spy network, detective, investigator, police captain, prosecutor, defense attorney, grand jury, the court system, judge, or jail. I feel God has performed a miracle in my life by revealing to me I was under investigation.

"When I was a teenager, I dreamed I was running through Fort Greene Park with my friend Darrin. There were snakes of all shapes and sizes falling from the sky. They were all over the ground. I was screaming and running, trying to get away from them. Then I felt something in my back. It was a vine, but it was moving. I was yelling at Darrin to pick up a tree limb, put it under my shirt, and pull it out of my back. That's all I can remember about the dream. I don't recall whether he pulled it out or not. However, I was always told, whenever you dream about snakes, that is an enemy. I feel that dream was a foretelling of what I would have to endure in this life. In essence, to be continuously surrounded by snakes in human form of all kinds and coming from all directions. But I feel God has watched over me. God wanted me to understand that he has walked with me through all of these horrible experiences. I also believe he will continue to walk with me throughout life as long as I continue to lean on him.

"Given that reality, I shall never let go of his hand, no matter what challenges I encounter. I believe God is giving me experiences to evolve my consciousness. Ultimately to be a better servant for him, no matter how difficult they might be for me. I believe I'm an ordinary person who God is using in an extraordinary way."

"But how do you function on a day-to-day basis?"

"It's similar to what the author Toni Morrison said: 'African-Americans must think about slavery all the time, but at the same time, they can't think about slavery all the time.' I have to think about being investigated all the time, but at the same time, I can't think about it all the time, or else I wouldn't be able to function. I feel there is a subtext to all my interactions in this world. I am always mindful of it, but to be honest, a lot of the stuff I push out of my mind and don't think about or just release it to God."

Ms. Sonnovia says, "Doug, you've talked about a lot of things during this session, but it's time for us to close. However, I have one last question for you. What about your friends?"

Doug says, "My friends mean the world to me. The people I'm closest to are Darryl, Ron, Rommie, Ryan, and Tommy."

"How is your relationship with Darryl and Ryan?"

"It's fine. I'm closer to Darryl, but I speak to Ryan more often. Ryan and I bump heads a lot. His way of being in the world just annoys me so much. We argue a lot, but they're both good people. I've known them for quite a long time."

"Okay, on that note, we'll have to end the session. Is this same day and time good for you next week?"

"Yes, it is."

"Good. I'll see you next week."

"All right, Ms. Sonnovia. Enjoy the rest of your day."

"Will do. You too."

Doug exits the room and goes downstairs to wait for the bus.

Once he leaves the building, Ms. Sonnovia immediately calls Bruce.

"This is Bruce."

"Hi, this is Judy. Doug just left our session."

"How'd it go?"

"It went well. Doug decided to take the antipsychotic, but he's still talking about being investigated. I told him Dr. Feinstein and I would get going on his Social Security Disability application right away. He also talked a lot about what he believes he's currently going through because of the investigation and his early childhood experiences. Given the traumatic nature of the events Doug mentioned, he was very calm and unemotional. He didn't cry, and his vocal inflection didn't change. Our session went a little over, but I let him continue talking. Did he stop at Starbucks before coming here?"

Bruce says, "Yes, they were able to put the drugs in his drink. So, he should start feeling the full effects within about fifteen minutes. Did he mention stabbing his father?"

Judy says, "No."

"That's good. We can have Doug's Social Security Disability application expedited. Typically, those decisions take two years, and eighty percent of the time, they get denied the first time, but we can do something about that on our end. Also, were you able to ask about his two friends, Ryan and Darryl?"

"Yes, I mentioned them near the end of the session."

"Great. Let's hope Doug has one of his 'aha' moments about them on his way home. I'll review the video of your session later and remind the team to look at it also."

"Yes, let's keep our fingers and toes crossed."

"Okay, Judy, thanks for touching base. I'll see you at our staff meeting tomorrow."

"All right, talk to you later."

Doug is about ten minutes from home when a slight shiver goes up and down his body. He immediately realizes what's happening and says to himself, "It must have been in my chai tea this morning."

Doug begins to get a queasy feeling in his stomach. Once the bus arrives across the street from his building, he stops at the store. Doug purchases a white candle then goes upstairs to his apartment. Once home, he immediately places the candle on his cedar chest and lights it.

After lying on his bed for about fifteen minutes with his eyes closed and one hand on his forehead, the thoughts begin to occur to him. The insights in his mind say, *I'm being watched, and my phone is tapped. Darryl and Ryan put spy cameras in my home and a listening device on my phone. I hate them. They are sleazy, untrustworthy, and have betrayed me.* After hearing these thoughts clearly in his mind, Doug gets up and swiftly walks to the snow globe Darryl gave him and puts it in the garbage. He goes to the clock in the kitchen, takes it off the wall, and throws it down the compactor chute. Doug then opens his phone, removes the listening device, and throws it in the garbage. Next, he unscrews the showerhead, finds the spy camera, and throws it in the toilet. Finally, he goes to the component system given to him by Ryan, which he now realizes has a receiver in it, and puts it in the downstairs trash bin.

Filled with rage, Doug starts writing nasty letters to both Ryan and Darryl. The team at base camp watches with undivided attention. They call Bruce.

"Hi, Bruce here. What's going on?"

Gary is the first to speak. "It looks like he's found all the cameras and the listening device."

Bruce says, "Amazing. What did he do with them?"

Whitney replies, "He threw them out."

"He found all of them, even the listening device, huh?"

"Yes," Tom replies.

Bruce says, "Simply remarkable. What's he doing now?"

Rich says, "He just finished writing nasty emails to both Darryl and Ryan."

Bruce asks, "What did he put in those letters?"

Vincent replies, "He let them know he realizes what they've done to him. He talked about their lack of decency, his feelings of betrayal, and their disloyalty. He also put some very personal and mean things about their families, just some very offensive stuff overall."

"Did he make any written threats in his letters?"

"No," Tom replies.

Bruce says, "That's good. This guy is something else. Our plan worked like a charm."

Whitney asks, "What was it?"

"We gave him the drugs this morning; then we had his therapist ask him about his feelings toward both of them near the end of his session. We wanted to see if this would spark any new insights or realizations about them. We tried to time the full effect of the dosing to when he would be on his way home. It worked perfectly."

Whitney asks, "So, what's going to happen next?"

Bruce says, "Since he didn't call the police or bring the devices in, we can't arrest them. We'll have to keep investigating them. By the way, what's he doing now?"

Logan responds, "He's lying in bed on his back with his eyes closed and one hand on his forehead."

"Let me know if anything changes. I'm going to hang up now."

"All right, will do. Talk to you later," Gary says.

"Okay, enjoy the rest of your day."

The team continues to observe Doug. Tom says, "He'll probably be in that position for a while, then he'll probably fall asleep."

Rich suddenly remembers he needs to call the hospital and check on Sherry. As the rest of the team watches the monitors, Rich goes outside to make his phone call.

The receptionist picks up after the third ring, "Peninsula General Hospital. How may I help you?"

Rich asks, "May I have the psych unit?"

The receptionist replies, "Sure, hold on a minute."

The phone rings a couple of times, then someone answers, "Psych unit. Nurse Fields."

Rich says, "Hello. Could you tell me how Sherry Martin is doing?"

Nurse Fields replies, "What's your name? I have to check and see if we have a preauthorization for you."

"My name is Rich Wilson. I don't think my girlfriend signed a preauthorization form. She was previously in the maternity ward and gave her doctor verbal authorization to speak with me."

"In that case, I can't tell you how she's doing. The psych unit is a separate division of the hospital. Due to HIPAA laws, I can't give you any information on our patients. Our visiting hours are from nine to eight during the week and eight to four on the weekend. If she gave you verbal authorization to speak with her previous doctor, I would suggest you first talk to him. He can expedite the process of you getting on the ward to see her and obtaining any information on her."

Rich says, "Okay. I'll try to get over there today."

Nurse Fields says, "In that case, enjoy the rest of your day."

"You too."

After hanging up, Rich looks at Doug's apartment for a moment. Uncertain of why he glances up there, he momentarily ponders the life of the young man he's investigating. Unsure of his feelings, he shakes himself out of his daydream and walks back into the store, ready to continue doing his job. Rich checks the time and thinks about his sons, who should be home from school by now.

Gerard and Vaughn have been home for about thirty minutes when their father thinks about them. This week has been uneventful. Each day seems like the day before. They come home, change their clothes, do their chores, and rush through their homework. Now they're sitting in front of the TV, watching their regular afternoon programs.

Rich, in the meantime, is back in the war room. Everyone sees Doug is now asleep and snoring.

Tom says, "Wow, he's knocked out."

Whitney says, "Yeah, he'll probably sleep straight through the night. He may not wake up until tomorrow."

Gary says, "Let's call Bruce and tell him Doug is asleep. Maybe he'll let us leave early again."

The team gathers around the phone.

"Hello. Bruce speaking."

Gary says, "Hey Bruce. Doug is sleeping hard now."

"How long has he been asleep?"

Rich says, "Probably about fifteen minutes, and he's snoring loudly too."

Bruce says, "So, I already know what this call is about. You'll want to leave early."

Laughing, Vincent says, "Yeah."

"If you can square it with your relief, then you're free to go."

Gary says, "Okay, Bruce. Thanks.

Bruce says, "All right, bye."

After the team hangs up, Logan asks Rich, "By the way. How's Sherry doing?"

"Not too good. You know she's in the Psych ward."

Logan says, "Yeah, I'm so sorry to hear that. Don't worry, man. I've got you covered. You can go now."

Rich says, "Thanks a lot, man. I appreciate that."

After gathering his things, Rich says goodbye to the team, walks out of the bodega, and gets in his car. He hasn't seen or spoken to Sherry in a few days. A little nervous about how she's doing and what condition she's in, he pushes the speed limit.

Rich suddenly remembers he needs to speak with Dr. Flores first and swiftly dials the hospital. The receptionist picks up.

"Peninsula General Hospital. How may I help you?"

Rich says, "May I have Dr. Flores's office?"

"Hold on a minute."

After a few rings, the secretary picks up.

"Dr. Flores office."

"Hi, this is Rich Wilson. May I speak to Dr. Flores?"

The secretary says, "Oh, I'm sorry he's not in today."

"When will he be in?"

"What's this about anyway?"

"My girlfriend was in the maternity ward then got transferred to the psych unit. Dr. Flores was her previous doctor, and I need him to get me in to see her. I planned on going to see her this evening."

"I'll check his schedule. Hold on a minute."

After a slight pause, the secretary picks back up.

"Dr. Flores won't be in for the rest of the week, but he'll be working all weekend."

Rich says, "Okay."

The secretary says, "Is that all you needed?"

"Yeah."

"All right, enjoy the rest of your day."

Rich says, "You too," and hangs up.

After ending the call, Rich changes direction and heads home. After about twenty-five minutes, he arrives in front of the building. Walking into the apartment, he finds Gerard and Vaughn in the living room. Without taking their eyes off the TV and with little enthusiasm, emotion, or even a stray look his way, they say, "Hi Dad."

Rich replies tersely, "Dinner'll be ready in thirty minutes."

Once in his bedroom, he changes into something more comfortable. After washing his hands, he goes into the kitchen. Looking in the freezer, he yells, "It's frozen dinners tonight!"

After heating their meals, Rich tells the boys, "Dinner is ready."

They say a silent grace and begin to eat. As usual, there is little to no conversation. Their father doesn't ask about their day, homework, plans for the future, or anything about their life. They awkwardly avoid eye contact and look at their plates or stare pass one another. After finishing his meal, Rich says, "Remember to clean up."

This evening he doesn't sit in the living room to watch the news. Glad he's gone, the boys eagerly clean up the kitchen, excited they have the TV to themselves tonight.

After lying in bed for fifteen minutes, Rich starts to feel drowsy and eventually falls into a light sleep. After resting a few hours, he gets up around eight and goes into the living room to check on the boys. Rich finds them asleep on the couch and nudges them awake, telling them to go to bed. He turns off the TV, decides to call it an early night, and goes back into his bedroom.

After a long and peaceful night's sleep, Rich feels refreshed. Just as Gerard and Vaughn are coming out of their room, Rich walks out of his bedroom. Like obedient soldiers, the boys say, "Good morning," on cue as they continue down the hall to school.

Once in the bathroom, Rich turns on the shower. As he lathers up, his thoughts turn to Sherry; questions pepper his mind, and he wonders how she's doing. Is her mental state the same? When or if she will get better? What does her condition mean for their relationship? Unsure of their future, Rich seeks answers without much success.

After showering, Rich gets dressed, grabs something to eat, and is in his car in fifteen minutes. Today Rich listens to music CDs. He decides to focus on songs instead of Sherry, Doug, or the boys. When he arrives at base camp, no one is outside, and Rich goes straight into the war room. He sees that Doug is still sleeping. Checking the time, he realizes Bruce is about to start the weekly supervisory staff meeting.

At the precinct, Bruce has just confirmed everyone's attendance.

In the conference room are Captain Kuntz, Judy, Detective Brooks, Detective Johnson, Investigator Wells, Michael, and Dr. Feinstein. Al, Ron, and Rommie are on the phone.

Bruce begins by saying, "Hello and welcome, everyone. I want to start with Judy first, but I want to ensure everyone has seen Doug's therapy session video. Is there anyone who has not seen it yet?"

No one raises their hand or says anything over the phone.

Bruce says, "Good. So we can begin the meeting. Oh, there's one more thing I must mention. We have two new investigators, Detective Brooks and Detective Johnson. They'll be discussing the investigation of Doug's friends, Ryan and Darryl. But I want to begin by asking Judy about her session with Doug."

Judy says, "First, I'd like to mention that Doug agreed to take the antipsychotic medication. So Dr. Feinstein and I are working on his Social Security Disability application. Doug also quit his temp job."

Bruce says, "I hate to interrupt you, but I'd like to ask Michael, our forensic accountant, a question. Does Doug have enough savings for six months of expenses because we plan on expediting his Social Security application. However, it's going to take about that long for us to get it done."

Michael says, "His monthly expenses are around $1600. He has around $20,000 saved, so he's good for at least six months, really a year."

"Excellent. Okay, Judy. Sorry, but I had to ask that. Please continue."

Judy says, "That's great, and I'm sure what Dr. Feinstein and I are putting in Doug's application will get him a favorable determination. Now, back to what I was saying about our session this week. Doug primarily focused on two things: what his beliefs are around our investigative teams. He refers to them as spy networks. He also talked about his early childhood experiences. Doug recounted a long history of physical and psychological abuse at the hands of his father. A lot of which I already read about in Dr. Ehnis's case notes. Doug is also convinced he's under investigation and is routinely being drugged and harassed by our investigative teams. He also believes they are trying to frame him. He went into quite a bit of detail about what he believes they have done to him. Doug also talked about having an anointing from God and being born unique with the gift of second sight."

Bruce asks, "What's second sight?"

Judy replies, "Second sight is the ability to perceive future or distant events, or clairvoyance. He also has a deep abiding faith in God. Not in a religious sense as someone who goes to church, reads their Bible, or prays all the time. But as someone who firmly believes God will protect him and he will always have this special relationship with God as long as he continues to lean on him."

Bruce says, "Interesting. How does he feel he's being framed?"

"You already know Doug believes his father put him on the police's radar when he was around eight years old. He thinks his father faked a break-in of the family home to start the surveillance. Then told law enforcement that Doug and his brother were responsible. Doug also believes his father had the entire family put under surveillance. But later, his father honed in on him as the fall guy for the molestation of his sister. Doug also didn't go into specifics on how our investigative teams are trying to frame him. He talked more about the harassment.

"Nonetheless, he firmly believes it's their purpose to ruin subject's lives. Doug feels that's the reason why his father started an investigation of him in the first place. He knew what it would portend for Doug's life, being well aware of how punitive and biased these investigations can be. Doug feels he knows this based on God's insight, personal intuition, and memory. I realize I'm probably repeating what you already know from the video. However, I would like to ask Dr. Feinstein a question. What are the side effects of the drugs we're giving him? He mentioned having concentration difficulties and ruminating a lot. I also saw this mentioned in his case files from Dr. Ehnis."

Dr. Feinstein says, "That's one of the main effects of the primary drug we give him. We want to see what he's thinking. So poor concentration is a direct result of the medication protocols ."

Judy says, "Can we give him a stimulant to improve his focus?"

Dr. Feinstein says, "He has never been diagnosed with ADHD or ADD. I can't give him a stimulant, but I can give him some nonstimulant medication that might help with that."

Judy says, "That's good. I'll mention it to him at our next session."

Bruce says, "On another note, I'd like to address the initial reason we started investigating Doug. Is there anyone who believes Doug is a child molester?"

Judy says, "No, I don't believe he is."

Al says, "Me either."

Ron says, "No."

Rommie says, "No."

Investigator Wells says, "We haven't found anything. Our investigative teams give him drugs to enhance his sexual urges. We also create street scenarios that would physically arouse him. We can see through our infra-red camera vans that he has the appropriate physical reactions. He is attracted to muscular men. However, I would like to explore further what he looks at sometimes and why he is looking at those things."

Bruce says, "I know what you mean, but we're not going to stop investigating him anyway. We can lower the investigative level but we can't go back to general surveillance as he continues to talk about being investigated. Okay, I have another question. Does anyone feel he's still a threat to his father?"

Everyone around the table and on the phone says, "No."

Bruce says, "So, I'm recommending we lower his investigative level, but we're not taking him off our radar. Now, I have a question for Al. Are our investigators finding other sexual abuse victims of the father?"

Al says, "We haven't found any victims within the family yet, but we have heard rumors that we are extensively investigating. I haven't spoken to his sister directly about what Doug said she told him. His sister also mentioned that she's worried about him because the family is turning against him since we told them what he's being investigated for."

Bruce says, "Unfortunately, we can't do anything about that, since he keeps talking about being investigated. You also need to speak to his sister about the allegation that their father molested her. Do that as soon as possible."

Al says, "Okay, I will. Doug also recently reached out to his sister and brother."

Bruce asks, "How did it go?"

"They both said it was a relatively short and general conversation, nothing deep."

"I mentioned last time that I want his friends and family to start reaching out to him more aggressively. Ron and Rommie, have you spoken to him lately?"

Ron says, "I called him once, but he didn't answer or return my call."

Rommie says, "I also called, but he didn't answer or return my call either."

Bruce says, "So he's socially isolating. We have to get him more socially engaged. That will be our goal for the near future. Now I'd like for Detective Brooks and Detective Johnson to speak. They're the lead investigators looking into his friends Darryl and Ryan."

Bruce asks, "First. I'd like to ask, did either of them respond to the emails Doug sent yesterday?"

Detective Brooks says only Ryan wrote back. He said, "He felt like coming over to Doug's house and beating his ass, but he was holding himself back." His friend Darryl didn't respond.

Bruce asks, "What did Doug do?"

"He laughed when he read it."

Detective Brooks says, "We've been looking extensively at Ryan. Currently, he's employed as a leasing agent and has a friend visiting from Atlanta named Eric. Ryan set up spy cameras in Eric's bedroom and bathroom. Ryan also has another friend named Sean, who is monitoring Eric. Ryan gave Sean access to his home video monitoring system. They also put a listening device on his phone. Ryan also routinely looks through Eric's personal belongings when he's not at home. We also found out Ryan is HIV positive."

Bruce says, "Is Doug aware Ryan is HIV positive?"

Detective Brooks says, "Yes, he mentioned it in his letter. Doug didn't say he was happy about it, but he said it was karma for Ryan's wickedness toward him."

Bruce says, "Ryan's probably done electronic eavesdropping before. Maybe he's put these types of devices in some of the tenants apartments where he works? We need to look into that further."

"Yes. I was thinking that also."

Bruce says, "What about his friend Darryl?"

Detective Johnson says, "It's pretty much the same story. He gave Doug a snow globe with an audio and video recording device in it. We also found out he's done it to other friends. Some friends named Samuel and Ms. Archer."

Bruce asks, "What does he do professionally?"

"He's a hairdresser at a nursing home and a minister. He also has a serious heart condition."

Bruce says, "That's a damn shame. Two friends doing that to you is incredible. I know an individual who does bug sweeps for a living. He says thirty percent of the homes he goes into contain some type of electronic eavesdropping device. I guess people don't realize it's a serious felony and can get you between one to five years in prison. Did they collude on doing this, or was it done independently?"

Detective Johnson says, "From what we can tell, it was done independently."

Judy says, "Video voyeurism is a sickness. Besides, it's considered a sexual offense, and you would have to register as a sex offender if convicted. Honestly, the sickest people I've met were never in treatment. They thought nothing was wrong with them, even though they usually had more problems than the individuals I saw in counseling."

Detective Brooks says, "On that note I want to request reassignment."

Bruce asks, "What's going on?"

"I find working on this investigation is getting me in my feelings. Ryan doesn't realize how sick he is. He acts like he's got his shit together and can tell everyone else what to do, but he doesn't even have himself together. So many people hate him. He frequently irks me and gets on my nerves. I find myself hating the hypocrisy."

Detective Johnson says, "I feel the same way about his friend Darryl. They're both full of shit and very deceitful. They routinely gaslight Doug. I want to request reassignment too. What kind of minister would do that to anyone, let alone a friend? Unbelievable!"

Bruce says, "I can transfer their investigation to another team, and if you want reassignment, I can do that also. We must remain as objective as possible throughout this entire process. But I would like to say to anyone else on this investigation, if you want to leave because you're getting too emotionally invested, please feel free to speak to me. We can reassign you. I know the toll these investigations can take on you. Just come talk to me."

Bruce asks, "Okay, I've covered everything on the agenda. Is there anything else we need to discuss?"

Judy says, "I'm good."

Ron says, "I'm fine."

Rommie says, "I don't have anything."

Al says, "I know what I need to do."

Everyone else says no.

Before closing, Captain Kuntz remarks, "I usually sit in on these meetings and don't say anything. However, I would like to say, I've been doing these investigations for a very long time, and I've never seen a case like this before. It's so fascinating."

Bruce says, "Yeah, I know what you mean. I feel the same way."

After a long pause, Bruce says, "Okay, if there's nothing else, then the meeting is adjourned."

As an afterthought, Bruce says, "Detective Brooks and Detective Johnson, I will get to work on your requests right away. Call me in the week to let me know if you still want to stay on the team."

Detective Brooks says, "I will."

Detective Johnson says, "Will do."

Bruce says, "All right, everyone. Enjoy the rest of your day."

Back at base camp, everyone is watching the monitors. Doug continues to sleep but starts to stir around 1:30 p.m. Upon awakening and still slightly tired, Doug looks at the white candle burning on his cedar chest.

Invigorated by its light, Doug goes into the bathroom and splashes cold water on his face. His first thought is *How am I going to survive this?* Doug tries to remember how much money he has in the bank and anxiously wonders how long it will take and whether he will even get Social Security Disability in the first place.

Doug goes into the kitchen to make some coffee, then turns on the news. Still thinking about this question, Doug stands in front of the white candle to seek answers from God. Perplexed and unsure, he goes into the kitchen to fix his coffee. Seated at the table drinking his coffee, he spots the newspaper *New York Visions*. Deciding to look through it again, Doug notices the full-page ad for the National Alliance on Mental Wellness (NAMW). Suddenly, Doug gets an idea: "I'll start getting involved with some of their programs." Overcoming the internalized stigma and initial resistance to being labeled disabled with a mental illness, Doug decides to accept what he initially feared. He meditates on the word Incognito" and "You've got to stoop to conquer. Doug wholheartedly accepts that this is where God wants his journey to begin.

After arriving at these insights, Doug feels an overwhelming sense of peace, and his worry about the future diminishes. He continues to browse through the newspaper and sits on the couch with his coffee to watch the news. Doug is eager to call the NAMW later this week.

With nothing on his agenda and being still somewhat tired, Doug decides to take it easy. After forty-five minutes, Doug's phone rings. He sees it's his sister and picks up quickly.

"Hi, Marima."

"Hi, Doug. What's up?"

"Nothing. I got up late; I didn't go into work today. I wasn't feeling well. I'm just sitting here, watching the news."

Doug decides not to tell his sister what's actually on his mind. Instead, he says, "I'm fine."

Marima asks, "How's the job going?"

"It's okay. Boring as hell, though."

"I would imagine temping can be boring at times."

Doug says, "Yes, there's not much to do, and what they give me to do is not very challenging or takes very long to finish, but hey, it's a paycheck."

Marima says, "If it helps pay the bills, then that's what matters. On another note, I was calling to check on you but also to see if you still want to have dinner."

Doug says, "Yeah, I remember we were supposed to make plans. I have a pretty open schedule. Where do you want to go, and what's a good day and time for you?"

"I know you like soul food and enjoy going to Sylvia's in Harlem. This Wednesday at seven is good for me."

Doug says, "Perfect. That works for me also. By the way, have you spoken to our brother lately?"

"No, I tried reaching out to him late last week, but he didn't pick up or return my call, as usual."

Doug says, "Such a hard guy to catch up with."

"Yeah, I know. All I can do is make an effort."

Doug asks, "By the way, how's your job going?"

"It's okay. I feel a little overworked, and my supervisor is riding my back, but overall I'm good. All right, brother, I've got a couple of errands to run today and didn't want to keep you long. So I'll see you at Sylvia's this Wednesday at seven."

Doug says, "That's fine. See you then."

"Sure, take care and enjoy the rest of your day."

"Okay, you too."

After hanging up, Marima immediately calls Al.

"Hi, Al speaking."

"This is Marima. I just spoke to Doug. We agreed to have dinner this Wednesday."

"Good. What else did you talk about?"

"He asked me about my job and if I spoke to our brother lately. It was a short conversation, maybe five or ten minutes."

Okay, that's great, but I also need to talk with you about something else at a later date.

Marima asks, "What?"

Al says, "Your father."

Surprised, Marima holds her breath for a second before answering, "Sure, anytime."

Al asks, "What else is going on? How have you been otherwise?"

Marima replies, "I'm fine, but I'm sorry I have to go, something came up. I just wanted to keep you in the loop."

"Thanks for letting me know you spoke with Doug. Enjoy your dinner this Wednesday. Take care."

After Doug hangs up with Marima, he goes back to watching the news. Within the hour, he's stretched out on the couch with his eyes closed, taking a midafternoon nap. At base camp, Logan says, "He's out again."

Whitney and Gary start laughing. Tom asks, "Is he snoring?" Rich says, "Yes."

Vincent says, "He'll probably be gone for a few hours. Those drugs can take a while to wear off completely."

Now they don't have to monitor Doug as closely and start to relax. Tom and Vincent go outside for a smoke. Logan and Gary drink beers while Whitney and Rich continue to watch the monitors just in case Doug wakes up. Forty-five minutes into his nap, Doug's phone rings again. He's abruptly jolted out of sleep. Seeing Rommie's number, Doug picks up.

"Hey, Rommie."

"Hi, Doug. "What's going on? Long time no hear."

Doug stares at the white candle to seek God's guidance.

"I quit my job, and I'm temping now."

"Why?"

"Ehh, numerous reasons. None I'd like to go into now."

As Doug continues to stare at the white candle, it occurs to him that Rommie is an undercover investigator. He's aware that all his relationships have been contaminated in this way. However, this realization still brings a certain level of shock and sadness. It causes tension in Doug's shoulders and neck, and his stomach muscles tighten. Uncertain of what to say, he blurts out, "I think I'm under investigation."

Rommie asks, "Why would you be investigated?"

Not willing to go into details, Doug says, "I think so, and I don't feel like talking about it, but the whole situation is giving me a damn headache."

Genuinely caring for Doug and wanting to get the conversation back on track. Rommie asks, "Are you okay?"

Doug says, "I'm fine."

"Are you sure?"

Doug reassures him by saying, "No, I'm okay."

"If you say so. Have you done anything or been anywhere lately?"

Distracted, Doug says, "No."

Unfocused and unsure of how to proceed with this friendship, Doug decides to hang up. Thinking of any excuse to leave the conversation, he says, "Rommie, I'm sorry, but something just came up. Can I talk to you later?"

Rommie replies, "Sure."

Doug says, "Speak with you soon."

Rommie says, "Okay, bye," and he hangs up.

Tears begin to well up in Doug's eyes as he cuts off the TV, turns to look at the white candle, then faces the ceiling. Wearily closing his eyes, he puts one hand on his forehead and looks for answers from God about his life.

After hanging up with Doug, Rommie calls Bruce.

"Hello, Bruce speaking."

"Hi, this is Rommie. I just got off the phone with Doug."

Bruce asks, "How was the call?"

"Strange. It was short, and Doug seemed distracted. However, he did mention that he believed he was under investigation. When I probed further, he said he didn't want to talk about it."

Bruce replies, "He's previously mentioned that more or less everyone in his life is part of a spy network. But I'm glad you reached out; please continue to do so. I'll also send a reminder to Ron to call Doug soon."

Rommie says, "All right, I just wanted to touch base."

"Okay, take care and enjoy the rest of your day."

"You do the same. Bye."

After thinking for a while, Doug falls back asleep. At base camp, Logan says, "He's out again."

Rich says, "Yeah, he's gone; he'll probably sleep the entire day. I'll be leaving soon anyway. By the way, guys, I'm going to visit Sherry tomorrow."

Whitney asks, "Yeah, how's she doing?"

Rich replies, "Not good. Sherry's condition hasn't changed."

Logan says, "I hope she gets better soon, man."

Gary says, "Yes, tell her I said hello also."

Rich says, "I certainly will. Thanks, everybody. I think I'll head home a little early this evening. Who's taking over for me today?"

Logan says, "I think it's Vincent."

Rich goes outside to find Vincent and Tom smoking.

Rich says, "Hey, Vincent, I want to take off early. Is that okay?"

Vincent says, "Sure, man. Enjoy the rest of your day."

Once home, Rich finds Gerard and Vaughn in their usual spot on the couch. Surprised at their father's early arrival, the boys say, "Hi, Dad." Rich walks past the living room without returning the greeting and goes to his bedroom. He puts his things down, and changes out of his work clothes. After washing his hands, he goes into the kitchen to prepare dinner.

It takes about twenty-five minutes to warm up the meal. Afterward, Rich puts the boy's food on the table and takes a snack tray into the living room. After Gerard and Vaughn finish their meal, they clean the kitchen then join their father. The evening ritual doesn't change much tonight. Their father controls the TV until he falls asleep. Then the boys take control of the remote and watch their shows until bedtime. Since they don't have school tomorrow, they stay up later tonight. They eventually go to bed around 10:30 p.m. and leave their father sleeping on the couch. Rich wakes up a couple of hours later, turns off the TV, and goes to bed.

The next day Rich wakes up first. After looking at the clock he sees it's 9:35 a.m. Thinking about Sherry, he remembers that visiting hours begin at eight. He decides to get an early start. On his way to the bathroom, Rich notices that Gerard and Vaughn's door is still closed. He assumes they haven't woken up yet.

Hearing the shower, Gerard and Vaughn wake up. As Rich leaves the bathroom, he notices the boy's door is now open. He pokes his head inside, saying, "I'm going to visit Sherry. You know the routine. Follow it and don't let me find anything wrong when I get back. Am I clear?"

Gerard says yes, and Vaughn nods his head. Rich goes into his bedroom to finish dressing then heads out the door.

Upon arrival at the hospital, Rich makes his way to the doctor's office. After greeting the receptionist, he asks, "Is Dr. Flores in?"

The receptionist says, "No, he's out making his morning rounds. He should be back in about fifteen minutes. May I ask what this is about?"

Rich says, "My girlfriend was in the maternity ward, then got transferred to the psych unit. I need Dr. Flores to get me in to see her."

The receptionist responds, "Oh, okay. He'll be here any minute. You can have a seat."

Rich is the only person in the waiting area. After a few minutes, he starts to look through a magazine.

After a while, the doctor arrives. Rich greets him, "Hello, Dr. Flores."

Dr. Flores shakes his hand and says, "Mr. Wilson. Correct?"

Rich says, "You remember my girlfriend, Sherry Martin."

Dr. Flores says, "Yes, of course. Wait here a few minutes. I have to take care of a couple of things first; then I'll have my receptionist send you in."

"Okay," Rich says.

After about five minutes, the receptionist says, "Mr. Wilson, you can go in to see the doctor now."

Rich gets up quickly and walks into the doctor's office.

"Have a seat. How may I help you?"

Rich says, "As you know, my girlfriend, Sherry Martin, is in the psych ward. They won't let me get any information on her because she didn't sign a release-of-information form for me."

"Yes, I remember when we transferred her. I can walk you over there and get you onto the ward."

Rich says, "That's great."

Dr. Flores says, "We can go over there immediately."

The doctor gets up and Rich follows him out of the office. They arrive at the psych unit in minutes. Dr. Flores rings the bell. A nurse sees the doctor's white coat and opens the door. She lets them in, asking, "How may I help you?"

Dr. Flores says, "I work in the maternity unit. I transferred a patient here a few days ago. Her name is Sherry Martin, and this is her boyfriend, Rich Wilson. He would like to speak with her doctor. Let him see Ms. Martin first, then ask if she would sign a release-of-information form so he can speak with her psychiatrist."

The nurse says, "Will do. I know the patient. Please follow me."

At this time, Dr. Flores says, "All right, I need to get back to my office."

He shakes Rich's hand, saying, "I hope everything works out for you and Ms. Martin."

Rich says, "Yeah, thanks, Dr. Flores. I appreciate your help."

The doctor says, "No problem," before turning to leave the ward.

The nurse takes Rich to the visiting area.

She says, "Wait here. I'll go get Ms. Martin."

After a few minutes, Sherry walks into the visitor's area. Rich is shocked. Her hair is standing up all over her head, her skin looks pale, her eyes are empty and absent, and she drags her feet. She looks like a zombie.

She takes a seat next to him and, speaking in a low, monotone voice, says, "Hi, Rich."

"Hi, Sherry. How're you feeling?"

She says, "To be honest, I feel numb."

Sherry's arms remain by her side as Rich wraps his arms around her in a tight embrace. After a while, he gently grabs her hand reassuringly, saying, "I know this is difficult, but we'll get through this."

Sherry turns to look at him with tears beginning to form in her eyes.

Suddenly, remembering to tell Sherry about his coworkers, he says, "The guys on the team say hello and send their love."

Sherry smiles blandly and continues to stare straight ahead. As they sit in silence, unable to find the words to convey what they both feel, the nurse comes down the hall.

Standing in front of Sherry, she asks, "Ms. Martin, do you want to give your boyfriend permission to speak with your doctor?"

"Yes," she says.

The nurse gives Sherry the clipboard with the release-of-information form. After putting a pen in her hand, she points to the signature line. Sherry scribbles her name, barely looking at the paper before signing it.

The nurse takes the clipboard and walks back to her station.

Rich searches for words to fill the silent pauses between them.

"Who's your doctor?"

"I think her name is Harris."

"How do you spend your day?"

"I stay in bed."

"How's the food in here?"

"It's okay."

"Did you eat breakfast yet?"

"Yes."

"Overall, how're they treating you?"

"Okay. How are Gerard and Vaughn?" Sherry asks.

"Fine."

Sherry asks, "When will I get out of here?"

"I don't know. Maybe I can speak with your doctor. Let me go to the nurses' station. You said her name was Dr. Harris. Right?"

"Yes," Sherry says.

As Rich gets up to leave, he says, "I'll be back as soon as possible."

Walking down the hall, Rich suddenly stops as if tapped on his shoulder. He turns around and sees Sherry sitting there with a sullen look on her face, vacant eyes, a flat affect, and staring straight ahead. For a half-second, Rich thinks about Brenda before continuing down the hall. Once at the nurses' station, Rich asks for Dr. Harris.

The nurse replies, "She just got in about an hour ago. I don't believe she's meeting with anyone at the moment. Go to the end of this hall, make a right, and her office should be the third door on the left."

"Okay, thanks."

He sees the sign "Dr. Harris" on the door. After he knocks, a woman with a strong, clear, and assertive voice says, "Come in."

Rich enters and sees a middle-aged woman with caramel skin, straight shoulder-length black hair, bright eyes, and full lips. She's wearing horn-rimmed glasses.

She asks, "How may I help you?"

"Hi, I'm Rich Wilson, the boyfriend of Sherry Martin."

Dr. Harris replies, "Yes, I remember her; actually, the nurse recently gave me a release-of-information form to put in her chart. I think it was probably for you. Before we start talking, let me check her file. Have a seat."

Dr. Harris looks through some folders and finds Sherry Martin's chart.

She looks at the release-of-information form and says, "You said your name was Rich Wilson."

"Yes, that's correct."

"Okay, here's the form with your name on it."

Rich says, "I just finished visiting Sherry, and she asked me, 'When am I going to be released?'"

"I remember when she was first transferred onto the ward, she was suicidal. However, she hasn't expressed a desire to kill herself recently. We have her on two antidepressants and an antipsychotic. I understand she's still very depressed, but it's a normal reaction to losing a child. Situations can change, but as of now, we plan on discharging her in a few days. We want to keep her a little while longer for further observation and monitoring. I would suggest you encourage her to sign up with an outside therapist once she leaves. Do you live together?"

"No, but I plan to marry her in about six months to a year."

"Do you have keys to her apartment?"

"Yes."

"I would encourage you to check on her frequently, make sure she's eating, bathing, taking her medications, going to her therapy appointments, and getting out."

"How long will she be like this?"

"To be honest, she may never be the person she was previously. Losing a child is very traumatic, and it's something you never really get over. Individuals respond to these medications differently, but they usually start working in about four to six weeks. The severity of the depression should start to lift somewhere around then."

Rich says, "That long, huh."

"Yes, these medications take a long time to kick in. You said you just met with Ms. Martin. How does she seem to you?"

"There's certainly a change in her demeanor. Previously, she smiled and laughed a lot. Now she seems sad and distant. I asked her several questions, and she gave very brief one-word answers."

Dr. Harris says, "She'll probably present that way for a while. Always be gentle and patient with her."

"I will."

After a long pause, Dr. Harris asks, "Is there anything else you want from me?"

"No, I'm good. Thanks for your time Dr. Harris."

Rich gets up and extends his hand.

Dr. Harris gives him a firm handshake, saying, "Nice to meet you. Enjoy the rest of your day."

Rich walks out of the office and back down the hall. Sherry still sits in the same chair, staring straight ahead. She barely turns her head when Rich sits next to her.

Speaking softly, Rich says, "I met with Dr. Harris. She said you should be getting out in a few days."

A half smile appears on Sherry's face.

Rich, feeling uncomfortable with the fragmented conversation and Sherry's overall demeanor, wishes to leave. Before departing, he asks, "Is there anything else you need from me?"

Sherry slowly shakes her head from side to side and says, "No."

"Okay, then I'll go. I just wanted to check on you. Take care and enjoy the rest of your day."

Sherry doesn't answer, and Rich gets up, kisses her on the forehead, and starts to walk away.

"Tell the boys I said hello."

Rich says, "I will."

In the hallway, Brenda's image starts to appear in Rich's mind. Instantly dismissing those uncomfortable memories, he quickens his pace and begins to distract himself by focusing on the rest of his day.

Arriving home, Rich searches for Gerard and Vaughn in front of the building. After going upstairs, he finds the apartment quiet. Assuming the boys are playing in the back of the development, he chooses to enjoy his time alone and turns on the TV, deciding to make it a lazy weekend.

Rich is asleep when the boys come back upstairs. The noise from the door slamming wakes him from his nap.

Annoyed, he snaps, "Goddamn, do you have to let the door close like that?"

Gerard says, "Oh, sorry."

While standing in the hall with their bikes, Vaughn says, "Dad, I'm hungry. What're we having for lunch?"

Rich says, "I don't know. Go in the kitchen and see what's in the fridge. I think there's some sandwich meat. Fix me something and remember to wash your hands first. Be careful with those bikes and don't scratch up the walls!"

The boys continue down the hall. Vaughn is eager to eat and washes his hands quickly. Once in the kitchen, he opens the fridge and finds some bologna and sliced ham.

"I found some bologna and ham!" Vaughn yells .

"That's good. Fix me a sandwich with some ham, a couple of slices of cheese, and put some mayonnaise on it. What's there to drink?"

"Coke, Sprite, and orange juice."

"Give me some Coke. I know there are chips on top of the fridge; get me a bag of corn chips too."

Vaughn starts fixing his father's plate. After getting out the ham and cheese and putting it on the bread, Vaughn spits on the sandwich. He then gets the corn chips, pours his father some Coke, and takes everything along with a snack tray into the living room. Vaughn is finishing his sandwich when Gerard walks in.

Vaughn asks, "What took you so long?"

"I decided to change my clothes. I was sweaty from all that bike riding."

"What're you fixing?"

"I'm making a ham and cheese sandwich. There's also some bologna in the fridge."

Gerard says, "I think I'll have some bologna and cheese with some potato chips. What's there to drink?"

"Oh, there's some Coke, Sprite, and orange juice in the fridge."

"I think I'll have some Sprite."

Gerard and Vaughn eat their food in the kitchen. In the living room, Rich's thoughts return to Sherry. Previously, he spoke to her at least two times a day. Her absence makes him feel very alone and lonely—the weight of not having anyone else to talk to begins to weigh on him. Rich turns on the TV to distract himself from these painful realizations.

Suddenly remembering, Rich yells into the kitchen, "Sherry asked about you boys and said to tell you hello!"

Vaughn says, "Tell her I said hi."

Gerard says, "Tell her I said hello too. When are we going to see her again?"

"She should be getting out in a few days."

Gerard says, "I like Ms. Sherry. She's nice."

Rich says, "Yeah, she's good people."

Vaughn remains silent. After the boys finish eating, they head to their room.

Gerard asks Vaughn, "Do you want to play Scrabble?"

Enthusiastically, Vaughn says, "Yeah, let's play."

Gerard finds the game and sets it up on his bed. After a while, the boys become engrossed in the competition and lose track of time.

Falling asleep after eating his lunch and waking up a few hours later, Rich looks at the time and decides to fix something to eat.

Laughing to himself, he thinks, *My life is not much more interesting than Doug's.*

While the food is warming up, he walks down the hall and knocks on the boys door, "Dinner'll be ready in about fifteen minutes," he yells.

Gerard and Vaughn are still engaged in their board game when their father knocks. Startled by the sudden interruption, they look up momentarily, listening to what their father says, then continuing to finish their game. Returning to the living room he turns on the news. The boys finish their game, go to the kitchen, and see their plates on the table. The food is cool, but they don't say anything and eat their meals in silence. Once finished, they clean up the kitchen then go back to their room.

Rich turns in around ten o'clock. Walking down the hall, he sees the light out in Gerard and Vaughn's room. Assuming they're in bed, he goes to bed without opening their door to check on them tonight.

After a good night's sleep, Rich wakes up around eight. He finds the house quiet and goes back to bed.

Up in the Bronx, Doug is awake and has already made his Starbucks run. While he's relaxing, watching the news and drinking his chai tea, his phone rings, and he sees that Ron is calling. Pausing before he picks up the phone, Doug looks over at the white candle and briefly closes his eyes to seek answers from God before speaking with Ron.

Doug picks up and says, "Hi, Ron."

Ron says, "Hey, buddy."

"How've you been?" Doug asks.

"Okay, I haven't spoken to you since church. What you been up to?"

"Yeah, I know. I just recently quit my job."

Ron says, "I didn't know that. Why'd you quit, and what're you going to do for a living now?"

"I just got tired of their shit, and I do mean everybody. I was temping for a minute, but I quit that also."

"So, how're you going to support yourself?"

Doug thinks about whether to tell Ron he's in the process of applying for disability, knows he's under investigation, and believes more or less everyone in his life is part of a spy network. Doug decides to be truthful, feeling Ron is genuine and has a sincere love for him.

Doug says, "To be honest, I'm applying for Social Security Disability. I also realize I'm under investigation, and I believe everyone in my life is more or less part of a spy network, including you, Ron. I do, however, believe you care for me, but you must understand I have a lot to think about."

"Investigation. Where did that come from?"

"I've been thinking it for a while."

Ron says, "I'm not going to challenge you on what you believe. You think what you want to think. I'll give you your space. I was initially calling to see if you wanted to go to Unity today. However, I guess given what you've said, you wouldn't want to go now, but I feel compelled to ask: you still taking your medicine?"

"Goddamn it, yes. And I'm tired of everyone always asking me that. I'm keeping a low profile this weekend. My mind has been so cluttered lately."

"Well, I'll say goodbye and let you get on with the rest of your day. Don't worry. You'll be all right, and I'll be Ok. We'll get through this," Ron says encouragingly.

Doug smiles to himself and says, "Yes, I'll keep the faith. Take care, my friend."

Ron says, "All right, buddy. Will do. Bye."

After hanging up, Doug looks at the white candle and continues to lie on his couch with his eyes closed and one hand on his forehead, seeking answers from God and strength for the way forward.

At base camp, Logan remarks, "He frequently gets in that position when he burns that white candle. I wonder what he's doing? Is he thinking or praying?"

Gary says, "I don't know."

Vincent says, "Let's call it his thinking, praying position."

Tom says, "He's usually like that for a very long time."

Whitney says, "Yeah, sometimes he stays in that position for hours. Eventually, he'll probably fall asleep, wake up, turn on the TV, then get something to eat. Didn't he tell his friend Ron he was keeping a low profile this weekend?"

Logan says, "Yeah, in general, he doesn't go out that much. He's supposed to have dinner with his sister on Wednesday."

Gary asks, "Hey, where's Rich? I didn't see him today. Is he coming in?"

Whitney says, "No, I think he's off."

"Oh, okay," Gary says.

Whitney says, "Actually, I think he's off the entire weekend."

Rich gets up very late today. On his way to the bathroom he doesn't see the boys in their room and assumes they're outside. After washing up, getting dressed, and going into the kitchen, he wonders how he'll spend the rest of his day.

As he's thinking, he hears the boys in the hallway and walks into the living room just as they open the door.

He barks, "Be careful with those bikes. I still see scuff marks on the wall."

As the boys walk through the living room, Rich says to Gerard, "I need you to go to Stop and Shop. I'm creating a list now."

Gerard says, "Okay," as he continues down the hall to put his bike away.

Vaughn looks at his father for a moment, then grabs his chain, retracing the words "He shall give his angels charge over thee."

Once in their bedroom, Vaughn sits on the side of his bed. Gerard goes back into the living room to get the list and go to the store.

Rich asks, "What else do we need? I see we're getting low on bread, orange juice, corn flakes, milk, and butter."

Gerard replies, "I don't know."

"All right, that's all I can think of for now, and don't forget to pick me up a paper."

After opening the window in their bedroom, Vaughn continues to sit quietly on his bed. After about fifteen minutes, he runs into the living room, shouting, "Gerard got hit by a car on Beach Channel Drive!"

Rich immediately runs into the boy's room. Vaughn follows close behind. Once in the bedroom, Rich rushes to the window and looks out. He turns his head in the direction of the grocery store; not immediately seeing any traffic accident, he leans out of the window even farther. Vaughn stands quietly in the farthermost corner of the bedroom. As Rich continues to look out the window, Vaughn runs as fast as he can and, with all his strength, pushes his father from behind. Taken off guard and disoriented, Rich loses his balance and tries to grab onto the outside window ledge. He can't catch hold of the frame and falls to the ground below. Vaughn hears the body hit the ground just as a woman begins to shriek loudly. Vaughn runs back to the corner and turns his back to the window. Unaware of the chaos below, Vaughn starts to cry and shiver. Outside, people scream and cover their mouths in shock and horror. A few minutes later, Vaughn hears the sirens from the cop cars and ambulance as they start to arrive.

After a few minutes, Vaughn hears pounding on the apartment door and runs to see who it is. Three police officers in uniform and one man in plainclothes stand there. The man in plainclothes is in front, and the rest of the officers stand behind him. The man asks, "Are there any adults home?"

Vaughn shakes his head as tears begin to stream down his face. Then he says, "My dad jumped out of the window."

The man in front asks, "What's your father's name?"

"Rich Wilson."

"What's your name?"

"Vaughn Wilson."

"Well, I'm Detective Falconi." Pointing to the other two policemen, he says, "This is Officer Willis and Officer Jackson. The man in the back is Sergeant Williams. Can we come in and talk to you?"

Vaughn nods and opens the door wider. The three officers and the detective walk in, and Detective Falconi bends down to hug Vaughn. Sergeant Williams begins to look around the apartment.

Talking in a comforting and soft voice, Detective Falconi asks, "Where's your mother and do you have any sisters or brothers?"

Vaughn says, "My mother died and I have one brother. He's at the grocery store. He wasn't here when it happened."

"What's his name?"

"Gerard"

"What store did he go to?"

"Stop and Shop."

Detective Falconi asks, "Could you show us a picture of your brother?"

Vaughn takes Detective Falconi into the living room and points to a class picture of Gerard.

Detective Falconi turns to Sergeant Williams and says, "You need to get some officers into that store and find his brother."

Sergeant Williams takes the picture and goes downstairs.

Detective Falconi then asks Vaughn, "Could you take us to where your dad jumped out of the window?"

Vaughn leads the rest of the officers to the boys' bedroom. Detective Falconi turns to Officer Willis and says, "Call Child Protective Services and tell them we need someone here right away."

Detective Falconi says, "Tell me what happened."

Vaughn says, "We were in the living room, when all of a sudden, Dad got upset, started crying, shaking, and talking to himself. I followed him into my brother and I's room, where he opened the window, sat on the ledge, then jumped off the windowsill. After he did it, I was scared, so I went into the corner and started crying. I didn't move until I heard someone knocking at the door."

Detective Falconi hugs Vaughn again and gently pats him on the head. Then he asks Officer Jackson, "Can you and Officer Willis sit in the living room with Vaughn until the CPS worker arrives?"

Officer Jackson takes Vaughn's hand and says, "Come with me," and leads him into the living room."

After about ten minutes, Vaughn hears his brother crying in the hall. Gerard enters the apartment with Sergeant Williams. Vaughn runs over to Gerard and begins to cry into his big brother's arms.

Sergeant Williams walks to the boys room and tells Detective Falconi, "We found his brother. They're both very upset and crying. Officer Willis and Officer Jackson are with them."

Sergeant Williams says, "I have one question that still bothers me."

"What?"

Sergeant Williams says, "When we examined the body, it looked like Mr. Wilson fell out of the window headfirst. Most suicides by jumping out of the window are feet first. It almost seems like he was pushed out of the window."

Detective Falconi says, "There was no one else in the apartment besides his son, and he said his father jumped off the windowsill."

"Yeah, I know, but it's a question that keeps haunting me."

Detective Falconi says, "There's a distinct possibility that Mr. Wilson could have changed position in the air. What other explanation could there be?"

Just as they're talking, Officer Willis walks into the bedroom. He tells Detective Falconi, "The CPS worker has arrived. She's a social worker, and her name is Mrs. Anderson. We debriefed her already. Right now, she's waiting for authorization from you to take the boys back to her office."

Detective Falconi asks, "Have they started notifying the next of kin?"

Officer Willis says, "Yes, and the boys need to come back here and get some clothes. They're also saying Mr. Wilson was a police officer."

Detective Falconi shakes his head, saying, "He was one of ours, huh. This job can certainly get the best of you sometimes. I'm glad the CPS worker is here. I think it's better that the boys not be around while we finish our investigation. Sergeant Williams, you can finish up back here while I go up front."

Detective Falconi walks into the living room and sees a short, plump brunette woman in a navy blue business suit and white blouse. She has piercing black eyes, and her hair is in a bun. She sits on the couch next to the boys and quickly stands up as Detective Falconi approaches.

"My name is Mrs. Anderson, and I'm from Child Protective Services."

She shows him her badge and says, "I need authorization to take Gerard and Vaughn Wilson off the premises and back to my office. Are you finished with them? I have to get back to my office soon.

Detective Falconi says, "Yes, that won't be a problem. You can leave with the boys as soon as you're ready."

Sitting with their heads down, Gerard and Vaughn look up as Detective Falconi approaches. He says, "All right, young men. I truly am sorry for your loss. You can go with Mrs. Anderson. She'll be helping you from now on."

He then touches each boy gently on the shoulder before turning to walk away. The boys hold back tears as Mrs. Anderson leads them to the back of the apartment. She moves as if time is of the essence. Once in their bedroom, she tells the boys to take about a week's worth of belongings. Following Mrs. Anderson's lead, they rush and throw their clothes into shopping bags. After getting their things, they immediately leave for the office.

Once they're seated in her cubicle, she asks Gerard and Vaughn what school they attend and their closest relatives' names. Gerard speaks for both of them, telling her they attend P.S. 105. He next mentions their grandaunt on Long Island and some cousins. Seeming uninterested in the conversation, Vaughn interrupts, saying, "Can I speak to my grandmother?"

Mrs. Anderson says, "I will call her soon, but I need to speak with her in private first. What's her full name and phone number?"

Vaughn says, "Her name is Veronica Davis, and her number is 919-485-8865."

"I'd like you boys to sit in the reception area for a few minutes while I speak to your grandmother in private."

Once they're outside, Mrs. Anderson dials the number. After three rings, a woman picks up.

"Hello. May I please speak to Mrs. Veronica Davis?"

"Yes, this is she."

"Well, this is Mrs. Anderson from New York City Child Protective Services."

Gasping, Veronica asks, "Did anything happen to Gerard or Vaughn?"

Mrs. Anderson says, "No, the boys are fine, but I have some sad news to report."

With rising anxiety and tension in her voice, Veronica asks, "What happened?"

"I'm sorry to report that Rich Wilson died today."

Shocked, Veronica instantly drops the phone. Mrs. Anderson starts to yell into the phone, "Hello, Hello, Hello! Mrs. Davis. Are you still there?"

Mrs. Anderson can hear Mrs. Davis crying loudly in the background. After a few minutes, Veronica picks up the phone. Still sobbing, she asks, "What happened?"

Mrs. Anderson says, "He jumped out of the window."

Veronica screams, "What? I can't believe it! Why would he do something like that? I can't believe it! Where are the boys?"

Mrs. Anderson says, "They're waiting in the reception area. They're safe and calm, but I want to speak with you first before I put them on the phone."

Veronica screams, "Those boys have been through so much. Their mother just recently passed away, and now this!"

Mrs. Anderson says, "Yes, that's a tragedy, and I'm truly sorry for your loss. My heart bleeds for those children too, but I also have a question to ask."

"What?"

"Who in the family is willing to take the children now that both parents are deceased?"

Veronica says, "Oh, that won't be a problem. I'll come and get them. I'll raise them. I'll be up there as soon as I can get a flight."

Mrs. Anderson asks, "Where do you live?"

"Raleigh, North Carolina."

"Then I will start on the paperwork right away.

Veronica implores, "Yes, I certainly will do that. But I have a favor to ask; can I please, please speak to my grand-babies now?"

Mrs. Anderson says, "Hold on a minute. I'll go get them."

Both boys look up with sad eyes as Mrs. Anderson approaches. She says, "I have your grandmother on the phone. I'll let Vaughn speak to her first; then you can talk to her next, Gerard."

Vaughn has tears in his eyes when he answers the phone. "Hi, Nana."

"Hi, Baby. I just heard about your father. I'm so sorry. Nana will be up there as soon as I can get a flight. Would you mind living with Grandma permanently?"

"No. I wouldn't mind."

Sobbing again, Veronica says, "Oh, how my heart aches and bleeds for you and your brother. First, your mother, and now your father. I feel so sorry for you boys. I can only imagine how devastating this must be for both of you. I won't keep you long. I'm sure you don't feel like talking much, but remember to pray whenever you start feeling sad or need someone to talk to; speak to God. You can put your brother on the phone now. Take care and remember Nana loves you."

"I will, and I love you too, Nana."

Vaughn walks back into the reception area with his head down and, shuffling his feet. He speaks in a slow, barely audible voice, saying to Gerard, "You can talk to Nana now."

Gerard ambles into Mrs. Anderson's office.

He picks up the receiver and says, "Hi, Nana," then starts crying into the phone."

"I'm so sorry for your loss. You boys have lost both your parents in one year; that's rough. You have been through so much. I'm coming up there as soon as I can get a flight. Would you mind staying with Nana from now on?"

"You mean to live in Raleigh forever?"

"Yes."

Gerard says, "I wouldn't mind."

"Well, the social worker is working on the paperwork to get that done. I know you probably don't feel like talking, but I'll tell you what I told Vaughn: remember to get on your hands and knees and pray. Whenever you start feeling sad and need someone to talk to, speak to God."

"Okay, Nana."

"All right, I'll be praying for you. I love you."

"And I love you too, Nana."

After hanging up, Gerard starts walking back to the reception area when Mrs. Anderson says, "Have a seat."

She then goes to the reception area and motions for Vaughn to follow her.

Mrs. Anderson says, "Your grandmother said you can stay with her in Raleigh. Is that okay with you boys?"

Both Gerard and Vaughn say, "Yes."

"Well, that makes things a little easier. I can get started on the paperwork right away. Your grandmother said she'll be taking the first flight up. I understand you have a grandaunt in Long Island. I'll call and see if she can keep you until your grandmother arrives. What is her name and phone number?"

Gerard says, "Ruth Barber, and her number is 516-248-6514."

Mrs. Anderson says, "Hold on a minute while I call her."

After one ring a woman answers the phone. Mrs. Anderson says, "May I please speak to Ruth Barber?"

"Speaking."

"This is Mrs. Anderson from Child Protective Services. I have some sad news to report."

Mrs. Barber interrupts, "Does this have anything to do with the death of my nephew Rich Wilson? My daughter just told me. I'm so upset. Those boys lost their mother not too long ago."

"Yes, it does. I'm so sorry for your loss, and it's definitely a tragedy. I have Gerard and Vaughn Wilson here in my office. Their grandmother said she's flying up from Raleigh as soon as possible. She agreed to have the boys live with her permanently, but in the meantime, we're looking for relatives to keep the boys until she gets here."

Mrs. Barber says, "That won't be a problem. They can stay with me until she arrives."

"I'll have one of my coworkers drive the boys out to you as soon as we finish here, and I want to thank you for your kindness and support."

"No problem. That's my family. By the way, how're they doing anyway?"

"They're okay. I just let them speak with their grandmother. I'll contact my coworker, Mr. Hamilton, as soon as I get off the phone. He'll be arranging transportation for them to get to your house. They should be there within the next two hours."

"Give them my love anyway, and I'll see them when they get here."

"Okay, bye. And you take care."

"You do the same."

After getting off the phone with Mrs. Barber, Mrs. Anderson calls a coworker named Mr. Hamilton, the transportation coordinator.

"Mr. Hamilton speaking."

"Hi, Mr. Hamilton. I have two children here. I was hoping you had a driver available to take them to their grandaunt in Long Island."

Mr. Hamilton says, "I'm a little short-staffed. I can take them. What's the address?"

"78 Thorens Avenue, Garden City Park. The boys are in my office. Come over when you're ready."

"It's seven o'clock now. I can be over there in fifteen minutes."

After speaking with Mr. Hamilton, Mrs. Anderson remembers she needs to make one more call. She says to the boys, "Your Grandaunt Ruth sends her love. I must talk with your grandmother one more time before you leave. Excuse me for a moment."

Veronica sees it's Mrs. Anderson calling and picks up quickly.

"Hello."

Mrs. Anderson says, "I have some new information; Gerard and Vaughn will be staying with their grandaunt on Long Island until you arrive. Her name is Ruther Barber. Let me give you her phone number and address. Do you have a pen and paper?"

"Yes," Veronica says.

"Her number is 516-248-6514, and her address is 78 Thorens Avenue, Garden City Park. You can coordinate with her about picking the boys up, but you have to stop by my office first to sign some papers before going to get them. Let me give you my address. It's 100 Livingston Street, Brooklyn. Do you have a flight yet?"

"Yes, I'm taking the first flight into New York tomorrow morning. It leaves around six and should put me in the city around seven-twenty."

"Well, that's good."

Just then, Mrs. Anderson notices Mr. Hamilton standing at her door.

"Oh, I'm sorry to be so short, but I have to go. A coworker of mine just walked into my cubicle. He'll be taking the boys to Long Island. All right, see you tomorrow."

"Okay, speak with you soon. Bye."

After hanging up, Mrs. Anderson says, "That was faster than I expected. Here are Gerard and Vaughn Wilson. Their grandmother will be in the city at seven-twenty tomorrow morning. She's coming from Raleigh, North Carolina."

Mr. Hamilton looks down at the boys and extends his hand. Gerard and Vaughn shake his hand unenthusiastically. He then looks at Mrs. Anderson and says, "I'm ready whenever you are."

"Okay, give me a minute."

Then turning to Gerard and Vaughn, she says, "As you've heard, I've talked with your Grandaunt Ruth and your grandmother. Your grandmother's flight gets in tomorrow morning at seven-twenty. I don't know what time she will be at your grandaunt's house, but it should be some time before twelve. You boys have been through so much. You have my deepest sympathy for the loss of your father. Mr. Hamilton will be taking you to your grandaunt's house. Take care and be well."

After the boys say, "Thank you," Mr. Hamilton instructs them to follow him with their belongings. He tells Mrs. Anderson, "I'll speak with you later."

"All right, thanks, Mr. Hamilton. I'll see you when you get back."

The boys mumble goodbye as they get ready to leave Mrs. Anderson's office. They walk in lockstep behind Mr. Hamilton on the way to his car.

Once on the road, there is little conversation, and Mr. Hamilton turns on the radio to disrupt the uneasy silence within the car. The ride is shorter than expected, and they arrive in front of their grandaunt's house in a little over an hour.

The house is as they remember it: a big tan-colored bi-level house, situated on the corner with two brick columns holding up a portico. The door is mahogany with beveled glass side panels and two regular-sized and one bay window on top, as well as two large windows at ground level. There are three bedrooms on the first level and one bedroom downstairs.

Before Mr. Hamilton reaches the door, a tall, older-looking, brown-skinned woman with a round face, oval-shaped eyes, thin lips, and a short gray and white-haired afro opens the door. She has a concerned look on her face as she sees Gerard and Vaughn coming up the walkway. Cautiously she says, "Hello, Mr. Hamilton."

"Mrs. Barber, I'm from Child Protective Services. As you know, I'm here to drop off Gerard and Vaughn Wilson. Do you have any identification on you?"

"Hold on a minute while I get my pocketbook."

It takes about two minutes before Mrs. Barber comes back to the door with her driver's license.

Mr. Hamilton takes a brief look at the picture and says, "Okay, boys, take good care of yourself."

He pats each boy gently on the head as they walk by. He immediately steps out of the way as Gerard and Vaughn run toward their grandaunt. Since she's the first family member they've seen since their father's death, they easily melt into her arms, feeling reassured and at ease.

"I fixed you something to eat, thinking you'd be hungry by now. Let me show you to your room first."

The boys take their shopping bags and walk to the larger back bedroom. Eager for a meal, they put their belongings at the foot of their beds and wash their hands before going back into the kitchen.

Once in the kitchen, they see two place settings with a delicious-looking meal of fried pork chops, rice, collard greens, cornbread, and Coke. They salivate at the sights and smells of the food. As the boys eat, their grandaunt sits at the table with tears forming in her eyes and her voice cracking. She says, "I feel so, so sorry for you boys. I can't imagine how you must be feeling right now. Your father and mother were such good people. I'll never understand this. You truly have my sympathy."

She then reaches over and lightly caresses both boys' hands. Overcome with emotion, Gerard puts down his silverware and starts to cry. Vaughn remains emotionless as he continues to eat his food slowly. The boys communicate through overcast eyes that remain downcast and glassy, nervously avoiding eye contact with one another. They sit silently with hunched shoulders that bear the weight of their emotional burdens.

After occupying this sad space for a while, the phone rings. Ruth walks into the hallway and clears her throat before answering; not wanting to sound too emotional or upset, she casually says, "Hello."

"Hi, Ruth."

"Yes, Veronica, I was expecting your call. The social worker, Mrs. Anderson, called and told me you would be coming in soon."

"My flight should be arriving around seven-thirty in the morning. I have to first stop at the Child Protective Services office in Brooklyn to sign some paperwork. I don't know how long that should take, but I don't imagine it would be over an hour. I should be at your home by eleven at the latest."

"That should be fine. What day were you planning on going back home?"

"I have an open ticket. I intend to stay with my niece in Queens. She has lots of room."

"Why not stay here? I have four bedrooms."

"Are you sure that wouldn't put you out too much?"

"No, not at all. I consider you family also."

"Well, that's very nice of you. I really do appreciate that. Are you sure it wouldn't be too much of an inconvenience?

"No, not at all."

"In that case, I think I'll take you up on the offer."

"Sure, no problem. No problem at all."

Veronica asks, "How're the boys doing?"

"I guess the best that can be expected under the circumstances. They're eating now."

"I'm still in a daze."

"Me too. I can't believe it. I don't know what to do or say to the boys or even myself."

"Have they been asking questions?"

"No, they've been quiet. Gerard started crying at the table when I mentioned how sorry I am for the loss of their father. Vaughn didn't start crying, but both of them looked very sad."

"Well, if they start asking questions, be as honest as possible. Don't sugarcoat the truth. They're probably going through a range of emotions right now."

"They're probably still in a state of shock."

Veronica says, "Ask them what they want to do. If they say they want to talk about it, then speak with them about it; if they say they have questions, then answer them; if they say they want to watch TV, then let them do that; if they say they want to go to bed, then make it an early night. Let them take the lead."

"Well, I appreciate your advice and look forward to seeing you tomorrow, but I don't want to leave the boys alone too long. I think it's time I go back into the kitchen."

"All right, I just wanted to let you know around what time I'll be getting in tomorrow, and thanks again for the offer; take care."

"No problem. You do the same. Good night."

After hanging up, Ruth walks back into the kitchen. Seeing both boys have finished, she asks if they want dessert.

Gerard says, "I'm full."

Vaughn says, "Me too."

"I just spoke to your grandmother. She'll be here by noon tomorrow. I told her she could stay here until you all are ready to go back to Raleigh."

Gerard and Vaughn's eyes grow wide; they're glad their grandmother will be arriving soon.

As an afterthought, Ruth asks, "By the way, what time do you boys normally go to bed?"

Gerard says, "Nine o'clock."

"Well, it's eight-fifteen now. You have about forty-five minutes left. What do you want to do for the rest of the night?"

Gerard says, "I want to watch some TV."

Breaking their nightly tradition, Vaughn says, "I want to go to bed."

"Well, take a bath. Then change into your pajamas. Oh, and don't forget to say your prayers."

In addition to saying his prayers tonight, Vaughn retraces the words "He shall give his angels charge over thee" before falling asleep. Approximately a half hour later, Gerard is in his bed, sleeping. Both boys settle into a long night's rest after a very trying and tiring day.

Unexpectedly, in the middle of the night, Vaughn sits up in bed. His eyes remain closed, and he's unsure if he's dreaming or awake. He sees his mother's image, dressed all in white with a dead white snake in both her hands, standing before two freshly filled in graves. She bows before him with the snake and utters the words, "It is done." Confused about whether he was actually in the presence of his deceased mother, Vaughn sinks into his pillow as if drugged and continues to sleep undisturbed and peacefully throughout the night.

The following day Gerard is up first. Vaughn wakes up shortly thereafter. After washing up both boys get dressed and go into the kitchen. Their grandaunt has placed a box of Cheerios with two bowls, a few slices of toast, and orange juice on the table. As Gerard gets some milk; Vaughn appears right behind him.

A few minutes later, Ruth walks in and says, "I thought I heard someone in the kitchen."

As she starts to fix her breakfast, she asks, "How did you sleep last night?"

"I slept well," Gerard says.

"Me too."

"What do you boys want to do until your grandmother gets here?"

Vaughn says, "I want to watch TV."

Gerard asks, "What's on Nickelodeon?"

Vaughn replies, "I don't know."

Ruth says, "That's fine; both of you can watch TV in the living room until she arrives

Not used to being home in the morning, Gerard turns to Nickelodeon. They feel like they've hit the jackpot because one of their favorite shows, *SpongeBob SquarePants*, is on. After a while, the doorbell rings. The boys eagerly turn away from the TV and wait for their grandaunt to open the door, hoping it's their grandmother.

Their grandaunt walks quickly to the door and opens it. She sees Veronica standing there with weary eyes and a tired look on her face. Ruth immediately reaches for her suitcases, wanting to relieve Veronica's load and help her into the house. After the bags are in the foyer, they hold each other for a minute, not speaking but communicating reassurance through the warmth of a comforting hug. By this time, Gerard and Vaughn have walked into the entryway. They scoot around their grandaunt to welcome their grandmother.

"How're my grandbabies?" she asks as the boys jump into her arms. "You've been through so much."

The boys enjoy the full-bodied embrace of their grandmother. After a few minutes, Ruth says, "I know your grandmother must be tired. Let her sit down for a moment."

Then Ruth asks Veronica, "Would you like something to eat?"

"I'm not hungry. I ate something on the plane, but you were correct; what I want is some rest right now."

"That's not a problem, not a problem at all. I've already prepared a room for you."

"All right, let Nana take a nap," Veronica says to the boys.

Vaughn says, "Okay, Nana," as both boys stop following her down the hall and go back into the living room.

Continuing down the hall, Ruth asks, "Did you contact the boys' schools yet?"

"The social worker already has that information. She said she'd do it later on today."

Suddenly thinking about the arrangements, Veronica asks, "Who's Rich's next of kin?"

"I am. Rich was an only child, and both his parents are dead. I had one brother and one sister, and they're all deceased now."

"Have you heard anything from his job yet?"

"No, they haven't called."

"You might want to give them a call sometime today."

Ruth replies, "That's a good idea. I was also thinking about the funeral. I first need some information on Rich's insurance. I hope he made me his beneficiary so I can start making plans for the service."

"Yes, I had my mind on the very same thing. I was also thinking about Gerard and Vaughn. Since they've lost both parents so close to each other, I wonder if it's even a good idea to have them attend the funeral. They're still so young and vulnerable."

"I know what you mean, but we can always ask them. Let them make up their own mind."

"Yes, that's definitely something to consider."

By this time, Ruth has ushered Veronica into the other guest bedroom, saying, "Okay, I know you must be exhausted. Take a load off and enjoy your nap. We'll talk when you wake up."

Veronica smiles as she kicks off her shoes and wearily lies down on the covers.

Meanwhile, in the Bronx, Bruce receives a call on his cellphone. He must report to the captain's office immediately. He believes this has something to do with Doug's case, and his mind instantly goes in a million directions.

As soon as Bruce gets in, he goes to see the captain. Captain Kuntz is seated at his desk with a sad look on his face. He says, "Good morning, Bruce. I have some very sad news to report."

Bruce asks, "What's going on?"

Captain Kuntz says, "We lost one of our own yesterday."

"Who?"

"Rich Wilson."

Bruce's eyes grow wide and his mouth drops open.

With intense emotion in his voice, he yells, "What happened?"

"I got a call from Central Ops last night saying Rich committed suicide."

Jumping out of his seat, Bruce says, "What? I can't believe it!"

"An acquaintance from Central Ops told me he jumped out of the window."

Feeling both shocked and perplexed, Bruce says, "What, you must be kidding me. Why did he do it? Did he leave a note?"

"Everyone's been asking the same question. Nobody understands it. He must have been carrying something heavy no one knew about. He didn't leave a note."

Shaking his head in disbelief, Bruce asks rhetorically, "Wow. How am I going to tell the guys at base camp?"

"Yeah, I understand how you're feeling. Rich had only been on the force a short time. I'm stunned. You know the force offers grief counseling and psychological services."

"Yeah, I know, but I still can't believe it. Give me a minute to process all this."

Captain Kuntz says, "Take as much time as you need."

"I need a smoke right now," Bruce says.

After taking a few puffs outside, Bruce walks back into the captain's office and says, "I have to tell the team immediately. I've got to go up the hill and tell the guys in person."

As Bruce begins to leave, Captain Kuntz gets up from his desk. He pats Bruce on the shoulder, saying, "I totally understand. Take care and speak with you soon."

Bruce looks at his watch and sees it's eleven-fifteen. The ride up to base camp takes about ten minutes. Logan and Whitney are outside. Surprised to see Bruce, they immediately notice the solemn look on his face.

Walking past them without making eye contact, Bruce says, "I need to talk with the entire team."

Perplexed, Logan and Whitney follow him downstairs. Everyone looks up as soon as Bruce enters the room. Noticing the expression on his face, no one says anything and waits for him to speak.

"Look, team, I have some very unfortunate news to report. I know it's going to shock you because it shocked me. Rich committed suicide yesterday."

Whitney says, "I don't believe it."

Tom says, "You've got to be kidding me, man."

Vincent says, "My God. What happened?"

Logan says, "How'd you find out?"

Tears start to gleam in Gary's eyes as he bites his upper lip in an attempt to hold back his emotions.

Bruce says, "Captain Kuntz told me this morning. Central Ops told him yesterday Rich jumped out of the window."

"Jumped out of the window!" Whitney exclaims.

Gary says, "I can't even find the words to express how I'm feeling right now. Man, this is too much!"

Vincent says, "I can't help but think about Sherry and his boys. They must be devastated."

Bruce responds, "I intend to leave a message with the people at the facility where Sherry is staying once I get back to my office. I don't know what's going on with his kids. I need to look in his file and call his next of kin soon."

Logan says, "Damn, those boys lost their mother recently too!"

Tom says, "We've got to do something for the family."

Whitney says, "I had a cousin who committed suicide a few years back. It tears up a family."

Gary says, "I'm going to visit Sherry tomorrow. I want to see how she's doing and offer some support."

Vincent says, "That's a great idea, Gary. I'm sure she'll need it."

Bruce says, "Yeah, that's very nice of you."

For the time being, everyone forgets about the investigation until Bruce notices the monitors and asks, "I see Doug isn't home. Where is he?"

Tom says, "He's at that mental health organization today."

Bruce asks, "What time is he coming back?"

Tom says, "I'm assuming he'll be back around three."

"Okay, well, I'm getting ready to go back down the hill. I'm sorry to have to bring you such tragic news; I wanted to deliver it in person. I have to go back to my office to call Rich's family and fill out some paperwork. I can see some of you guys are really broken up over this. You know the force offers free grief counseling and psychological services. Seriously, we don't need another tragedy. I encourage all of you to seek help for yourself if any of this starts affecting you too deeply or you're carrying something, anything, that's weighing on your heart and mind too heavily. Seek support, and I do honestly mean that. No one else has to know. Please do it for yourself or your family."

After pausing for a minute and looking around the room to assess their reaction to his statement, Bruce says, "All right, on that note, I think I'll leave now. Reach out if you need me."

Gary says, "Thanks, Bruce."

Logan says, "All right, man."

Vincent says, "Take care."

Tom places his hand on Bruce's shoulder and says, "You be good."

Whitney shakes his hand and says, "Appreciate you."

Bruce leaves the war room, feeling appreciated, believing they care as much about him as he cares about them. After he's in his car, he focuses on calling Rich's family.

At the precinct, Bruce looks through his files and locates Rich's emergency contact information. It was updated after his wife's death and lists Ruth Barber, his aunt, as his new emergency contact. Wanting to get this over quickly, he reaches for the phone and dials the number listed.

After a few rings, a woman picks up.

"Hello."

"Hi, this is Detective Bruce Rodriguez from the New York City Police Department. May I please speak to Ruth Barber?"

"Yes, this is she."

"First, I'd like to express my condolences for the loss of your nephew, Rich Wilson. I was his direct supervisor, and he was a great police officer and an even better friend."

A lump begins to develop in Ruth's throat, and her voice cracks a little as she says, "Thank you for saying that."

"How are you and the family doing? How are his sons especially?"

Ruth says, "Well, we're doing the best we can. It's so soon, and everyone is still in a state of shock."

"Yes, everyone on our team is devastated. Rich was a good guy, and I know how much he loved his family and how much you all meant to him. I really feel so sorry for those boys; they recently lost their mother too."

"Yes, I know, but we have our arms wrapped tightly around them. They're very sad but are handling it okay for now. We were planning on having the funeral Saturday. I was going to start making arrangements right away. I'm also going to need keys to the apartment to pick up more things for the boys and locate some of his papers."

"Well, that can be arranged. I'll get the keys and have them here at the precinct. That way, you can come and pick them up whenever you have the time."

Ruth says, "Okay, that's good."

"Please let me know when you make the arrangements. The guys on the team and I certainly want to be there."

"I definitely will do that."

Bruce says, "All right, I won't keep you long. I know you have a lot to do, but I did want to reach out and give you my condolences."

"Thank you. I was intending to call someone at Rich's workplace today anyway, but you saved me the trouble, and I appreciate that. Be blessed."

Bruce says, "If there's anything else you need, feel free to call me. I can give you my number. Do you have a paper and pen handy?"

"Yes, It's right here."

"It's 914-792-1793."

"Okay, take care, and thanks again."

"All right, you too. Bye."

Veronica walks into the hallway after Ruth hangs up, saying, "That phone woke me up."

Ruth says, "Oh, that was Rich's job. His supervisor called to give his condolences. He's going to leave the keys to the apartment at the precinct."

"That's convenient."

"Yes, I appreciated the call. Sorry for interrupting your sleep. You can go back to bed if you wish."

Looking at the clock, Veronica says, "Nah, I'll stay up. Wow, I was only asleep for twenty minutes. It certainly didn't feel like it. Felt more like a couple of hours."

"That just goes to show how tired you were. The boys have been watching TV in the living room for the last half hour."

ERIC FERGERSON

"I think this is as good a time as any to discuss whether or not they want to go to the funeral."

Ruth says, "Okay, we can do that."

As they walk into the living room, Ruth says, "All right, guys, we need to talk to you about something."

Gerard and Vaughn look toward their aunt as she picks up the remote and turns off the TV. Veronica and Ruth sit on the couch opposite the boys.

Veronica begins with, "First, I'd like to ask how you boys are doing?"

Gerard says, "Fine."

Vaughn says, "Okay."

"No, I mean, how're you really doing?"

The boys look puzzled as Veronica explains, "Look, we know you've been through a lot this past year with both your parents passing. I can only imagine how tough this must be for the two of you. To lose one parent in a year is upsetting enough, but to lose both parents in one year is unimaginable pain."

Ruth says, "I want to know how you're handling all this. I mean, are you sad, mad, confused, numb, or unsure of how you're feeling? What's really going on inside?"

Tears begin to form in Gerard's eyes as his lips start to quiver. He says, "I feel mad. It just seems unfair that I would lose both my parents so early in life and so close to each other."

Veronica says, "I can't explain it either, but we're still here, and you do have a family. Reach out whenever you start feeling bad. You can talk to me anytime, day or night, and you can always speak to God."

Ruth turns to Vaughn and asks, "How're you feeling?"

"I feel sad."

"I want you to do the same thing Veronica told Gerard to do. Reach out and talk to us whenever you start feeling bad, and of course, you can always talk to God. Now you both know we need to have the funeral service. I have a question I need to ask. It's an important question, and I want you to think carefully before answering."

Veronica asks, "Do you boys want to go to your father's funeral? Don't feel obligated to do it for your Aunt Ruth or myself but for yourself."

Vaughn immediately says, "No."

Surprised at Vaughn's quick response, Gerard says, "Then I don't want to go either."

Ruth asks, "Are you sure?"

Vaughn says, "Yes," as a lone teardrop slips from his eye, beginning its slow journey down the right side of his cheek."

Looking at his brother sympathetically, Gerard says, "Yes, I'm sure."

Veronica breathes a deep sigh of relief. The boys make the decision she was hoping for.

Ruth says, "I hope you don't feel like you're letting us down. We're more concerned about you boys than you should be about us."

Veronica adds, "We'll be able to go back to Raleigh in a couple of days. After I wrap up a few last-minute things around here."

Veronica walks over to the boys and gives them each a big hug, saying, "It'll be all right. You guys will be fine."

Ruth says, "Please try to focus on the more joyful memories you have of your parents, not how they left here. Always keep those more positive recollections in your heart and mind."

Veronica says, "That's where the true beauty of their existence will always be, in memories. Funerals are just a formality for the living; it's a ritual. Both your parents are already with God."

The boys don't say anything and stare at their grandaunt and grandmother with unreadable expressions. Ruth tries to change the subject by saying, "Now, I'm getting a little hungry. I'll be in the kitchen making something to eat."

Veronica turns back on the TV and gives Gerard and Vaughn one last long and compassionate look before following Ruth into the kitchen.

Back at base camp, everyone is still upset over Rich's passing but begin to focus on the monitors, as Doug has returned home. Once in his apartment, he throws the bag full of NAMW brochures, pamphlets, and flyers on the kitchen table and starts looking through the information on support groups, psychoeducational classes, the speaker's bureau, art/music therapy, and writing workshops. While he's looking through the materials, the phone rings. Doug looks at the number and sees it's Ron.

He says, "Hey buddy."

"Hi, What's going on?"

Doug says, "Just a lot on my mind, an awful lot."

"Tell me. What's going on?"

Doug says, "I, for one, am just over everything as of late. I'm seeing a new therapist, Ms. Sonnovia. Dr. Ehnis moved to Michigan."

"Okay, well, how do you like her?"

"I like her a lot."

"Well, that's good because I know you liked Dr. Ehnis and were seeing him for a long time."

"Did he tell you why he was moving?"

"No."

"Oh well, they say the only thing that's permanent is change."

"Good luck with the new therapist."

"Thanks."

"Well, how have you been otherwise?"

"All right, I guess."

"All right, you guess. That doesn't sound too confident."

"Yeah, I know, but that's the way I feel. I went to the National Alliance on Mental Wellness today to get some information on their programs."

"I've never heard of them."

Doug says, "I just found out about them myself. I was looking through a newspaper for people with mental illness at my therapist's office and found a full-page ad for them. They offer many groups, programs, and classes for people living with a mental health diagnosis. I intend to check out one of their support groups soon. They seem like a great organization."

Doug is on the fence about mentioning the investigation again, believing in the back of his mind that Ron is also a police informant. Thinking about this is starting to give Doug a headache.

Ron asks, "By the way, have you heard from Rommie lately?"

"Yes, I heard from him about a week or so ago."

"How's he doing?"

Sarcastically, Doug says, "He's doing okay. The same ol' Rommie."

Trying to lighten up the mood, Ron starts talking in a British accent, saying, "He's so dignified and proper, wearing his ascot. He kills me sometimes."

Laughing, Doug says rhetorically, "He's quite a character, isn't he?"

After giggling together for a minute, Ron says, "Yes."

Wanting to change the direction of the conversation, Ron asks, "So, what has Doug been doing for Doug lately?"

"To be quite honest, nothing really."

Doug starts feeling frustrated and wants to end the aimless chitchat. He says abruptly, "I hate to be rude, but something just came up. I've got to go now."

Taken off guard, Ron says, "That's fine. I'll let you get on with the rest of your day."

"Okay, take care and speak with you soon."

"All right, I will."

After getting off the phone, Doug goes into his cabinet and gets a white candle. Placing it on the cedar chest, he lights it while bowing his head and closing his eyes. He seeks answers from God and goes to bed resting on his back, with his eyes closed and one hand placed on his forehead.

Logan says, "He's in that thinking, praying position again."

Whitney says, "He might be in that same position for hours."

Vincent says, "Well, it's almost time for us to change shifts anyway."

Gary says, "Yeah, it's actually past the time for me to leave. Let me get out of here."

Tom says, "I still can't believe Rich is gone—and those boys."

Whitney says, "I know what you mean, man."

Vincent says, "That's the most shocking news I've heard in a while."

Gary says, "It does take your breath away. I'm still going to check on Sherry tomorrow morning just to make sure she's okay. I'll let Bruce know I'll be in a little late."

Tom says, "Definitely. Let us know how she's doing and, most of all, give her our regards."

Gary says, "Yeah, I'll tell her the whole team sends its condolences."

As Gary walks out the door, Tom says, "All right, enjoy the rest of your evening."

Gary says, "Okay. Bye, guys."

Waiting for shift change, the team gets restless watching Doug rest. They do the usual when bored: smoke cigarettes, drink beers, read the newspaper, occasionally check the monitors, and look through magazines until it's time to leave. Although everyone is still thinking about Rich and Sherry, Tom asks, "I just wonder how his sons are handling all this?"

Ruth is looking in her cupboards, trying to find something for dinner, while Veronica sits at the kitchen table.

Veronica says, "Given that the boys are not going to the funeral, I better hurry up and make our reservations to go home."

Ruth says, "Yeah, I need to go to the house and get the insurance papers so I can start planning the funeral. I plan to have the service Saturday. You're welcome to come with me to get the boys' clothes."

"Okay, whenever you're ready, just let me know. I plan on leaving for Raleigh within the week."

"That's fine. We can go tomorrow."

Becoming disinterested in the TV, Vaughn walks into the kitchen for something to drink.

Ruth says, "Dinner will be ready in about thirty minutes."

Veronica says, "We'll probably be going back to Raleigh this week."

Vaughn says, "Okay."

After finishing his soda, Vaughn doesn't go back into the living room; instead, he goes toward his bedroom. Veronica senses something is wrong and follows him. When Vaughn enters the room, he gets in bed and turns his back away from the door. Two minutes later, Veronica walks in and gently places her hand on his shoulder.

"I know this is hard," she says.

Startled by her touch, Vaughn turns around to look his grandmother in the eye. He sits up with tears streaming down his face, hugging her tightly; he begins to sob quietly.

"I told you we'll get through this. I love you and your brother, and as I said before, you can always come and speak to me or Aunt Ruth about anything. And of course, you can always talk to God."

Vaughn doesn't say anything, but his grandmother feels his pain by looking through his tears and seeing into his soul.

After hugging for a few minutes, Veronica decides to leave and, wishing for a white candle, says, "I'll let you get some rest."

Vaughn lies in bed until his grandaunt comes to get him for dinner. Hungry, he looks forward to his meal. Walking into the kitchen, he sees everyone is already seated at the table, and the spread of barbecued spareribs, rice, and turnips makes his mouth water.

Veronica says, "Let's say grace. I'm ready to dig in. Everything looks so good."

Ruth smiles contentedly and asks, "Gerard, do you want to say grace?"

Bowing his head and closing his eyes, Gerard says, "Dear Lord, we thank you for this food we are about to receive, for the nourishment of our body, and for Christ's redeeming sake. Amen."

Veronica adds, "And dear Lord, we pray for the departed souls not at this table. We ask for your strength, mercy, and grace on the way forward to heal broken hearts at the loss of loved ones, gone too soon."

Everyone starts to eat, and after a couple of mouthfuls, Veronica says, "Oh, this food is even better than it looks. You really put your foot in it this time, girl."

Ruth laughs and says, "Thank you," then she asks the boys, "Are you enjoying your meal?"

They both eagerly say, "Uh-huh," and nod their heads in agreement.

"One thing about me is I love to see people appreciate my cooking."

Veronica says, "Judging by everyone here, that goal has definitely been reached."

"Since you cooked, I'll clean up the kitchen this evening," Veronica says.

"Thanks. I'm a little tired tonight anyway. I'm turning in early."

Veronica says, "You boys can go back in the living room and continue watching TV. I think you usually turn in around nine or so."

Gerard says, "Yeah, but I'm going to bed early tonight. I'm tired."

Veronica says, "It's all that food you ate. You guys really wolfed it down."

Vaughn says, "I want to watch TV."

Veronica says, "Well, you have it all to yourself tonight."

Gerard walks out of the kitchen and says, "Goodnight."

Veronica replies, "All right, baby. Goodnight," as she takes her plate to the garbage can.

Gerard goes into the bathroom to wash up. Ten minutes later, he changes into his pajamas and gets in bed.

Ruth says, "I'm going to read for a while, then I'll probably turn in. If I fall asleep, I'll just see you in the morning. Have a good night, everyone."

Veronica says, "Okay, good night," as she starts clearing the table. Ruth picks up a magazine in the hallway and goes to her room.

After he's done, Vaughn goes into the living room and turns on the TV. Twenty minutes later, Veronica is finished. Intending to sit with Vaughn, she walks into the living room and finds him fast asleep. Smiling to herself, she nudges him awake and says, "Go to bed."

Bleary eyed and on unsteady legs, he walks to his bedroom and changes into his pajamas before falling asleep. Not wanting to stay up by herself, Veronica turns off the TV and makes it an early night.

The house is resting peacefully when, around two in the morning, a commotion in the boy's room wakes Veronica from her sleep. All of a sudden, Gerard jumps out of bed and lands on the floor. Vaughn wakes up immediately and asks, "What happened?"

"I had a nightmare; there was a rat on my pillow and a snake on fire was coming down the hall."

By this time, Veronica has come into the room. She finds both boys awake and asks, "What's going on?"

Vaughn says, "Gerard had a nightmare and jumped out of bed."

"What was it?"

"I had a dream there was a rat on my pillow and a snake on fire was coming down the hall."

Vaughn asks, "What does it mean, Nana?"

Veronica's facial expression changes from one of concern to serious reflection, and she says, "Honestly, I don't know, but what I want you both to do right now is get on your hands and knees and repeat the twenty-seventh Psalm after me.

"The Lord is my light and my salvation—whom shall I fear? The Lord is the stronghold of my life—of whom shall I be afraid? When the wicked advance against me to devour me, it is my enemies and my foes who will stumble and fall? Though an army besiege me, my heart will not fear; though war break out against me, Even then, I will be confident. One thing I ask from the LORD, this only do I seek: that I may dwell in the house of the Lord all the days of my life, to gaze on the beauty of the Lord and to seek him in his temple. For in the day of trouble he will keep me safe in his dwelling; he will hide me in the shelter of his sacred tent and set me high upon a rock. Then my head will be exalted above the enemies who surround me; at his sacred tent I will sacrifice with shouts of joy; I will sing and make music to the Lord. Hear my voice when I call, Lord; be merciful to me and answer me. My heart says of you, 'Seek his face!' Your face, Lord, I will seek. Do not hide your face from me, do not turn your servant away in anger; you have been my helper. Do not reject me or forsake me, God my Savior. Though my father and mother forsake me, the Lord will receive me. Teach me your way,

Lord; lead me in a straight path because of my oppressors. Do not turn me over to the desire of my foes, for false witnesses rise up against me, spouting malicious accusations. I remain confident of this: I will see the goodness of the Lord in the land of the living. Wait for the Lord; be strong and take heart and wait for the Lord."

After repeating this scripture with the boys, Veronica says, "Only God knows the true meaning of a dream, but I do know that if you continue to lean on him throughout life, no harm will ever come to you." She then goes over to Gerard and Vaughn and gives them each a big hug, saying, "Now, go back to sleep."

Secretly Veronica knows what she believes the dream means but makes a vow never to give voice to it. She goes back to bed with a restless spirit and sleeps uncomfortably the rest of the night.

The following day, Gary gets an early start. It takes about forty-five minutes for him to drive from Brooklyn to Far Rockaway. Walking into Peninsula Hospital, he immediately locates the information desk. Eager to see Sherry, he quickly walks up to the receptionist and asks for the psych unit. The young man directs him to the seventh floor. After getting off the elevator, he sees two heavy-looking locked doors on either side of the floor with a small glass window and a phone outside each door. He dials the number for the nurse on duty.

A woman with a strong West Indian accent picks up. "Ward A," she says.

Gary says, "I'm here to visit Sherry Martin."

"Oh, let me buzz you in."

After walking onto the ward, Gary immediately sees the nurse coming down the hall. She motions for him to start walking toward her and goes back to the reception area to wait for him. After he gets to the desk, the nurse opens the visitor logbook.

"Sign here," she says. "I'll take you to her."

Together they walk farther down the hall to a small room with a locked door and a small mesh window. Gary cannot see clearly through the window but notices there is someone in there. After the nurse opens the door, he enters the padded room. It contains two chairs, one empty and another with a woman seated in a strait jacket. The woman turns around to face him. He's stunned by what he sees, and his mouth drops open. Trying not to seem surprised, he closes his mouth quickly. Momentarily speechless, he tentatively says, "Sherry," unsure if the person he is looking at is even the person he came to see.

Her hair is unkempt, standing wildly all over her head yet matted and missing entirely in other spots. Sherry appears lighter and has lost a lot of weight. Her affect is flat, and there is no spark of recognition in her eyes when she sees him. She appears to look through him, not registering Gary's presence at all.

After a couple of minutes, he tries to engage her by saying, "This is Gary. Remember me?"

She doesn't respond and continues to look straight ahead. Unsure of what to say or how to proceed, Gary says, "I'm here to support you."

Water instantly forms in Sherry's eyes, eventually becoming tears that stream down her face.

"I'm so sorry for your loss. The team sends their love…Is there anything we can do for you?…How're you feeling?…Do you want anything to eat?…Do you want me to do anything for you?"

Sherry doesn't answer, and after making a couple more comments and asking a few more questions, Gary realizes his attempts to elicit a response are futile. Sherry continues to communicate through tears and doesn't say a word.

After waiting a few more minutes, with water forming in his eyes, Gary decides to leave. He gently places his hand on her arm and says, "Take care, Sherry, and you will always be in my thoughts and prayers."

Despairing, he hangs his head down and slowly walks out of the room. As he passes the reception desk, the nurse calls him over.

She talks in hushed tones, almost whispering, "I know I'm not supposed to let you on the ward or speak to you about our patients without preauthorization and a release-of-information form, but I feel so sorry for Ms. Martin, and I'm glad someone came to visit her so soon. A man from her boyfriend's job called yesterday and told us the news. I hope you are aware she recently lost her baby. Then the man she was supposed to marry dies by suicide; one tragedy right after the other. It's unimaginable."

Gary says, "Yes, I worked on the same team with her boyfriend, Rich. We're all devastated."

"After Ms. Martin found out, she became hysterical. She was crying, screaming, throwing things, and tried to climb out the window. She even tried to attack the doctor. They had to give her several shots, and it took three orderlies to subdue her. After a while, she just became very quiet and started staring into space with this blank look on her face."

Gary says, "Wow, I knew it wasn't going to be pretty. I had no idea it would be that bad. That's why I came to visit as soon as I could."

"We were going to release her before all this happened, but the doctor says she'll probably need long-term care. Our policy states, if a patient doesn't improve in a reasonable amount of time or needs more comprehensive treatment, they must go to our facility upstate."

"How long will they keep her?"

"We don't know. It all depends on how Ms. Martin responds to treatment. We tried to help her, but these things happen. I'm so sorry about everything."

"I appreciate you telling me."

"Do you know if she has any other family? Her boyfriend was the only contact listed?"

"I'm not sure."

"She's going to need a lot of support."

"Yes, I'll tell the team. We'll keep in touch. We won't forget about Sherry."

"Okay, that's good. I've talked long enough. I'll let you go."

"All right, take care."

"You too."

Gary gets in his car, feeling slightly disoriented, trying to process what he's seen and heard; it makes him drive slower. The ride to work takes longer than usual this morning. He arrives at base camp and finds Logan and Whitney having a smoke. As he exits his car, Logan yells, "How's Sherry?"

Gary shakes his head, saying," "Not good, man, not good at all."

Whitney asks, "What's going on?"

"I'll tell the entire team when I get to the war room."

Eager to find out what's going on, Logan and Whitney follow Gary down the stairs.

When he walks into the room, Tom is the first to ask, "How'd it go?"

"I was just telling Logan and Whitney that Sherry is not doing well at all, and I do mean not at all. Man, Sherry doesn't even look like herself. She lost all this weight, her complexion has changed, and her hair was standing up all over her head. I didn't even recognize her at first. They had her in a strait jacket, man."

Vincent says, "That's rough."

Gary says, "Yeah, I know. I was totally shocked."

Logan asks, "Well, did she say anything? Could you get her to talk?"

"No, I told her the team sends their regards and asked if she wanted anything, but she just kept staring straight ahead. The entire time she didn't utter one word. She was like a damn zombie."

Whitney says, "It must have been hard to see her like that."

"Yeah, it was."

Tom asks, "So, what's going to happen to her?"

"They say they're going to transfer her to an upstate facility for more long-term and intensive treatment."

Vincent says, "So, she's not coming back to work anytime soon?"

Gary says, "Definitely not soon, maybe never."

Logan says, "Man, to lose a baby and then your boyfriend in the space of a few weeks is hard as hell. Life can really be a bitch sometimes."

Whitney says, "I know just what you mean. It all seems so unfair."

Gary reiterates, "Very unfair."

Tom asks, "Did you hear anything about his boys?"

"No, I don't know what's going on with them. I think Bruce would know, and he also should have information on the service."

Logan says, "He'll probably fill us in when he gets all the details."

Gary says, "Yeah, I'm sure."

After a slight lull in the conversation, Gary asks, "How's Doug doing? Where's he at anyway?"

Vincent says, "He's at Starbucks."

Gary asks, "How long ago did he leave?"

Whitney says, "About twenty minutes ago."

Gary says, "So, he should be returning home any moment now."

Vincent says, "Yeah."

After about five minutes, the team gets a call from Starbucks telling them that Doug is on his way up the hill. The team members position themselves. Logan sees him exit the bus and walk across the street to his building. After getting off on the third floor, Doug hears his phone ring. Not expecting a call, he hurries to open the door. Seeing his sister's name on the caller ID puts a smile on his face, and he picks up quickly.

"Hi, Marima."

"Hi, Doug."

"How's it going?"

"Same ol', same ol'."

"Well, I guess that's good.

"I'm just calling to remind you about our dinner date tomorrow at seven at Sylvia's." Marima says.

"Okay, thanks. But I didn't forget."

"I don't want to keep you long. I've got to get back to work. So I'll see you tomorrow evening."

"Yep. All right, take care. Enjoy the rest of your day."

After hanging up, Doug feels like doing something different today. Kind of tired of his Starbucks routine, TV, eating, and sleeping, he tries to think of a more creative way to spend the rest of his day. Overwhelmed by the thought of living in a fishbowl, Doug gets an idea, deciding instead to read a book and walk around the reservoir later on. Feeling the topic is apropos to his current life situation, he chooses a text from his psychology class, *Trauma, and Recovery* by Judith L. Herman. Searching for any context to better understand the trauma he's currently living through.

At base camp, Tom says, "Oh, he's reading today. That's a change of pace."

Logan says, "No TV, sleeping, burning a white candle, or praying, thinking. I'm surprised."

Whitney says, "He use to read a lot more before he started talking about our investigation."

Tom says, "Yes, he did, but I bet you he'll read a while then go back to bed. Boring-ass Doug."

The team is laughing as the phone rings.

"Hey, Bruce."

"Hi, team. How's everything?"

Whitney says, "Doug is reading."

"Okay, that's fine. I just finished speaking with Rich's aunt and mother-in-law. They dropped by with Rich's boys to pick up keys to his apartment. His aunt said the funeral service would be this Saturday, but the arrangements have not been finalized yet."

Gary asks, "How do they seem to be handling his death?"

"They seemed fine. Rich's mother-in-law mentioned his sons would be moving down to Raleigh to live with her. Rich's aunt said the boys would not be at the funeral. The family felt it would be too traumatic, since they lost both parents so close to one another."

Surprised, Vincent says, "So, they're not going to their father's funeral."

"Nope, apparently it was a family decision."

Logan says, "That's strange. But being so young, I guess I can understand."

Gary says, "It's unusual but I get it."

Bruce says, "All right, I just wanted to keep you guys in the loop. I'll let you know when I get more specifics on the service."

Gary says, "Please do. We all want to pay our final respects. Rich was a good guy."

Vincent says, "Yeah, I really want to be there."

Logan says, "He wasn't with us long, but he came and just fit right in."

Bruce says, "Well, I'll definitely pass the information along as soon as I get it. Take care, guys. Enjoy the rest of your day."

Gary says, "You too, Bruce."

After Veronica, Ruth, and the boys leave the precinct, they head straight to Rich's apartment. Once inside, Veronica immediately notices the chill in the air, remarking, "I should've brought my coat instead of this light jacket."

Ruth says, "Yeah, it's freezing in here. It's colder in here than it is outside."

Veronica says, "I'll go in the bedroom and help the boys get their things together."

"I'll be in Rich's room, looking for the insurance papers."

Veronica is the first to walk into the boys' room. She immediately notices the window is open.

As if reading her mind, Vaughn immediately walks over and closes it.

Veronica says, "All right, I want you boys to put everything in these bags. Remember, we're leaving tomorrow, and you won't get another chance to come back here."

Gerard asks, "When does our flight leave?"

"I haven't called the airline yet. I have an open ticket, but I want a morning flight."

After a few minutes, Ruth walks in, saying to the boys, "I found this bag at the bottom of your father's closet. It contains dark glasses, a false beard, and a hat. I was wondering if this was part of you guy's Halloween costume?"

Vaughn grabs the bag and looks in it. A frown immediately appears on his face. He says, "It's mine," snatching it and putting it in the bag with his clothes.

After an hour of helping the boys clean out their closet and chest of drawers, Veronica goes into Rich's bedroom, asking Ruth, "Having any luck?"

"Not really. I've found some papers, but not the policy. I still haven't looked through everything. I need to go through some stuff at the top of this closet and look through the night-stand."

Veronica starts to look at the junk on Rich's bed. Spotting the empty candles, she picks them up and notices the residue of black wax. An instant chill goes through her body.

"I can search his nightstand while you concentrate on his closet."

After a few minutes, Veronica says, "I didn't find anything."

With excitement in her voice, Ruth suddenly says, "I just found a folder at the top of the closet. I think this is probably it. It says 'Met Life' on it."

After spending a few moments looking in the folder, Ruth exclaims, "Eureka! I've found it. Let me check to see who the beneficiary is."

Ruth turns to the last page and sees her name listed as the primary beneficiary. Relieved, she breathes a deep sigh of relief, saying, "Thank God."

Veronica says, "Great. Let me go check on the boys."

She walks into the bedroom, asking, "Have you finished packing up your things yet?"

Vaughn says, "Yes."

Gerard says, "I'm almost done."

"That gives me a few minutes to make our airline reservations. I'll meet you guys in the living room when you're finished."

By this time, Ruth has walked into the boy's bedroom. She says, "I'll help them finish up."

After about ten minutes, Ruth and the boys walk upfront, announcing, "Packed and ready to go."

Veronica is still on the phone and holds her hand over the receiver. "One more minute," she whispers.

Ruth says, "We'll meet you in the car."

Veronica nods and mouths the word "Okay" as Ruth and the boys leave the apartment.

They struggle but manage to take everything down in one trip. After they've put the bags in the trunk and just as Ruth gets in the car, she sees Veronica walk off the elevator.

Ruth starts the car as Veronica opens the passenger side door.

Once inside, Veronica says, "Our flight leaves at eleven in the morning from JFK."

"We should be home in about forty-five minutes. I have some leftovers. You and the boys can have a quick dinner then pack your luggage."

Veronica is happy to be going back to Raleigh with her grandsons and smiles, saying, "Sounds like a plan."

Back at base camp, Doug has been reading for the past two and a half hours. He starts to feel tired and changes his mind about going for a walk. Looking at the clock, Doug decides to fix something to eat. Walking into the kitchen and looking in the freezer, he finds one frozen dinner and quickly heats it up. After finishing his meal, he turns on the TV and sits in the living room, watching the evening news.

Tom says to the team, "I bet it'll be lights out within the next half hour."

Gary says, "Yeah, you're probably right, but I leave in about ten minutes. So I'll be home by then; let the next guys watch him sleep."

True to form, after about forty-five minutes, Doug falls asleep on the couch.

Tom says, "See? I told you. Well, it's time for me to leave anyway."

As Tom walks out of the war room, he says, "Enjoy the rest of your evening, guys."

Around midnight, and still on the couch, Doug wakes up, gets in bed, then suddenly remembers the white candle. Going to the cedar chest, he lights it and starts to contemplate his life. While he prays, the phrases "You've got to stoop to conquer," and "Incognito." reverberate in his mind. Thinking about his future, Doug suddenly recalls the NAMW support group meeting. Checking the *New York Visions* newspaper, he sees their support group meetings are at six on Wednesdays. Again realizing that this is where his healing journey must begin, Doug decides to check out NAMW. He's annoyed that it's so close to the time of his dinner date with Marima. Nonetheless, Doug decides to go to the meeting and change his plans for tomorrow.

The next morning Ruth gets up early. Wishing to send Veronica and the boys off with a big breakfast, she decides to make bacon, eggs, toast, grits, and hash browns. Awakened by the smell of the food, Vaughn goes into the bathroom and washes up. After getting dressed, he goes into the kitchen. After saying good morning, he sits at his place setting, drinking a glass of orange juice. A couple of minutes later, Gerard walks in, and a few minutes after that, Veronica follows.

After greeting everyone, Veronica says to the boys, "Breakfast isn't ready. Go in the living room until you're called."

While still at the stove, Ruth says, "I decided to send you all off with a full stomach this morning."

Veronica says, "I appreciate that, and I'm sure the boys do too."

"Did you finish packing?"

"Yes, we're all done. All I need to do is make sure we arrive at the airport on time. Do you need any help?"

"No, I'm fine."

"I'll sit in the living room with the boys until you're ready."

"It shouldn't be long."

Veronica walks into the living room and sees the boys have turned to the Disney channel. Overriding their TV choice this morning, she says, "Let's watch some news."

After watching *The Today Show* for a few minutes, Ruth yells from the kitchen, "Breakfast is served!"

After a quick blessing, the family digs in.

Ruth says, "Your flight leaves at eleven this morning. Right?"

"Yes, but I like to be at the airport early with a little wiggle room. So after we finish eating, we'll need to get on the road."

"That's fine. I'll be ready soon. I'm sorry I had to see you all under such tragic circumstances."

"Yeah, I know, but it couldn't be avoided. I just thank you for your hospitality."

"No problem. No problem at all," Ruth says obligingly.

Gerard and Vaughn finish their meals in a hurry.

Veronica says, "You can go and get your things, boys. I'll get the kitchen together while you get ready, Ruth."

Eager to leave, they hurriedly get up from the table and walk back to their bedroom. Gerard and Vaughn gather their things, struggling with their luggage as they bump along in the hallway, making their way into the living room. Veronica is finished in the kitchen at the same time Ruth is coming out of her bedroom.

As they pass each other in the hall, Veronica says, "I'll be ready in five."

Ruth says, "I'll help the boys put their belongings in the trunk. We'll be waiting in the car."

"Okay, I won't be long."

The boys sit on the edge of their seats, inwardly excited about their journey to a new home and life.

Ruth walks into the living room, saying, "All right, it's time to go."

As the boys get up from the couch and pick up their stuff, Ruth turns to Vaughn and says, "Let me take a couple of your bags."

Without hesitation, Vaughn hands two of his bags to his grandaunt. Before walking out, Ruth shouts down the hall, "The door has a slam lock! All you need to do is close it."

Veronica yells back, "Okay! I'm practically done now."

While Ruth and the boys are putting their luggage in the trunk, Veronica walks out of the house with her suitcase. She helps them put all the bags in the trunk. Then they all get in the car together.

Veronica puts fifty dollars in the cup holder located between the front driver and passenger seat.

Ruth says, "You've got to be kidding me."

She takes the money out of the cup holder and gives it back to Veronica.

Veronica asks, "Are you sure?"

"Yes, I'm sure."

"You were so gracious."

"Like I said before, anytime. As I mentioned over the phone, we're family. I could never accept any money from you for this."

Veronica smiles, reaches over, and pats Ruth's hand.

"By the way, we better get going. You said you like to be at the airport a little early, and we're traveling during rush hour, so traffic might be heavy."

With those words, Ruth cranks the ignition, and the small, packed blue Toyota Corolla begins its journey to the airport. Typically, the trip would take about twenty minutes, but this morning, it takes longer because of congestion on the highway. Thirty-minutes into the trip, Veronica asks the boys, "Everything okay back there?"

Gerard says, "Yes."

Vaughn doesn't respond, and Veronica turns around to look him in the eye, asking again, "How about you, Vaughn?"

Deep in thought and distracted, he replies, "I'm fine."

Once at the airport, Ruth finds the domestic terminal, then Veronica helps her locate Delta.

After finding a place to park temporarily, Veronica searches for a redcap to assist them with their luggage. Ruth also starts helping them take their bags out of the trunk, and with tears in her eyes, stretching out her arms, she says to the boys, "Here, come give me a hug."

Squeezing them tightly, she closes her eyes as if to hold on to the experience longer, saying, "Now, you take care of yourself and don't give Nana any problems. Remember, I don't want to hear any bad news about you boys."

Patting Gerard and Vaughn on the head in a sign of reassurance, Veronica walks over to Ruth, saying, "We've got to run, but I did want to give you a quick hug and thank you again for putting us up. And don't worry; I won't forget to keep in touch."

Ruth says, "I'm looking forward to it. We can't chat long; I know you've got a flight to catch but have a safe trip back."

"Yeah, I know I'm holding up the works. You take care too, Ruth."

"You do the same, Veronica."

Veronica looks up and sees impatience in the redcap's body language and eyes. She walks over, saying, "I'm sorry. I'm ready to go now," and with those words, Veronica, Gerard, and Vaughn close one door and open another as they leave one life behind and begin their journey into a new chapter of their lives.

At base camp, Doug is still sleeping when the call comes in from Bruce.

"Hi, team. We've decided to try some truth serum on Doug today. We know he's having dinner with his sister this evening. We'll have some agents in the restaurant, and they'll put the drug cocktail in his food. As usual, we want you to be on the lookout for any changes in his behavior tonight. Make sure you double-check the listening devices we put in his clothes when he leaves for Starbucks this morning."

Vincent asks, "What's going on?"

"We're going to see if we can create a more authentic conversation between him and his sister. There are some very serious issues they need to discuss, and we want to make sure we can hear them. What's Doug doing now anyway?"

Logan says, "He's sleeping."

"What did he do yesterday?"

Tom says, "He read for a while, fell asleep on the couch, and then got up around midnight to light a white candle and pray before going back to bed."

Looking at the monitors, Gary says, "It seems like he's waking up right now."

"By the way, I also have the information on Rich's service. I apologize for the late notice. I already emailed it to everyone on the team."

Gary says, "I'm so glad you did that. The rest of the team and I intend to be there."

Bruce says, "Yeah, a lot of people from the force should be there too."

Vincent says, "Rich was such a great asset to the team."

Tom says, "Yes, he was."

Bruce says, "Well, that's everything I wanted to tell you. I'll let you get back to your job."

Logan says, "All right, take care, Bruce. Enjoy the rest of your day."

"You too, guys."

The first thing Doug does after getting out of bed is pick up his phone. Eager to speak with his sister, he dials her cellphone immediately.

"Good morning, Marima."

"Good morning, Doug. This is a surprise."

"Yeah, I wanted to get you earlier, but I slept later than I intended. I wanted to tell you I need to change our plans. Can we have lunch today instead of dinner? I have an important appointment at six that just came up."

Marima says, "Yes, that's fine."

"What time do you usually have lunch?"

"One o'clock."

"That's good for me."

"We're not going to be able to make it to Sylvia's? Do you feel like Chinese?"

"That's fine."

"There's a restaurant around here called Chow Buffet. Their food is good. We can go there instead."

"All right, I know you're probably busy, so let me let you go; that's all I wanted to ask. I'll see you soon."

"You have my address, don't you?"

"Yes. You still work on Fifty-seventh Street, don't you?"

"Yeah. All right, take care."

After hanging up the phone, Doug starts to get ready. At base camp, the team wonders what appointment Doug is talking about.

Vincent then remembers: "Last night, he looked at that newspaper from that organization before he went back to sleep. Maybe he's planning on doing something with them today."

Logan says, "He was just there a few days ago. We'd better let Bruce know."

Bruce picks up on the first ring.

"What's up, team?"

Tom says, "Doug just called his sister and said he has an appointment at six, so he has to change their dinner date to a lunch date at one."

Bruce says, "That's vital information. I'll let our agents know. Where's his appointment at?"

Gary says, "We're not sure, but we think it could be at that mental health organization he went to a few days ago."

"Oh, you mean the National Alliance on Mental Wellness."

Vincent says, "Yeah. When he got up around midnight, he looked at that newspaper for a few minutes."

"Well, you can check out the newspaper and see if there are any activities scheduled around that time for today. What's Doug doing now?"

Logan says, "He's washing up."

Bruce says, "He'll probably be leaving soon. We'll have to change our plans about giving him the drug cocktail. He'll probably go to Starbucks then get on the train. I'll let our agents know. They'll dose his chai."

Gary says, "He's getting dressed now."

"Okay, thanks for telling me. I need to let our agents know right away. You won't have an opportunity to double-check the listening devices. I just hope they're working. What restaurant is he going to with his sister?"

Logan says, "Someplace near her job called Chow Buffet."

Bruce says, "We'll get some agents in there to listen to their conversation. Again, thanks for the update."

"Doug will probably be at Starbucks in about ten or fifteen minutes. He's putting on his shirt now," Tom says.

"All right, gotta go. I have to get on this right away. Thanks, guys. This was crucial information."

Doug puts on his pants as Bruce hangs up. Eager to meet his sister, he exits his building and starts walking down the hill. Stopping at Starbucks, Doug gets his chai and runs upstairs to wait for the downtown train. The train rumbles into the station ten minutes later. Without waiting, he changes to the express at Ninety-sixth Street. The ride downtown takes about twenty minutes.

Once at Fifty-seventh Street, Doug feels a slight shiver go up and down his body. He realizes what must have happened.

Checking the time, Doug sees it's now 12:45 p.m. He finds his sister's job and waits in the lobby. After about five minutes, he recognizes Marima's walk before he can discern her face. Having not seen her in a long time, Doug immediately notices the resemblance to their mother. After greeting one another, Doug says, "You look so much like mom."

Marima says, "Oh, you think so?"

"Not so much when you're up close, but definitely from a distance. It also looks like you lost a little weight."

Laughing, Marima says, "Now that's what I want to hear." Realizing the clock is ticking, she says, "We better get going. The restaurant is only two blocks away, but it might be crowded."

After walking for about five minutes, they approach the large building located in the middle of Fifty-ninth Street with the words "Chow Buffet" written in large script above the entrance. Doug sees the food is served buffet style and the line is not too long. Looking around the eatery, he sees it's busy, noisy, and colorful, with a giant Chinese dragon hanging from the ceiling and paintings of daily life in ancient China posted on the wall. Since he's only had chai for breakfast, Doug's hunger grows after seeing the large selection of steaming, hot food placed in bins situated around the large cafeteria.

Doug says, "Quite a spread."

"Yes, that's why I like to come here. Do you know what you're getting?"

"Not yet, but the whole thing looks so good, and I feel so hungry. I'll probably get a sampling of everything."

"Well, we'd better hurry. I only have an hour."

"I know what I want, so I'll probably be finished first. Then I'll get our seats."

Doug starts to notice his speech is getting slurred, and he starts to feel a little drowsy. He immediately thinks about this morning's chai tea then rolls his eyes and shakes his head, saying to himself, *What a life.* Deciding not to focus on the wherefores or whys or play his three-card monte mental mind game, he just tries to concentrate on lunch with his sister.

After finding a booth for the two of them, Marima waits patiently for Doug. After a few minutes, Doug comes with a heaping plate of food. Looking at his serving, Marima laughs, saying, "Did you leave food for anyone else?"

Doug smiles and says, "What can I say? I was hungry."

Doug says grace, and they start eating. Marima notices his pupils look enlarged and says, "Are you taking any special medications? Because your pupils look dilated?"

Feeling slightly dazed and deciding to be unusually truthful and authentic today, Doug says, "As a matter of fact, I am."

"You are?"

"Yes, as a matter of fact, sis, there are a lot of things about my life you don't know and I have chosen not to share with you. First, I quit my temp job, I'm applying for Social Security Disability, I know I'm under investigation, I'm routinely being drugged and surveilled, and yes, I do take medication for my quote-unquote condition."

Doug knows he has hit a nerve, as Marima's eyes grow wide, and she sits up, leaning forward in her seat.

"Why'd you quit your job and decide to go on disability? How are you going to support yourself? And how do you know you're under investigation?"

Doug says, "I just got tired of the bullshit, even as a temp. My therapist and psychiatrist thought it would be a good idea if I applied for Social Security Disability given my new diagnosis of schizophrenia. I can live off my savings for a year, and by that time, they should have determined my eligibility. As for being under investigation. It's a long story how I know, but trust me, I know."

"It's your life; hey, I'm not going to argue with you about your choices. I also had no idea you were in therapy, seeing a psychiatrist, have been diagnosed with schizophrenia, and are taking medication for it. Wow, this is all so shocking!"

Doug mockingly says, "Yes, I know, but to be honest, we've never really been much of a family, and as we've gotten older, I've watched us drift further and further apart. We don't even have real conversations very often."

"What do you mean?"

"There are three topics we never talk about: my homosexuality, your drug abuse, and our father."

Marima says, "Your homosexuality is your business, and I don't feel the need to discuss that with you. It's none of my business. As for my drug abuse history, that's my business, and it's also part of my past. I don't see what relevance it has on our relationship now. As for our father, I remember I told you some things he did to me growing up. He is dead to me now. I don't wish to discuss him."

Doug raises his voice a little. "You said 'some things,' but it's not just some things. Goddamn it, he molested you!"

Marima starts to tear up, and her voice begins to quiver. "I just can't talk about him or that, and you need to respect my wishes. I told you about that in the strictest confidence."

"But he needs to be exposed for the devil that he is. There could be other victims out there."

Marima asks, "Did he mess with you also?"

"No, but I'm concerned about you and others. You're my sister. He really shouldn't be walking around. He should be locked up in the bottom of someone's prison. The man is wicked. Not just for doing what he did to you but for a lot of the shit he put us through growing up. You have no idea!"

Emphatic and annoyed, Marima says, "Do you really think this is the time and place for this discussion? You've dropped a lot of heavy stuff on me this afternoon. Is this why you wanted to have lunch?"

"No, I actually just wanted to reconnect."

"Well, you've seen me, and you've hardly eaten any food."

Doug says, "I'll stop, but this is a conversation we need to have, and if you don't talk to me, you need to discuss it with someone else."

Marima looks at her watch and says, "I've got about twenty minutes."

Changing his tone, Doug says, "I understand."

Still aggravated, Marima says, "I'm glad you do."

After the heated exchange, Doug lowers his head and starts to eat. They avoid eye contact and finish their meals in relative silence. The walk back to Marima's office is quiet, and they part ways with unenthusiastic and somewhat cold goodbyes.

Doug decides to go to Starbucks for the next few hours before his NAMW meeting.

Back in her office, Marima feels the heaviness of the conversation still weighing on her. She calls Al right away, and after a couple of rings, he picks up.

"Hi, this is Marima."

"I saw your name on the caller ID. How're you?"

"I just had lunch with Doug."

Al asks, "How did it go?"

"He triggered me."

"What do you mean?"

"He kind of bowled me over."

"What did he say?"

Marima says, "Doug told me he quit his job and was applying for disability. He surprised me when he mentioned seeing a therapist and psychiatrist for schizophrenia and taking medication for it. He also told me he was being drugged and surveilled. Did you know all this?"

"Yes, we knew."

"Why didn't you tell me?"

"You should know by now that's not how it works. I can tell you some of the things we know, but much of our information must remain confidential. Now, if Doug chooses to tell you something, that's up to him."

Marima says, "He also brought up being gay, my drug abuse history, and our father. He really was like a steamroller, just so truthful and authentic this time. I told him his homosexuality and my drug abuse were not topics for discussion. They are private matters and have no bearing on our relationship in the present. He didn't argue the point."

"What about your father?"

Sensing Marima's disdain, Al says, "Look, you probably realize we know about the child molestation. We're still investigating it, but to be honest, we're finding other victims within your family."

Marima yells, "What? Who're they?"

"I'm not at liberty to say. When did it happen to you?"

"I can't talk about it. The memories are too painful and upsetting."

Al says, "We can't do anything about it as long as you refuse to tell us about it."

Marima's voice cracks as she says, "I'm just not ready."

"I understand, and I'm sympathetic to what you've been through, but we can't wait forever."

Shaking her head after a long pause, Marima says, "I just can't do it right now." Then after another moment of silence, she says, "I need to get off this phone and get back to work."

Al says, "Okay, I'll let you go, but remember this conversation is not over."

Marima says, "All right, I'll talk with you later."

"You take care."

"You too."

After hanging up, Marima immediately starts back to work to distract herself from her worrisome thoughts.

Back at base camp, the team gets a call from Bruce.

"Hey, team. Our drug protocols got them talking. Doug opened up quite a bit and told his sister he quit his job, applied for disability, and is taking medication. He also mentioned seeing a therapist and psychiatrist for schizophrenia. He then talked about his belief that he was being drugged and surveilled."

Gary says, "That truth serum really worked."

"Yes, along with some other stuff."

Vincent asks, "Did he mention where he was going this evening?"

"No."

Tom says, "We checked that newspaper, and it looks like they're having a support group meeting today at six."

Bruce says, "I'm pretty sure that's where he's going. We'll have some agents in there; no need to worry."

Logan asks, "What's he doing now?"

"He's at Starbucks. Doug should start moving soon to be at the meeting on time."

Vincent says, "How's he been occupying his time?"

"The agents say he's been reading, drinking a cup of coffee, and walking around the Village for a while."

Logan asks, "I don't usually ask about this, but how's that investigation of his father going?"

Vincent says, "Yeah, Doug said their father molested his sister. Didn't he?"

Bruce says, "Yes, and actually, they're finding other victims—both within and outside of the family."

Gary asks, "So, what're they going to do about it?"

"It's hard to prosecute these cases because the victims say it occurred twenty to twenty-five years ago, and the statute of limitations has run out, but we'll certainly keep our eyes on him. We could try and get around that if we can establish a pattern of abusive behavior but we need his sister's cooperation.

Tom says, "That's a damn shame."

"It is, but I'll be discussing with my supervisors how we should proceed. A lot of what Doug put in his letters has been substantiated by our other investigative teams."

Gary says, "It would be a fucking disgrace to let that man get away with that."

Bruce says, "I know what you mean."

Bruce's cellphone starts ringing, and he looks at the number and picks up, saying to the team, "Hold on. I'll be back in a minute."

After getting on the speaker again, he says, "I just received word that Doug is on the move. I must go. All right, I just wanted to fill you in. Talk with you later."

Gary says, "Thanks for the information."

After hanging up, Tom says, "Man, those drugs are something else."

Logan says, "Quite a secret weapon."

Vincent says, "They're like a magic potion."

By this time, Doug is on the downtown 1 train. After getting off the subway he walks two blocks west on 34th Street to Eighth Avenue, then walks one block north to 35th Street. The building has construction scaffolding which obscures the 505 building address, but Doug finds it easily, nonetheless. He walks inside the small, dingy lobby, locating which floor the NAMW office is on quickly. He takes the elevator to the tenth floor, finds the door number, and walks in. Doug is immediately greeted by a short, dark-skinned woman with a curly afro, big eyes, and a high-pitched voice. She's seated at a reception desk.

She greets him with, "How may I help you?"

Doug replies, "I'm here for the support group meeting at six."

The receptionist points him to a conference room with ten individuals seated around a large table. The room is lined with bookcases filled with books, computers, and a large TV at the front of the room. A petite, white woman with shoulder-length wavy, black hair, olive skin, glasses, a pleasant smile, and a comforting, warm voice says, "Welcome. We'll be starting in about ten minutes."

Doug is still feeling the drugs' effects. He looks around the room, immediately noticing the diversity of facial types, body sizes, races and genders seated around the table. Searching everyone's face, Doug starts to play his three-card monte mental mind game, trying to figure out who the undercover investigators are in the room.

After what seems like five minutes instead of ten, the petite white woman introduces herself as Pat. She welcomes everyone and starts the meeting, calling it the "Client Support Network." Pat outlines the meeting's format, highlighting the reading of the agenda and group guidelines, then going into the check-in, general discussion, and closing.

After reciting the agenda and group guidelines, Pat begins to go around the room and asks everyone to check in. As each person checks in, Doug looks deeply into their eyes and tries to discern their spirit.

Taking mental notes, he decides that Renee, Deirdre, George, and Heidi are all undercover investigators. Because he's caught up in his thoughts, Pat asks him twice to check in. Doug begins with his name, describes his guilty pleasure as watching true crime TV shows, and says he comes to the meeting to both give and get support. He doesn't disclose his diagnosis.

Pat next asks for volunteers to get the discussion going.

A woman named Tanya starts talking about her symptoms of depression. She says, "I've really been struggling a lot lately. It seems like there is a dark cloud hanging over my head. I can't seem to find the motivation to do anything besides brush my teeth and wash my face, and even that is a struggle. My bed has become both my best friend and my worst enemy."

Pat asks, "Can anyone relate to what Tanya is going through?"

Mary says, "Yes. When I start having bad symptoms, I stay in bed and cry all day. I also develop suicidal ideations."

Pat asks, "What do you do to cope?"

Tanya says, "I tell myself that feelings are temporary and this too shall pass."

Larry says, "I try to do one or two things everyday that give me a sense of accomplishment, or I'll reach out to a friend. They don't have to be big things. They can be simple, like washing dishes for ten minutes or making my bed."

Pat asks, "Does anyone exercise or meditate?"

Rose says, "I walk thirty minutes on my treadmill every day. I believe that if I practice healthy habits when I can, the force of the habit will build up resilience in me so that, when I'm having a bad day, the force of the routine will give me a gentle nudge to do something."

George says, "I try to meditate, but I have a hard time controlling my thoughts."

Pat says, "Meditation is not about controlling your thoughts. It's about watching your thoughts and releasing them. Does anyone else have the same issue?"

Esther says, "I have the same problem. My thoughts don't just float by. They grab me, and I can't seem to let them go."

Doug sits quietly, listening to everyone share, and he is genuinely enjoying the conversation, but normal ruminations typically in the back of his mind begin to dominate his thinking, *I'm under investigation. They're out to get me. I'm not safe here. This meeting is a setup. I see wickedness and evil intentions in their eyes.* These thoughts cause Doug to become agitated and nervous. He gets up and excuses himself to the bathroom, then leaves the office. As he exits the building, he hears in his head, *Home is the only safe place for me.*

As Doug gets on the train, he thinks about options for his life but can't seem to come up with any. He only focuses on getting to the safety and security of his apartment. Doug doesn't think about tomorrow; he just wants to be home and alone.

Once home, Doug lights a white candle and goes to bed, where he gets into his thinking, praying position.

Gary says, "He's home earlier than I expected. How long was that meeting supposed to last?"

Logan says, "An hour and a half."

Tom says, "He'll probably be asleep within the hour."

Whitney says, "Bruce says those drug cocktails can knock you out for a very long time."

Tom says, "Once he goes to sleep, he'll probably be gone until tomorrow."

As everyone is discussing Doug's next move, Bruce calls up to base camp.

"Hi, team."

Gary asks, "Hi. Why'd Doug come home so early?"

Bruce says, "We're not sure. Our agents said everything seemed to be going well, then Doug just excused himself to the bathroom and left the meeting. What's he doing now?"

Tom says, "He came home, lit a white candle, then got into bed."

Vincent says, "So, our work is light this evening."

Bruce says, "Seems like it is. The drugs will probably knock him out for the rest of the night. He'll most likely sleep until tomorrow."

Tom says, "Well, I'll be leaving soon anyway."

"Okay, I'll say goodbye then. I think it's time for some of you guys to change shifts anyway. I was just checking in. Enjoy the rest of your evening."

As predicted, Doug starts snoring about an hour to an hour and a half later. He sleeps straight through the night. Waking up the following day, he still feels groggy and tired. Unsure about his future, Doug stares at the white candle for inspiration and encouragement. After a few minutes, he gets up and makes some cereal. After washing up, Doug sits in the living room to watch the morning news. Doug then remembers his appointment with Ms. Sonnovia and starts to feel a bit better. Even though he believes she works for the police, he's still eager to tell his story to someone he feels understands the conundrum of his life. Having slept past his usual wake-up time, Doug looks at the clock, realizing it's almost time to get going. He gets dressed, exits the building, and walks down the hill to wait for the bus to Riverview. Not wanting to be late, he skips Starbucks and arrives at his appointment fifteen minutes later, ready to unpack on Ms. Sonnovia.

She answers the door with a quickness that startles him. Ms. Sonnovia's pace seems a little rushed this morning. After he sits down, she begins with, "How've you been?"

Doug replies, "Not good. Not good at all."

"Well, I have some good news for you. Dr. Feinstein and I were able to finish your disability application. Given what we wrote, you shouldn't have any problem getting qualified. So that should help put your mind somewhat at ease. Also, Dr. Feinstein is going to prescribe you some off-label medication to improve your concentration."

Doug sarcastically replies, "Gee, whoopee. But I'm still annoyed."

"Tell me what's going on."

"I don't know how I'm going to live or have a life with this investigation going on."

Ms. Sonnovia asks, "What do you mean?"

Doug says, "All of these drugs, surveillance, and undercover investigators are getting on my nerves. They're messing up my life."

"You still believe you're under investigation."

Doug says emphatically, "Yes, I know I am. I met my sister this week, and I believe they drugged and surveilled me. I went to the NAMW meeting yesterday and believe the drugs were still affecting me. I often ask myself, 'Is this going to be every-where and forever?' The sum total of my life."

Ms. Sonnovia says, "I can see how that can be upsetting. To be honest, I don't know how to help you with that. Do you still believe I'm an investigator?"

Doug says, "Yes, I do."

"How do you think the police are drugging you?"

Doug says, "I believe they come into my apartment and put drugs in my food and drink all the time. I also believe they have agents at Starbucks that put drugs in my chai tea?"

"Why do you keep going there then?"

"They would just put it in something else, it's the police. I think it's government sanctioned terrorism."

"Why do you keep coming here then?"

"I see fairness and kindness in your eyes, and I believe you understand the complexity and are sympathetic to the situation I find myself in. If I didn't come here, I think I'd explode. Just being able to talk helps me. It doesn't solve the problems, but it does help."

Ms. Sonnovia says, "Well, I'm glad to know that. How was your conversation with your sister?"

Doug says, "It was stressful. I brought up three things I never discuss with her: my homosexuality, her drug abuse his-tory, and our father."

"How did that go?"

"She said my homosexuality and her drug abuse history were private matters and not open for discussion, which I can respect. However, I told her she needs to start telling the story of what our father did to her."

"How did she react?"

"She said it was too painful, and she couldn't talk about it, but I pushed. I told her she needs to tell someone, first, to process the pain, second, because he could still be abusing other children, and third, his cloak needs to be removed and he needs to be held accountable for what he's done. People need to know the devil that he really is."

Ms. Sonnovia says, "Good show. I would've given pretty much the same advice."

"It was our most authentic and challenging conversation in a very, very long time. I also went to a NAMW meeting.

How'd that go?"

"It was good in the beginning, but after a while, I started getting very intense thoughts in my head telling me to leave."

Ms. Sonnovia asks, "Were those thoughts coming from inside or outside of your head?"

Annoyed, Doug says, "I told you before I don't have visual or auditory hallucinations. They were coming from inside my head, not voices outside my head."

"What were they saying?"

"I'm under investigation. They're out to get me. I'm not safe here. This meeting is a setup. Wickedness and evil intentions are in their eyes. Home is the only safe place for me."

"Did they command you to leave?"

"No, I just got agitated and decided to leave. I felt my home was the only safe place for me."

Ms. Sonnovia asks, "What did you do once you got home?"

"I burned a white candle then got into bed."

"What do the white candles signify?"

Doug says, "It's a ritual I perform to facilitate a conversation with God. I think God talks to me through my thoughts when I pray to him with a white candle burning."

"What has God been saying to you through this ritual?"

"That I need to be a part of NAMW and embrace my mental health journey, but whenever I get drugged, I start believing the people in these spy networks are out to get me, and I leave."

Ms. Sonnovia says, "So you feel God is telling you to do one thing, but the drugs make you do something else."

Doug says, "Yes, that's it."

"That's quite a dilemma."

"I feel the people in these spy networks are going against God's plan for my life, and there will eventually be consequences for that."

"What kind of consequences?"

"I don't know, but you can't go against what God has ordained to manifest. I'll let God handle that. I'll just keep being his servant."

"Interesting. So what goals do you have for your life now."

Doug says, "I'm just taking it day by day and letting God be God."

Ms. Sonnovia asks, "What does taking it day by day mean? Goals are the fuel that ignites our engine every day, our passion."

"Yes, you're right. However, if I'm not allowed to have a life, what other choices do I have? There's nothing I can do about it. So I throw the situation up to God and let him handle it."

"It amazes me how you keep going given your perception of reality that more or less everyone in your life is part of a spy network."

Doug says, "God's grace."

"Okay, so on that note, I'll have to end our session a little early because I have a personal errand to run."

Doug says, "So, I'll see you next week."

"Is this day and time still good for you?"

"Yes, enjoy the rest of your day, Ms. Sonnovia."

"You too, Doug."

After Doug walks out of her office, Ms. Sonnovia calls Bruce. He picks up on the first ring.

"Hi, Judy."

"Hi, Bruce. My session with Doug just ended."

"How'd it go?"

"It was fine."

"What're his plans?"

"We specifically talked about that. Doug said he doesn't have any plans and will take life one day at a time. I think he feels somewhat trapped. I'll talk more about that at our next staff meeting."

"Okay, Judy. I'll remind the team to watch the video of the session before our staff meeting tomorrow."

"All right, will do. Talk with you later."

"Okay, speak with you soon. Goodbye."

Doug is halfway home when Judy gets off the phone with Bruce. Feeling very jumpy after his session and unsure of why his thoughts and feelings are so intense, he's puzzled about how they got the drugs into him this time, thinking to himself, *I didn't stop at Starbucks, so what's going on?*

He shrugs his shoulders and says to himself, "Maybe it was in the milk this morning."

Once home, Doug finds it hard to settle down. His nervousness and anxiety continue to grow. He turns out the lights, closes the blinds, and tries to relax by lying in bed on his back with one hand on his forehead, and his eyes closed, but he still can't get comfortable or calm down. Seeking reassurance from God, Doug gets up and lights a white candle. He walks around his apartment with the white candle, saying, "He shall give his angels charge over thee."

At base camp, the team is puzzled by Doug's behavior.

Gary says, "I wonder what's going on with Doug?"

Tom says, "Yeah, he's acting very strange."

Vincent says, "I wonder if they gave him another drug cocktail and forgot to tell us."

Whitney says, "Let's call Bruce."

Bruce picks up immediately.

"Hey, team. What's up?"

Logan says, "Doug is acting very bizarre, and I was wondering if you gave him a new drug cocktail and forgot to tell us about it?"

Bruce says, "No, we didn't give him anything. What's going on?"

Gary says, "Doug is very restless and almost frantic. His apartment is dark, and he's burning a white candle and walking around, saying, 'He shall give his angels charge over thee.'"

"I don't know what that's about, but we didn't dose him again. Maybe it's the aftereffect of the previous dosing. It could still be in his system. Well, in any event, keep a close eye on him."

Vincent says, "We will."

Tom says, "He just picked up the phone."

Bruce says, "I'll let you guys get back to work. Let me know of any other significant changes in his behavior."

Gary says, "Okay, will do."

Bruce says, "All right, take care."

After hanging up, the team listens carefully to Doug's conversation.

"Hi, Ron."

"Hi, Doug. How are you?"

"For one thing, I'm tired of these fucking investigators and damn keystone cops messing up my life."

"What do you mean? What's going on?" Ron asks.

"They follow me, drug me, and harass me. In essence, I have a life in name only, not in the true sense of the word! They should be following these damn terrorists. That's what they should be doing—and leave me the hell alone!"

"You already told me you believe you're under investigation and feel I'm an investigator too. Have you been taking your meds?"

Doug says, "Please don't get on my nerves by asking me about those meds."

Ron says, "I'm just curious."

"Yes, I've been taking my meds."

Ron asks, "What caused all this?"

"I'm not sure. I think it's the drugs they put in my food and drink."

Ron says, "Well, this certainly doesn't sound like you. You're always so peaceful and reserved. I've never seen you like this before."

"Yeah, but even I'm allowed to have a moment. I'm telling you these investigators better leave me alone and start following these damn terrorists."

Ron says, "I don't know what to say to you right now. I'm at a loss for words."

Doug says, "You don't have to say anything. I realize you're one of them too. That's what I mean; it feels like I've been living a dream. Nothing is real or authentic anymore or never was."

"I'm sorry you feel this way, but the fact we had a relationship is a reality."

"Yes, I know that."

Doug starts to feel even more rage and says, "Look. I'm getting off the phone. Thanks for letting me vent, but I'm just not in a good place right now! Ron says, "All right, Take care."

Doug hangs up without saying goodbye and then stands in front of the cedar chest, looking at the white candle.

Gary says, "I've never seen him this distressed."

Vincent says, "Yeah, he was talking loud."

Whitney says, "Practically yelling, really."

Logan says, "Something is definitely going on with him."

Tom says, "Maybe he really is losing it this time."

Logan says, "I remember Bruce said, 'sometimes subjects become unhinged on these drugs.'"

Whitney says, "He's in that thinking, praying position again."

Vincent says, "He'll probably be in that position for hours."

Logan says, "Look, he's lit two more candles."

Vincent says, "He's never done that before."

Gary says, "I hope he calms down and doesn't wind up in some mental ward tonight."

After tossing and turning a long time, Doug finally settles down, before he goes to sleep he says, as if in a trance, "Something bad is going to happen tomorrow."

Tom says, "It looks like he's finally going to sleep."

Logan says, "Yeah, but I wonder what he meant when he said, 'Something bad is going to happen tomorrow.'"

Vincent says, "Knowing him, I think something bad will happen tomorrow."

Gary says, "You're probably right. This is one crazy case."

Laughing, Whitney sarcastically says, "Him being a psychic and all."

Once Doug is asleep, the team relaxes and looks away from the monitors, content to enjoy a night of easy conversation.

The following day Doug sleeps later than usual. Around eight, Bruce starts the weekly supervisory staff meeting. In the conference room are Captain Kuntz, Judy, Michael, and Dr. Feinstein. Al, Ron, and Rommie are on the phone.

Bruce begins by saying, "Hello and welcome, everyone. First, I want to make sure that everyone has seen Doug's therapy session video. Has anyone not seen it?"

There is silence, so Bruce begins the meeting.

"I want to start by saying that I transferred Doug's friends'— Ryan and Darryl's—case to another team. Also, investigators Brooks and Johnson will no longer be with us. I'd like to begin with Al by asking how the investigation of Doug's father is going?"

Al says, "We're finding other sexual abuse victims both within and outside of the family. I was very frank with his sister. I told her we know she reported being sexually abused by her father and she needs to tell us more about it. She said she's not ready. I was very firm with her and said she needs to get ready. She was adamant in saying that she just can't deal with that right now. I told her we would revisit the issue."

Bruce asks, "Is there any way we could proceed with the victims we have?"

Irritated, Al snaps, "No, it happened too long ago, and the statute of limitations has run out. I swear we should call the auto mechanic. These men get away with murder, and there's nothing legally we can do about it. It just pisses me off!"

With those words, the room gets very quiet for a couple of minutes.

Bruce interrupts the uncomfortable silence by asking Judy, "How was your session yesterday?"

Judy says, "It was briefer than usual because I had an important errand to run, but he talked about being drugged, harassed, followed, and not being allowed to have a life. He also mentioned that more or less everyone in his life is part of a spy network: family, friends, coworkers, and neighbors. It seems like he feels trapped."

Bruce says, "So a lot of the same stuff he's spoken about before. I'm just amazed at how he's handling it."

Judy says, "So am I. He just says it's God's grace."

Ron interrupts, saying, "He called me yesterday, very troubled. I think it was after he met with you, Judy."

"That's interesting because he was so calm during our session."

Ron says, "Yeah, Doug was definitely different. He was talking loud and said I was an investigator and the police should stop harassing him and go after these damn terrorists."

Bruce says, "The team at base camp said the same thing. That's so interesting because we didn't give him anything new yesterday. So, it was all him. I told them maybe the previous dosing didn't fully wear off yet. Rommie, have you heard from Doug lately?"

"No, I haven't heard from him in a while."

Bruce asks Michael, "How's Doug doing financially?"

"He's staying within his budget."

Just then, the team hears a commotion outside, and someone knocks loudly on the door. Officer Perez opens the door and yells, "A jet just hit the World Trade Center!"

Captain Kuntz says, "What?"

Officer Perez repeats, "I said a plane just hit the World Trade Center!"

Bruce says, "We can adjourn the meeting early. There is really not that much more we need to discuss anyway. I'm turning on the news."

As everyone's attention is riveted to the TV screen, other officers walk into the large conference room. Open mouths, wide eyes, gasps, and stunned silence convey the shared reactions. People in the precinct immediately start to call their loved ones.

Within the next two hours, people watch in horror as another jet hits the second tower and both buildings collapse. Dazed and confused, Bruce thinks about Doug and gets in his car to ride up to base camp. Doug is still asleep, and Bruce beeps his horn aggressively to wake him up.

Doug hears the blaring horn, gets up, and casually turns on the news. Still in a haze, he briefly glances at the TV and sees there's a big fire somewhere in the city. Not yet grasping the full import of what's happened, Doug starts his daily routine of orange juice, cereal, and coffee. As the cobwebs begin to clear, he sits on the couch with his coffee. The reporters replay the series of events with the two planes hitting the World Trade Center and the buildings collapsing. Doug feels like he's watching a movie and does a double-take, unsure of what he's just witnessed.

Disturbed by the images and still in a state of shock, Doug finishes washing up and goes outside, unable to stay in his apartment. He gets on the bus and rides to the end of the line, then he turns around and returns home.

The team at base camp is beside themselves. When Bruce walks into the war room, he's hardly noticed. Everyone is laser-focused on the news and Doug.

Vincent says, "Doug said yesterday 'something bad would happen tomorrow,' and he also mentioned terrorists!"

Gary says, "Yes, we all heard him!"

Whitney says, "The guy is really a psychic, some kind of God walking on earth!"

Once Doug returns home, he tries to call his sister and brother but gets a busy signal.

After lighting a white candle, Doug gets in his thinking, praying position, turns on the news, not watching it, just listening to it. He stays in this position for a couple of hours.

At base camp, Bruce says, "I was amazed before; now I'm in awe."

Unsure of what to do or say, everyone in the war room stays fixated on the TV and Doug.

After two days, Doug gets in touch with his sister and brother. He's glad to know they're both okay, and they're happy to hear that he is too.

September 11th has changed the world forever. As days turn into nights, the world is still in a daze. Speculation of who was behind the attack is confirmed. President Bush vows to catch the perpetrators and hold them accountable. War in Afghanistan is launched to destroy Al-Qaeda and kill Osama bin Laden.

Slowly the world comes out of its fog and starts to resume its everyday rituals again. The stock market recovers, the economy still struggles, a war is begun, and people continue to go to work in a new post-September 11th world.

After a couple of weeks, Al decides to call Marima. Marima sees who's calling and hesitates to pick up but decides to answer on the third ring.

"Hello, Marima speaking."

"Hi, this is Al. How're you?"

"As well as can be expected under the circumstances. You know the world has been turned upside down since the World Trade Center terrorist attacks."

Al says, "You don't have to tell me. I'm well aware. But really, how are you doing? I'm sure you remember we have a conversation to finish."

"Yes, I remember our last talk."

"Well, we still need to resolve the issue."

Marima says, "Al, I'm really not in the mood for this discussion."

Raising his voice, Al says, "Well, goddamn it. Get ready!"

Marima shouts back, "Don't curse at me!"

"You're getting on my nerves. There are other lives at stake besides your own. Your father needs to be held accountable for what he's done to you and others."

"I realize that, but now is not the time."

Al says, "And it never will be if you don't make the time."

"Yes, he did it! Is that what you want to hear?" She yells.

"That and more. You need to come, speak to the police, and have an in-person interview."

Marima starts to sniffle, saying, "I just can't do it right now. It's just too painful."

She then abruptly hangs up the phone.

Al immediately phones back, but Marima lets the call go to voicemail. Al angrily says, "I know what I must do," and slams the receiver down.

He calls Bruce and says, "Doug's sister and I just got into a heated argument about her coming down to interview with the police about being molested."

Bruce asks, "What did she say?"

"She can't do it now; it's too painful."

"Does she understand the seriousness of the issue?"

Al says, "I guess she does, but she keeps saying she's not ready."

Bruce says, "Damn, I hate that these guys get away with murder due to uncooperative victims."

"I know what you mean."

Al asks, "By the way. How's Doug?"

"Actually, not that well."

"What's going on?"

Bruce says, "The guys say, for the past three weeks, Doug's been acting very strange; he's not going out or getting out of bed; he's keeping the blinds closed, tossing and turning in his sleep, appearing to have conversations with himself, shuffling his feet when he walks, moving his head in an unusual manner, and has an absent look in his eyes. He also started carrying a knife around and is not taking Ron's or Rommie's calls."

Al asks, "I'd be particularly worried about the knife. He's not mentioned killing his father, has he?"

"No. I'm also concerned because Doug's appointment with Judy is today. If he even goes, I'm wondering if he's going to take the knife. I'll call and let her know. There's always so much to think about and do with this case. Still, I've got to go; the captain is having a community meeting, and he wants me in attendance."

Al says, "All right. I was just keeping you in the loop."

Bruce says, "No problem. Take care, man."

"You too."

An hour later, Doug gets out of bed and takes a shower. The team is surprised.

Logan says, "As I've said before, you know; Bruce said some people become unhinged on these drugs. Maybe he's becoming seriously mentally ill, for real."

Gary says, "Well, I don't know. You might be right, but in any case, it appears he's getting ready to go somewhere. I think he has an appointment with his therapist."

Whitney says, "I wonder if he'll take the knife. If he does, we need to tell Bruce."

After Doug puts on his clothes, Tom says, "He's definitely going somewhere."

Vincent says, "He's probably going to his therapy appointment."

Whitney says, "Yeah, I'm sure you're right."

Tom says, "Well, he put on his jacket with the knife in the pocket. We better call Bruce."

As the team huddles around the phone, Bruce picks up on the first ring.

"Hey, team."

Gary says, "Doug is leaving this morning. We think he's going to his therapist. He put on his jacket with the knife in it."

Bruce says, "I already spoke to his therapist about the knife. She's not worried and is going through with the appointment."

Tom says, "Okay, we just wanted to tell you. But I have one other question about Rich. How're his boys doing?"

"Oh, I heard from their grandaunt last week. She called me to get some information on benefits for his kids. She said she heard from their grandmother recently and the boys are adjusting well to their new home in Raleigh. She said they're doing well in school and don't really talk much about their father."

Gary says, "Well, I'm glad to hear they're doing okay."

Logan says, "Me too."

Whitney interrupts, saying, "Doug just left his apartment. We have to get in place."

Bruce says, "All right, talk with you later."

Gary says, "Take care."

The guys are in position and watch Doug go down the hill. Everyone assumes he'll wait for the bus to Riverview at 231st Street and Broadway. However, he makes a right turn at Broadway and starts walking north. The surveillance team is surprised and continues to follow him.

To the investigators, it looks like he's on his way to the precinct. The agents call ahead to let Bruce know. Bruce rushes into Captain Kuntz's office.

"You'll never guess who's on his way to the precinct!"

"Who?"

"Doug."

Surprised, Captain Kuntz says, "I wonder why."

Bruce says, "I don't know."

Captain Kuntz says, "I'd really like to see him in person. Maybe he's coming to the community meeting."

"Could be," Bruce says.

"In any event, we'll be starting soon. As a matter of fact, I think it's time for me to go in there now."

As the captain walks into the meeting room, Doug enters the precinct. Bruce eyes him and immediately notices his disheveled appearance, flat affect, and absent look. Bruce stares at Doug from a distance. Seeming to know where he's going, Doug walks toward the meeting room. Once there, he takes a seat in the back. After a couple of minutes, the captain introduces himself and calls everyone to order. There are approximately twenty-five people in the room. The secretary passes out the agenda as the captain states the meeting should last between an hour to an hour and a half. During the introduction, Bruce quietly slips into the row behind Doug. The captain first reads through the agenda:

Call to Order
Roll Call
A. Open Discussion
   1. Crime Statistics update
   2. First quarter report on the budget
   3. Implementation of "action items"
B. Approval of minutes from previous meetings.
C. Letters and Communications

D. Old Business

E. New Business.

As the meeting progresses, Doug doesn't move, make any comments, or ask any questions. He seems to be in a trance, intensely looking at the captain. After the meeting ends, the captain is shaking everyone's hand as they leave. Doug is the last person in the room, and as he's shaking the captain's hand, he looks intensely into his eyes and then suddenly takes out the knife and stabs the captain in his chest. Standing behind the captain, Bruce is shocked, but his quick reflexes kick in, and he tackles Doug to the ground. Hearing the commotion, other officers swiftly walk in, gain control of Doug, and render assistance to the captain.

Doug is immediately handcuffed and put in a chair. He doesn't resist and is easily subdued. The captain is wheeled out of the precinct on a gurney. After his initial shock, Bruce calls base camp and tells them Doug just stabbed the captain. Everyone on the team is shocked and in a state of disbelief.

By this time, Doug has been fingerprinted and is being taken downtown for pre-arraignment custody. At the jail, Doug makes a call to Marima explaining what's happened. Marima promises to come as soon as she can. After a few hours, Doug is interviewed by a forensic psychologist named Dr. Gilberto. Doug is brought into a small, dingy, gray and white room with peeling plaster and a table with two chairs and a phone. He is handcuffed to the chair. Dr. Gilberto sits opposite him with a pen and a long, yellow legal pad. He starts taking notes on Doug's unkempt appearance and overall presentation. After introducing himself, the doctor asks a few basic questions, such as Doug's name, address, age, race, family size, and occupational status. He then starts the interview.

"Do you know where you are?"

"Yes."

"Where?"

"Jail."

"Do you remember what happened at the precinct?"

Doug replies, "Yes."

"Why did you assault the captain with a knife?"

"A voice commanded me to do it."

"Were the voices coming from inside or outside of your head?"

"Outside."

"Do you see images outside of your head?"

"No."

"What were the voices saying?"

"Kill."

"How long have you heard these voices?"

"For approximately three weeks."

"Describe the attributes of these voices."

"One was a woman, and one was a little boy."

"Were they saying anything else?"

"Yes, sometimes they'd say 'revenge,' and sometimes I'd hear the woman say my name."

"But these voices were auditory command hallucinations telling you to hurt someone."

"Correct."

"Do you want to hurt yourself or anyone else now?"

"No."

"Did you take any illegal drugs recently?"

"No, I don't use drugs."

"Do you take any medications?"

"Yes, I take Zyprexa and Wellbutrin."

"What is your diagnosis?"

"Schizophrenia."

"You said you just recently started hearing voices."

"Yes."

"You never heard any voices before these last three weeks?"

"No."

"Are you seeing a psychiatrist or therapist, and if you are, what are their names?"

"Dr. Finkelstein and Ms. Sonnovia."

"Okay, Mr. Jordan. Those are all the questions I have for you."

After finishing Doug's interview, the officers come and take Doug back to jail. He spends the night with ten other inmates in a hot, cramped, and dirty cell. The following day Doug is brought to his arraignment. After the charges are read, Doug pleads guilty. At sentencing, he spots his sister in the courtroom and tries to muster a smile. The defense attorney states that Doug has a mental health diagnosis then presents the findings of the forensic psychologist. He asks Marima to speak on Doug's behalf. She says she recently found out Doug has a serious mental illness. She also states he has her full support, has no history of violence, and was doing very well until his diagnosis. The prosecutor said the state recommends Doug be remanded to a state mental hospital for criminal defendants. The judge agrees and orders Doug to a forensic placement for psychiatric diseases. Doug is taken out of court and put in a padded van for transport to Creedale Mental Hospital.

As the weeks and months pass by, Doug settles into his new reality. Marima is his only regular visitor. One afternoon Doug receives a frantic call from his sister. She is crying, and Doug tries to calm her down. Speaking between gasps of breath, she finally utters the words, "Dad is dead."

Doug says, "What happened?"

Marima says, "He had a car accident and died. It happened yesterday."

Doug starts smiling on the inside as the voice outside his head whispers, "Auto mechanic."

P lease feel free to contact the author about any questions or comments regarding this work of fiction at either efccny@juno.com or PO Box 490507, Atlanta, GA 30349.

CPSIA information can be obtained
at www.ICGtesting.com
Printed in the USA
LVHW011141300921
698967LV00004B/96